NO JUDGMENTS

Also by Meg Cabot

The Princess Diaries series
The Mediator series
The Boy series
Heather Wells series
Insatiable
Overbite
Ransom My Heart (with Mia Thermopolis)
Queen of Babble series
She Went All the Way
The 1-800-Where-R-You series
All-American Girl Series
Nicola and the Viscount
Victoria and the Rogue
Jinx
How to Be Popular
Pants on Fire
Avalon High series
The Airhead series
Abandon series
Allie Finkle's Rules for Girls series
From the Notebooks of a Middle School Princess series

NO JUDGMENTS

A Novel

MEG CABOT

WILLIAM MORROW
An Imprint of HarperCollins*Publishers*

This is a work of fiction. Names, characters, places, and incidents are products of the author's imagination or are used fictitiously and are not to be construed as real. Any resemblance to actual events, locales, organizations, or persons, living or dead, is entirely coincidental.

HarperCollins books may be purchased for educational, business, or sales promotional use. For information, please email the Special Markets Department at SPsales@harpercollins.com.

FIRST EDITION

Designed by Diahann Sturge
Title page and chapter opener art © pichayasri / Shutterstock, Inc.

Library of Congress Cataloging-in-Publication Data has been applied for.

ISBN 978-0-06-289004-7
ISBN 978-0-06-291357-9 (hardcover library edition)

19 20 21 22 23 LSC 10 9 8 7 6 5 4 3 2 1

In memory of Kady Elkins, Marilyn Furman, and Maureen Venti, fierce lovers of books and nature, and all taken too soon from this world

NO JUDGMENTS

CHAPTER ONE

Time: 8:18 A.M.
Temperature: 82°F
Wind Speed: 6 MPH
Wind Gust: 0 MPH
Precipitation: 0.0 in.

The hurricane was a thousand miles offshore when my ex-boyfriend called to offer me a ride to safety in his private jet.

"No, thanks," I said, cradling my phone against my shoulder as I wiped a jelly smear off the Formica counter. "That's really nice of you. But I'm not going anywhere."

"Sabrina," Caleb said. "There's a Category Five hurricane headed straight for you."

"It's not headed straight for me. It's headed for Miami."

"Little Bridge Island is only a hundred and fifty miles south of Miami." Caleb sounded exasperated. "The storm could change course at any time. That's why they call the hurricane track the cone of uncertainty."

He wasn't telling me anything I didn't already know. But it was typical of Caleb to feel it necessary to explain the weather to me.

"Thanks for your concern," I said coolly. "But I'll take my chances."

"Take your chances of dying? Do you really hate me that much?"

This was a good question. Caleb Foley had had his good points: like me, he loved a good painting. His family owned one of the largest private collections of nineteenth-century Impressionist works in North America.

He'd also been great in bed, always waiting politely to orgasm until after I did.

But when I'd needed him most—which was definitely not now—what had he done?

Ghosted.

And now he thought he could make it up to me with a free ride in his Gulfstream just because a hurricane might sideswipe the little island to which I'd fled in order to recover from my heartbreak?

Sorry. Too little, too late.

"It's nice of you to offer." I ignored his question. "But like I said, I'm not going anywhere."

I thought of telling him the real reason why—Gary, with whom my life had become inextricably tied, but who was in no shape to travel at the moment.

But what would be the point? I knew what Caleb would say about Gary. He wouldn't understand.

It felt a little weird keeping something that meant so much to me from this person with whom I'd once shared every little thing in my life.

But it also felt right.

"Besides," I added, instead, "no one here is evacuating."

It was true. Instead of panicking and running around, throwing all of their stuff into the backs of their cars the way I always imagined people would when a hurricane was in the vicinity, the residents of Little Bridge Island, population 4,700, seemed to be taking the news in stride. The café where I worked was packed with the usual breakfast crowd, and though a lot of people were talking about the storm, no one seemed alarmed, only vaguely irritated. . . .

Like Drew Hartwell, whom I could hear next to me informing someone over the phone that he wouldn't be replacing the hundred-year-old window sash they'd hired him to restore anytime soon.

"Because there's a storm on the way," Drew said, sounding a little testy as he dabbed more hot sauce onto his Spanish omelet, "and there's no way the glazing's going to dry before it gets here. That's why. If you want an inch of rainwater all over your bathroom floor, that's your business, but personally, I'd wait until it passes."

Normally I don't make a habit of eavesdropping on my customers' conversations, but then normally Drew Hartwell didn't use his cell phone in the café. He was good about following the rules that Ed, the Mermaid's manager slash owner, had listed by the cash register:

NO SHOES, NO SHIRT, NO PROBLEM.
USE YOUR CELL PHONE? GET OUT.

One person who isn't so good at following the rules? Me. The last one, anyway.

"Beckham!" Ed bellowed at me from behind the counter. I whipped around and saw him glaring at me. He jerked a thumb at my cell phone, then the glass side door. "Take it outside if it's that important." His irritated gaze fell on Drew, who happened to be his nephew, but whom he still treated like any other customer. "You, too."

Drew held up a calloused palm, nodding as he slid off his orange vinyl counter stool and headed toward the door, his phone still clutched to his chin. "Look," he said to whoever was on the other end of his call. "I get it. But you're going to have the window boarded up anyway. So it's not going to make any—"

The rest of his conversation was lost as he stepped outside.

Sorry, I mouthed to Ed. Then, to Caleb, I said quickly, "Listen, I'm at work. I never should have picked up in the first place. I only did because . . . because . . ."

Why *had* I picked up, especially since Caleb and I hadn't spoken in months? Maybe because it was eight o'clock in the morning, and he never called this early. I'd assumed it was an emergency, only not an emergency concerning him.

"Look," I said. "If that's all you wanted, I'll talk to you later, okay?" As in, never.

"No, Sabrina. I've got to talk to you now. The thing is, your mother—"

I knew it. My pulse quickened. "What about her? Is there something wrong?"

"She's fine. But she's the one who's been bugging me to phone, since you won't pick up when she calls."

My heartbeat slowed. Of course. I should have known. Caleb would never have called, let alone volunteered to fly fifteen hundred miles to get me of his own accord . . . not after the way we'd ended things. Or not we, exactly, considering the fact that I was the one who'd packed up my things, handed my keys to his doorman, and left, making me, technically, the one who had ghosted.

But not really. What else could I have done? What kind of relationship had the two of us even had? Not one I'd wanted anything to do with anymore.

Now I was heading for the door again—the Mermaid's side door. A rush of humid, saltwater-scented air greeted me as I stepped out onto the sidewalk, ignoring the glare from Ed as well as the curious looks my fellow servers, Angela and Nevaeh, threw me. Neither of them could imagine what was so important that I'd dare take a call during the morning rush. I hardly ever got calls anyway, so this was a first.

A first that was probably going to get me fired.

"Caleb, look—"

"She's really worried about you, Sabrina. We all are."

It was all I could do to keep from bursting out laughing.

"You know your mom pals around with all those meteorologists from the station," Caleb went on. "She says they tell her this one is a real monster. If there were such a thing as a Category Six, this would be it. She says—"

"Tell my mom I'm fine," I interrupted, aware that Drew Hartwell was standing only a few feet away from me, his own cell clutched to his ear, having a not dissimilar conversation. I could hear him telling whoever was on the other end of the phone, "Well, for one thing, because I have other things to do right now than restore a century-old window you waited until the last minute to notice needed repairing. And for another, because I'm going to have to special-order the replacement glass, and there's no way it's going to get here before the rain does."

Except that Drew Hartwell didn't look particularly worried. He never did. Even now his free hand—the one not holding his phone—had crept beneath his well-worn, sun-faded Little Bridge Island Bocce League T-shirt to scratch lazily at his flat stomach, unconsciously revealing a trail of dark, downy hair that disappeared into the waistband of his cargo shorts . . . the sight of which caused my stomach to give a pleasant lurch, as if I'd just taken a spin on a Tilt-A-Whirl.

What was wrong with me?

Realizing I was staring, I glanced hastily away, remembering the whispered warning my coworker Angela Fairweather had given me on my first day of work: "Stay away from that one. There was a time when that old pickup of his was parked in front of a different house every week. For a while, it was a different house a *night*."

Because apparently Drew Hartwell—with his lean six-foot frame, tousled dark hair, permanent deep-sea tan, and summer-sky blue eyes—was as much of a player as Caleb and his friends, just of a different variety: Drew was the homegrown style.

Having been born on Little Bridge Island, Drew had never lived anywhere else, with the exception of a few years on the mainland.

Whereas Caleb and his best friend, Kyle—who'd turned my entire life upside down in a single moment—had been born in New York City and had traveled all over the world, thanks to their trust funds and wealthy parents.

And yet Caleb still didn't know a thing about women. Or at least the one he was currently speaking to.

"I can tell your mom that you're fine all you want, Sabrina," Caleb was saying into my ear. "But she isn't going to stop calling. She said to tell you that she thinks it's time you stopped being so stubborn and gave up on this little solo adventure to find yourself, or whatever it is, and come home. And that it shouldn't take a Category Five hurricane for you to realize it."

I smiled wryly. It sounded exactly like something my mom would say. "Well, do me a favor and let her know that I haven't quite finished finding myself, but when I do, she'll be the first to know. In the meantime, I'm perfectly capable of taking care of myself. I don't need help from her, or anybody else—especially you."

"Well, that's just great, Sabrina." Now Caleb sounded offended. "Excuse me for caring. You know, last time I talked to you, you were mad at me for not caring *enough*—"

I felt a different kind of spurt from my gut, far less pleasant than the one I'd experienced at the sight of Drew's naked stomach. "That's not what I said, and you know it. There's a difference between not caring and calling me a liar."

"I never called you a liar, Sabrina. I just said that maybe you were overreacting—"

"Overreacting? Really, Caleb?"

"Yes, overreacting. You know Kyle gets a little frisky when he's had too much to drink—"

A little frisky? I was so mad, I had to force myself to gaze past the harbor, out where the turquoise blue sky met the aquamarine sea, in order to steady myself. Something about the sight of that calm, azure water stretching as far as the eye could see always seemed to help me find my equilibrium. I'd taken to painting it during my time off from work—not, however, when anyone else was around—and it always soothed me.

"I don't want to get into it again, Caleb," I said. "I need to go back to my job, or I'll lose it."

"Oh, wouldn't that be a tragedy," Caleb sneered. "Your *waitressing* job at some *beach* bar in *Florida*."

I glanced hastily in Drew Hartwell's direction, fearful that he might have overheard—Caleb could be as overbearingly loud on the phone as he was in person.

But fortunately, Drew still seemed preoccupied with his own call.

"At least," I hissed at Caleb through gritted teeth, "I *have* a job."

"Oh, was that supposed to be a blow to my ego, Sabrina?" Caleb said snarkily. "Because I've never had a job, I'm somehow inferior to you? Excuse me for not rising to the bait. Look, if you won't come with me, at least let me send you a ticket for a commercial flight, since you can't seem to be bothered to buy one on your own."

"Don't even try it," I snarled into the phone, "because I'm not leaving Little Bridge Island. And it's Bree now, not Sabrina."

Then I hung up on him.

CHAPTER TWO

A hurricane is a rotating storm system that begins over the ocean and can span hundreds of miles across, at the center of which is a region of low pressure called an eye, from which rain bands spiral outward.

It wasn't until I was jamming my phone back into the pocket of my jeans that I realized how quiet it had gotten all of a sudden. I couldn't hear anything except that Drew Hartwell's conversation had ceased . . . and that his gaze was no longer on the harbor in front of us, but on me.

It was difficult to tell given the slant of the sun—it was shining full on into his face, and I'd left my sunglasses inside—but he appeared to be smiling, that sardonic smile for which Drew Hartwell was well known, and about which Angela had also warned me. I couldn't tell how much of my conversation he'd overheard.

Oh God, I thought, my heart thumping. Don't let it have been too much.

"First hurricane?" he asked.

I bristled. "What? No."

The last thing you wanted was for one of these native islanders to accuse you of being "Fresh Water"—new to the place. They took great joy in informing tourists that "conch"—a shellfish and local delicacy, served fried at the Mermaid in sandwiches, on salads, and on their own, hush-puppy style—was pronounced "konk" and not "konch," and that there were man-eating sharks along the reef, where tourists loved to snorkel (though the truth was that the sharks ate only other fish and were extremely shy, and there'd been only one reported shark attack in the past fifty years, and that had been when a tourist, showing off, had attacked the shark first).

Getting a sunburn or mosquito bite was a sure sign that you were "Fresh Water." All native-born Little Bridge Islanders woke up and applied SPF 100 and several layers of mosquito repellant first thing after showering. This was how they managed to avoid both melanoma and the various mosquito-borne illnesses that had been running rampant in South Florida for centuries. Whenever a beet-red, mosquito-stung tourist limped into the café, even my self-absorbed teenage coworker Nevaeh would shake her head and murmur, "Oh, poor thing."

Which was why I lied to Drew Hartwell.

"I went through Wilhelmina when I, uh, first moved here."

"Oh, Wilhelmina," he said, and nodded at the memory of the fierce Category 3 storm that a decade earlier had done so much damage.

I didn't mention that at the time I'd been sixteen and living in my parents' vacation rental, and that at the first hint of wind my mother had insisted on evacuating us to an exclusive resort and spa outside of Miami, where we'd ridden through the outer rain bands of the storm in a three-bedroom suite with full power, room service, and our own butler.

Technically, I'd still gone through Hurricane Wilhelmina . . . just not the way Drew Hartwell thought I had.

"So. You going to evacuate?" he asked.

"I wasn't planning on it," I said. "Though people in my family seem to think I should." I gestured toward my pocket to indicate my phone.

He nodded again.

"Family," he muttered, squinting at the horizon. He said it as if it were a dirty word.

It wasn't a total mystery to me why. Angela's warning about Drew Hartwell had been echoed by Nevaeh as well, just not for the same reasons. "He's crazy," Nevaeh had said.

And Nevaeh (Heaven spelled backward) would know, since Drew Hartwell was her uncle. It had been weeks before I'd learned that the only reason Nevaeh considered her uncle crazy was not because he'd done anything particularly outlandish, but because he'd once had a thriving carpentry career up north, which had included a partnership in a fledgling historic restoration company in "NoDo" (Nevaeh's grasp of Manhattan real estate was slim).

And yet he'd given it all up in order to move back to the island.

"Who would do something so nuts?" Nevaeh had asked me one morning as we were wrapping forks, knives, and spoons into paper napkins. "Who would leave an amazing life in New York City to come back here?"

I'd known what she was doing—fishing around for my reason for having done exactly that—but I didn't fall for it. Nevaeh was one of the biggest gossips in the café, which was forgivable, since she was fifteen and only working in the diner for the summer because its owners, Lucy and Ed Hartwell, were her great-aunt and uncle. For reasons that had never been fully explained to me, Nevaeh was living with her aunt and uncle instead of her parents, Drew Hartwell's sister and a man who was, according to Nevaeh, a famous baseball player who was someday going to come back and take her away from "all of this."

I'd said only, "Well, I'm sure your uncle Drew had his reasons for leaving the city," and left it at that.

But I'd been unable to keep from wondering myself, especially since the woman with whom Drew had moved back to Little Bridge from New York had apparently had trouble with the adjustment. Nevaeh had kept a sharp eye on her, envying while at the same time scorning her "big city" ways ("I heard she buys this special pink salt that comes all the way from Europe and costs twenty dollars a bottle. Who needs twenty-dollar European pink salt?" Nevaeh had shaken her head in wonder. "What makes it so much better than plain old white American salt?").

Drew was building his own house on beachside property left to him by his parents (who'd died under circumstances nearly as mysterious as Nevaeh's living arrangements . . . or at least, mysterious to me).

It wasn't long before rumors began to circulate that all was not well between him and Leighanne (the big-city girlfriend) out there on Sandy Point Beach.

"I heard she can't take the heat," Nevaeh informed me one morning as we were refilling ketchup bottles. "I mean, literally. Uncle Drew hasn't got the air-conditioning system installed yet. He says he might not install one at all. He doesn't like air-conditioning."

I was appalled. "It was eighty-five degrees last night. I wouldn't be able to sleep without AC."

Nevaeh nodded. "It's more than just that, though. I hear she's got island fever."

"Island fever?"

"It's like claustrophobia. It happens to people who can't stand living so far from the mainland. They have to get out. Just watch. Leighanne's gonna dump him and move back to New York. I already warned him, but does he listen to me? Nope."

A few weeks later, that's exactly what Leighanne did do—in a dramatic fashion we all got to witness, since she chose to do it at the café, storming in during the height of the breakfast rush and hurling a small object at Drew's chest as he sat at his usual place at the counter, sipping his coffee and reading the sports page of the local paper.

"Here," Leighanne had shouted. "You can have your damn keys back. I won't be needing them anymore."

Drew had looked confused . . . even more so when the

next thing she'd hurled at him was, of all things, a saltshaker. I knew this because I'd been standing beside him holding two orders of huevos rancheros when the object struck him in the chest, then landed at my feet, miraculously unbroken. The shaker was empty, except for a slight tinge of pink at the bottom.

"And you can have that back, too," Leighanne had shouted. "I don't want anything of yours. And you'll never have to worry about putting up with anything of mine again."

Then she'd turned and stormed from the restaurant, the glossy brown curls beneath her straw cowboy hat bobbing, while Drew only sat there, looking mildly astonished. At least until Nevaeh, now worried that she was losing her glamorous potential aunt-to-be forever, had cried, "Well, don't just sit there, Uncle Drew. Go after her!"

But Drew had chosen not to—which had probably been for the best, since even if he'd tried, it would have been too late, given the possible case of island fever. As Leighanne sped off, all of us could see that the back of her Mini Cooper was piled high with her belongings, most likely not only including the infamous salt, but also the heart that she'd reclaimed from him.

So I could understand why "Uncle Drew" might feel a little down on family at the moment, especially since Nevaeh had spent the better part of the following week bitterly informing anyone who would listen, "I told him she was going to dump him if he wasn't more careful. I told him!"

That didn't give Drew the right, however, to swing his unnervingly blue gaze on me and say what he did next, which was, "Although in your case, your family is right. You should evacuate, Fresh Water."

I was so stunned, I couldn't even summon up a suitably stinging retort before he turned and headed coolly back indoors to his breakfast.

Where did he get off, I wondered as I stood there, open-mouthed in the early morning heat, suggesting I couldn't handle myself in a hurricane? He barely even knew me. After three months of serving breakfast to him nearly every day—Spanish omelet, café con leche, no sugar—this was the longest conversation we'd ever had.

True, he'd always been a generous tipper—30 percent, and cash, even when he'd paid for the meal by credit card.

But still.

Maybe, I told myself as I grasped the handle to the café's side door, it wasn't that Drew thought I couldn't handle a hurricane, but that I'd been there to witness his humiliating breakup. Some men could be sensitive about things like that.

Although I had to admit, he'd never seemed too upset about it. I'd seen at least half a dozen attractive young women walk up to him in the café since and inform him that they had plenty of "salt" for his "shaker" anytime he needed some . . . not that he appeared to have taken any of them up on it, so far as I could tell.

It was tough to keep a secret in a place as small as Little Bridge. Though I'd managed to keep mine.

Back inside, the air felt pleasantly cool and scented with the smell of freshly cooked bacon, as it did every morning.

Something was wrong, however. I sensed it as soon as I walked in. The usual early morning sounds to which I'd grown so accustomed—the scrape of forks against plates, and the low murmur of conversation as folks discussed the headlines in the local paper—were gone.

For a second, I was worried I really had been fired—Ed was as well known for his fiery temper as he was for his ability to bake a truly outstanding key lime pie—but a glance at Angela's and Nevaeh's faces showed me this wasn't the case. Instead of looking at me, everyone's attention was glued to both of the television sets that hung from the ceiling, one at each end of the breakfast counter. Ed kept one tuned to Fox News, and the other to CNN, both with the sound off and closed captioning on. This seemed to keep all customers happy.

But today, out of deference to the storm, both televisions were tuned to the Weather Channel, with the sound up.

That's how I was able to hear the meteorologists announce that Hurricane Marilyn was making a turn, and now appeared to be heading straight for Little Bridge Island.

CHAPTER THREE

The high winds of a hurricane sweeping across the ocean can produce a dangerous storm surge, a wall of water that can cause massive flooding even hundreds of miles inland.

Some people like to say that Little Bridge Island was discovered by the Spanish in 1513, but of course that isn't true. You can't "discover" something that's already been occupied for thousands of years before you ever even got there. Little Bridge, a small island in a chain of similar islands off the coast of the tip of Florida known as the Florida Keys, was home to the Tequesta Indians for many centuries before the Spanish invaded it. The Indians were enslaved, and eventually the Keys were turned into U.S. territory.

Little Bridge got its name due to the fact that it's connected to the rest of the Keys by a bridge.

But since most of the Keys are connected to one another by bridges, it makes no sense that Little Bridge is named after the fact that it has a bridge.

But that's part of its quirky appeal, and probably what drew my father to it when he was a young man and began planning our family vacations. He liked quirky places, and Little Bridge, with its odd name and even odder residents, is one of the quirkiest.

So Little Bridge was where we vacationed every year, even though my mother was pretty vocal about the fact that she'd have preferred to go somewhere more cosmopolitan, such as the Hamptons, Paris, or Ibiza.

But like my father, I grew to love our vacation house on the canal, waking to the smell of the salt water, finding manatees drinking from the hose of our dock, watching egrets pluck their delicate way through the sand. I loved boating, the rush of wind through my hair, the glassy stillness of the water near the sandbars, the challenge of painting that water, making it look as mirrorlike and gleaming on my canvas as it did in real life.

And of course walking through the quaint, sun-drenched town, the historic buildings—by law none were allowed to be more than two stories tall, because anything higher might impede a neighbor's view of the sunset—each painted a different shade of pink or blue or yellow, stopping for ice cream or groceries at the locally owned shops. I could see why my father loved Little Bridge, why he would have moved there if his job as a successful defense attorney in Manhattan—and my mother's dislike of the town—hadn't made such a dream impossible.

I loved it, too. I felt safe in Little Bridge—not that, back then, I had any reason to feel unsafe anywhere.

It made perfect sense to me that it was to Little Bridge that I fled when my safety felt threatened. My father—if he hadn't passed away last year—would have understood.

But now the new comfortable, safe life I'd put so carefully together seemed to be crumbling. I knew it the minute I walked into my apartment after I got off work and found my roommate, Daniella, throwing clothes into a suitcase.

"Where are you going?" I asked, though I had a sinking feeling I already knew. "You're not evacuating, are you?"

"Sure am." She took a slurp from the frozen margarita she'd poured herself. I'd seen the pitcher from the blender sitting on the kitchen counter as I'd walked into the two-bedroom apartment we shared.

The place was tiny—each of the bedrooms hardly large enough to fit a queen-size bed—but I considered myself lucky to have found it . . . not the place so much as the person who'd come with it.

A curvaceous, good-humored ER nurse, Daniella was outgoing and bubbly—exactly the kind of person I needed to be around after what I'd gone through this past year back in New York, just like the job at the Mermaid was exactly the kind of job I needed now. I was up and out the door by five thirty every morning, even on my days off, since Gary was used to being fed that early and woke me like clockwork daily at dawn.

This worked out well since Daniella was a morning person, too—not to mention extremely social. She seemed to be friends with nearly everyone on the island, which wasn't surprising: at some point, she'd either given a stitch, shot, X-ray, or bandage to nearly all of them.

That's how she'd snagged her two-bedroom rental for such a (comparatively) low rate: because she'd treated the landlady's son for chronic asthma. Two-bedroom apartments were rare on Little Bridge—at least ones that were affordable to locals, since most living spaces on the island proper had been snatched up by vacation rental companies and were hawked at astronomical prices online to tourists.

But since our landlady, Lydia, like most people, adored Daniella, she rented to her at a discount.

"Mandatory evac for all city employees," Dani was explaining to me, with her usual infallible cheer. "That includes the hospital. I've been reassigned to beautiful, sunny, downtown Coral Gables."

"Coral Gables?" I lifted Gary, who'd rushed over to give me his customary greeting (sprawling supine at my feet, then rubbing his face all over my shoes), and took a seat. "That makes no sense. Why would they send you to Coral Gables when the hurricane is supposed to be headed here?"

"You're asking for local bureaucracy to make sense?" Daniella let out a delighted laugh. Dani found everything delightful, even medical emergencies. She loved making sick people feel better. "You should know better than that by now, Bree!" Then she sobered and said, "No, but really, it's because they don't want people thinking it's safe to stay here. If they know hospital and emergency services will still be staffed and up and running, no one will leave, because they'll be lulled into a false sense of security. So all of us—ER staff, police, the firehouse—have been assigned to work at hurricane shelters out of the direct path of the eye. They hope that by doing this, the good citizens of this fine isle will follow. They're sending us all out on buses later this afternoon. Which is why I'm drinking this." She wagged her margarita at me. "I don't have to drive."

I stared glumly at the sunlight streaming in through her bedroom window. Given the blue sky and steamy temperature outside, it was hard to believe any sort of storm was on its way.

But the Weather Channel, blaring in the other room, was telling a different story, as were the dozens of text messages piling up on my phone, many from Caleb. And my mother.

"What's bugging you?" Dani asked. "You're not upset about this hurricane, are you? Chances are it will lose a ton of steam over Cuba, you know. It's a terrible thing to say, and poor Cuba, but that's usually what happens. We'll just get a lot of wind and rain. But they have to evacuate us anyway, you know, just in case."

I smiled wanly at her.

"Not the storm," I said. "Just . . . whatever. My ex called earlier and offered to come pick me up in his private plane."

Dani, who knew most of what had happened between me and Cal—though not the most sordid details, which were hard for me to discuss—almost spat out the sip of margarita she'd taken. "I hope you told him to stick his plane where the sun don't shine!"

"Of course I did. Well, not in so many words. But I kind

of regret it now that everybody's evacuating. Drew Hartwell even told me I should go. He called me Fresh Water."

Now Dani did spit, or looked as if she wanted to, at least. "Drew Hartwell can kiss my butt. He thinks he's God's gift to the ladies. Hey, look, I've got an idea. Why don't you come with me? They're getting us all hotel rooms. I'm sure it will be super nice. Last time they put us up at the Westin. It had a pool and a generator and everything. And, oh my God, there were these firemen from Key West—you won't believe how we partied. It was like *The Bachelorette,* but on steroids."

I smiled again, but less wanly. "Thanks, but I can't. I've got this guy to worry about."

We both eyed Gary, who'd crawled off my lap and was now sniffing the side of Daniella's suitcase suspiciously. He either knew something was going on or was looking for a new place to curl up and sleep. Knowing Gary, it was the latter. His survival instincts weren't exactly stellar. A middle-aged gray tabby cat who had spent years living in an animal shelter farther up the Keys before I'd come along and adopted him, he wanted only to be in the presence of human beings at all times, no matter what they were doing . . . even something as mundane as packing.

"Bring him along," Daniella suggested. "I'm sure the hotel's pet friendly. Or, if not, we can smuggle him in."

"Thanks," I said. "But you know Gary doesn't exactly travel well."

It was true. Gary howled up a storm when in moving vehicles, even when medicated, and a four-hour bus ride to the mainland with him sounded like one of the circles of hell.

"And besides, I don't want to sponge off the city's dime. I'd feel guilty."

"Oh for God's sake." Daniella leaned over to sweep some jewelry off her dressing table and into a pouch. The minute her back was turned, Gary leaped into her suitcase and began sniffing the inside. "The administration said it was okay for first responders to bring their families on the bus, and into their hotel rooms. You're the closest thing I've got to family around here."

"Aw." I was genuinely touched . . . though relieved that she hadn't noticed what Gary was doing now, which was pawing through the clothes she'd neatly folded into the suitcase, in order to make himself a comfortable place to sleep. I stepped toward the bed and swiftly lifted his nearly twenty-pound girth from the suitcase, as he let out a tiny squeak of protest, then plopped him on the floor. "That's sweet. But I think Gary and I would be better off here, especially given his recent medical issues."

Daniella frowned, but I could tell she agreed with me. I hadn't meant to adopt a cat as needy as Gary, whose personality was a joy but whose health, from having spent so many years on the streets and then in the shelter, was a wreck. Just a week earlier I'd ended up shelling out twelve hundred dollars for the removal of every last one of his teeth due to his having something called feline stomatitis, a painful inflammation of the mouth.

And while he already seemed to be on the mend, in a lot

less pain (and a lot less smelly), I was in no hurry to take him on a weekend jaunt out of town, hurricane or no hurricane. He was still on antibiotics and several other medications and could eat only soft canned foods that I carefully mashed for him.

But it was all worth it. At night, after thoroughly grooming himself and making a careful inspection of the entire apartment, he climbed onto my bed, curled up close to me, and dozed off.

And for the first time since that last morning with Caleb, I was finally able to get a good night's sleep. It seemed to me that this was only because of the sweet, heavy, purring warmth beside me.

I hadn't wanted to mention any of this to Caleb, let alone my mother or any of my other friends back home. Only my dad, a fellow animal lover, would have understood.

But Dad was gone now.

Daniella looked down at Gary as he wandered over toward her laundry basket full of dirty clothes, sniffed it, then leaped inside, molding a soft nest out of her scrubs, pajamas, and underwear from the day before while purring so loudly we could both hear him.

"I get it," Dani said. "He's your boy, and he's not really travel ready at the moment, storm or no storm."

I smiled at her gratefully. She really was the perfect roommate. She'd been fine with my asking if it would be all right if I got a cat (my first, since my mom had never wanted animals in the house. "So dirty!" she always said. "And they scratch up the furniture"). Gary had instantly won Daniella over with his big green eyes, foot-to-face-rub greetings, and constant purring.

"But," she said, returning to her packing, "if you change your mind, you can always take my car and come up. It doesn't have much gas in it, but I'll leave it parked over at the hospital with the keys under the visor anyway. Otherwise I'd say grab a rental car, but I heard the tourists snaked all of those in a panic to get out of here early this morning."

"Oh. Well, thanks, Dani. I might take you up on that." I doubted I would, actually, but a car low on gas was better than no car at all.

As if she'd read my mind, Dani said, "Lots of people stay, you know, Bree, even with mandatory evacs. Locals worry about looters and want to guard their homes or businesses, or they're sick, or have loved ones who are sick, like your boy Gary, or they can't afford to leave, or whatever. Evacuating is expensive. If you want to stay, you'll be totally fine. Even though the hospital will be closed, there'll be plenty of people around, even a skeleton crew of emergency responders." She gave a mischievous grin. "But of course, a couple firehouses are going to be stationed up with us. I'm looking forward to meeting some fresh probies."

Smiling, I rolled my eyes. Daniella often complained that dating apps were useless on such a small island—you basically ended up having already slept with everyone or being colleagues with the rest. The only way to meet anyone new was to travel or hook up with tourists.

I didn't suffer from that problem—not because I was new to the island, but because I was on a dating hiatus. I wasn't sure when, or if, my lady parts would ever be open again for business.

"But, hey, this place—" Dani thumped the side of her fist against the bedroom wall. "Solid concrete. Once Sonny gets the shutters on, it'll be like a fortress. So you're good here."

Sonny Petrovich was our landlady Lydia's son, a boy who was so extremely fond of video games that he would talk to you about them ad nauseum if you expressed the slightest enthusiasm, so I'd learned it was best not to.

"The only thing you have to worry about," she went on, "is flooding."

"Flooding?"

"Yeah. I wasn't living here then, but I heard it happened during Hurricane Wilhelmina—not too bad, only a foot. But Lydia had to replace the fridge and stove and stuff—"

I stared at her. *Flooding?*

"But every hurricane's different," Daniella went on. "Some are rain events, some are wind. You just never know. If it's only wind, you're golden in this place."

"I think," I said, getting up, "I'll just go check my messages."

"Yeah." Daniella nodded. "You should. Also, you should probably go to the store and buy some supplies before they run out, just in case. Like bottled water. And food for Gary. And alcohol. I have a list the Red Cross gave us to hand out to people. Alcohol's not on it, of course, but I wouldn't even go through a tropical storm without tequila, let alone a hurricane."

I took the paper she plucked from the top of her dresser.

Many of the things we already had—canned goods, bread, a manual can opener. But others—flashlight, batteries—it had never occurred to me to purchase. Daniella must have read my expression since she laughed and said, "I have all that stuff in the closet by the kitchen. Bought it for the last storm that headed our way, then never used it because it veered out to sea. You just might want to buy fresh batteries. But you're welcome to the rest of the stuff."

I felt relief wash over me. "Thanks, Dani. You're a lifesaver. Literally!" Suddenly overwhelmed by how lucky I was to have found a roommate—and friend—like her, merely by answering an ad, I added, "I'm going to miss you."

"I'm going to miss you, too," she said, and opened her arms to give me one of her "Dani hugs," which she handed out frequently at the hospital (but never, she'd informed me, to the "drunk frat boys during spring break." Even Dani had her limits).

And then she was gone. Her last words to me were to be sure to look after her sourdough starter—Daniella was an avid baker—that she'd inherited from her grandmother, but which would spoil in the fridge if the power went out.

I swore I would.

She'd barely been out of the apartment for five minutes before I became convinced that I was never going to see her again.

CHAPTER FOUR

If your community calls for a mandatory evacuation, heed the warning.

I was being ridiculous. The reason I felt so down was because the apartment seemed so dark and lonely after Dani left. She was such a bright and energetic force.

Also it was *literally* dark, since Sonny Petrovich had come around outside and begun to shutter the windows with large stainless steel planks, each one of which had to be drilled into place along runners that were secured onto the walls of the apartment building with a number of long screws.

I kept the Weather Channel on for company as I ate lunch—leftover chicken salad from the café—though it was hard to hear over Sonny's drilling.

I soon regretted it. Not the salad, the news.

Because according to the news, everyone who lived in South Florida who did not immediately evacuate from the area was going to die.

Not only die, but die in a variety of ways, most likely

from drowning in the tidal surge Hurricane Marilyn was bringing with it, and also from the destructive force of its 170-mile-per-hour winds.

The forecasters couldn't be sure, since there was no power or communication in Saint Martin or the Virgin Islands or anywhere else Hurricane Marilyn had already struck, but they were predicting that hundreds in the storm's apocalyptic path were probably already dead, and that those who did not get out of its way now would soon be dead as well.

Since this seemed like information I could do without, I switched off the television and opened my laptop. I had dozens of emails and social media messages from friends and relatives wondering if it was true that I had not evacuated and if so, why not. My phone was the same way, only with text messages and voice mails.

Most of them were from my mother. Each held a note of mounting hysteria. Classic Justine Beckham:

> I think you should know that the governor of Florida has just issued a statement that anyone who doesn't evacuate from your area had better write their Social Security number on their arm so that their bodies can be identified after the storm.

My mom had always known how to lay on the drama. It was one of the reasons her radio show was number one in her time slot, even though it was about legal advice.

> I don't know what you're thinking turning down Caleb's generous offer. I know you're angry with him, but what happened wasn't his fault. Kyle was drunk—did you know he's in rehab now? You can't hold Caleb responsible for the actions of his friends. You of all people should know this, considering you went to law school—not, of course, that you bothered to finish.

Wow, Justine. Way to turn the knife.

That was interesting about Kyle, though. I hadn't known he'd gone to rehab. That was big. Huge, even.

Although it didn't change anything, it actually made me feel a little better. If Kyle was in rehab, it meant he couldn't come after me again. I'd sleep even better now, knowing this, despite the coming storm.

I wondered why Caleb hadn't mentioned it, although it didn't take a genius to know why: because then he'd have to admit his friend wasn't perfect after all, and that he'd been wrong to say I'd "overreacted" about what had happened.

Unfortunately, my mother went on:

> And I know you think you don't need to listen to me anymore after that ridiculous genealogy test. But there are some bonds that are stronger than DNA, Sabrina. What about the fact that I carried you around in my womb for nine months, and breast-fed you for six? Do those things count for nothing?

I hit delete without listening to the rest. I'd heard enough. I loved my mother—and I did consider her my mother, even if we weren't genetically related. She was the woman who'd given birth to me and raised me.

But sometimes she was a little much.

Since it was hard to concentrate on anything with all the drilling going on outside—and the throbbing going on in my head now that I'd listened to Justine's messages—I decided to go to the store to buy the supplies Daniella had recommended.

So, after carefully checking that Sonny was not right outside my bathroom window—he was a sweet boy, and not at all the Peeping Tom type, but I didn't want to flagrantly strip in front of him—I showered, washing the smell of bacon from my shoulder-length pink hair (it had been blond for most of my life, but on impulse I'd asked Daniella to help me dye it: new life, new hair), then changed from my work clothes into shorts and a T-shirt, and finally opened the front door to my apartment.

Sonny was carefully drilling a precut steel shutter to the front window of my apartment. The sunshine poured brightly into the front courtyard—my apartment was one of three other identical two-bedrooms, all built in Spanish-style stucco around a single decoratively tiled courtyard, in the center of which grew a large frangipani tree, currently in full bloom.

Gary, who could not resist any opportunity to both lounge in the sun and greet a visitor, darted past me to fling himself against Sonny's bare legs.

"Oh, hi, Bree." Sonny bent down to stroke Gary's ears. "Did you hear about the new version of *Battlefront?* They just put a new edition out this week. I'm already up to level sixty-eight."

"No," I said. "I can't say I knew about that. I'm more concerned about this hurricane. Do you think it's going to hit us?"

"Oh, no," Sonny said dismissively, straightening up. "But my mom is making us evacuate to Orlando anyway."

"But you don't think it's coming here?" I felt the alarm I'd been experiencing since watching the news—and listening to my mom's message—growing. Maybe I was making a terrible mistake. Maybe all the people who'd left me those messages, including my mother, were right.

Except that, honestly, what did they know? None of them lived in the cone of uncertainty, or even knew what one was, really. If Drew Hartwell wasn't evacuating (and he didn't seem to be), why should I?

"Well, we were going to go to Orlando anyway," Sonny explained. "They have a new park devoted to *Star Wars*. I want to see that! You know I'm up to level sixty-eight in *Battlefront?*"

"Yeah," I said. "You mentioned that. So when are you two leaving?"

"Later tonight, I guess," Sonny said. "As soon as she can find some gas. You know there's no gas anywhere on the island? Except maybe the Shell over by the high school, she says. But there's a three-hour wait."

Oh. Well, so much for using Dani's car. The impending

gasoline shortage was a problem they'd mentioned on the Weather Channel, but I hadn't thought it was something that would affect Little Bridge . . . until now. A previous but much less powerful hurricane that had hit Texas and the Gulf side of Florida the week before had been causing fuel shortages all up and down the Keys and throughout much of the Southeast. I supposed I should feel lucky that the scooter I drove required only three dollars' worth of fuel to fill the tank.

Not that you could evacuate from a Category 5 hurricane on a scooter. Well, you could, but you wouldn't get very far.

"Wow," I said to Sonny. "That's tough. But I'm sure you two will get out of here in plenty of time."

"Oh, yes," Sonny said, looking unconcerned. "Hey, you can come if you want."

"What?" I was shocked. "With you and your mom? To Orlando?"

"Yeah, why not? It will be a lot of fun! You like rides, don't you?"

"Um." If it had been any other guy, I'd have suspected him of hitting on me. But Sonny genuinely only cared about rides and games—of the amusement park variety. "That's so sweet of you. Thanks so much for the offer. But I can't, I'm afraid. I have to stay here to take care of Gary."

He looked down at my cat, who now was lounging in the shade of the frangipani, Gary's favorite place in the whole world, outside of my bed. A gecko—there were thousands, maybe millions of geckos, all over Little Bridge. You couldn't seem to walk a foot down the sidewalk without nearly stepping on one of the small, fast-moving lizards—darted toward Gary, who swiped a lazy paw at it. The gecko darted safely away.

"Oh, right," Sonny said. "They don't allow pets at Disney. Or at least, not the hotel where we're staying. That's why we've got to leave R2-D2 and C-3PO at home."

R2-D2 and C-3PO were Sonny's pet guinea pigs, of which he was not only inordinately fond, but quite proud. He spent hours every day brushing and caring for them.

"But you have someone to look after them while you're gone, don't you?" I asked.

"Oh, yes," he said. "My cousin Sean said he'd come over. He can't evacuate because he works for the electric company, and they need him here to turn the electricity back on if it goes out."

I knew Sonny's cousin Sean Petrovich. He performed the more complicated repairs around the building.

"Oh, good," I said. "Well, I'll look forward to seeing him around. And thanks for putting up our shutters. I'm headed to the store right now. Can I get you something there as a way of saying thank you?"

"Sure, orange soda," he said, brightening. "If they have it? And Sour Patch Kids."

"Oh, sure. Can do. Come on, Gary." I hoisted the cat up from the shade of the frangipani, though he let out a squeak of protest. "You have to go inside while I'm at the store."

"I'll watch him while you're away," Sonny offered. "I'm just gonna be right here."

I lifted a hand to shade my eyes from the strong summer sun as I studied his earnest expression. "Are you sure?" It was something Sonny had done several times before while working around the building, without incident, but never while a violent hurricane was sitting a thousand miles offshore.

"Yeah," Sonny said, nodding vehemently. "I like Gary. And Gary likes me."

This was true. Although it was also true that Gary liked everyone, including the postal and newspaper delivery persons, all of my neighbors, the exterminator, and anyone else who happened to wander through the courtyard gate.

What was even more true was that Gary, like me, had been hurt . . . but he was healing. He'd chosen me at the shelter just as much as I'd chosen him, shuffling toward me and butting his head against my feet as if to say, "Hey, down here. Look at me. I'm needy, but I'm also needed. You need me as much as I need you."

Because it had turned out to be true. And together, we were forging a new life, learning to trust when we each had so much reason not to.

"Well," I said to Sonny. "Okay. I'll leave my door open, so he can come inside if he gets hungry or thirsty. And feel free to help yourself to anything you find in my fridge, too, while I'm gone. Except the beige stuff in the pitcher. My roommate bakes with that. You probably wouldn't like it."

Sonny nodded appreciatively. He was beginning to sweat in the midafternoon sun. "Thanks, Bree."

I smiled as I headed toward the front gate. One of the

reasons I loved Little Bridge so much was because you could do things like this—leave your beloved cat and apartment in the care of your handyman, and not worry about it, whereas in New York this would never happen. Well, maybe it would, but not in my experience.

This was one of the many reasons for my leaving the city.

But now, given what seemed to be headed our way, I was wondering if I'd made the right decision.

CHAPTER FIVE

Have supplies on hand to help with everything you might need before, during, and after a hurricane.

Emergency Disaster Survival Kit Basics—Food

Gas or charcoal for the grill (warning: never use a grill inside)
Manual can opener
Nonperishable foods and beverages—7–10 days per person
Drinking water—at least 1 gallon per person per day
Plastic plates, cups, and utensils
Don't forget food/water for pets and babies!

The sun was still shining brightly when I headed out for Frank's Food Emporium to buy my hurricane supplies—on my purple no-speed bike with its large front basket, since I wanted to save what little gas was left in my scooter—Daniella's list tucked in my hip pocket. I'd convinced myself after the two o'clock bulletin from the National Weather Service that we probably weren't going to get anything but a few rain bands, but it wouldn't hurt to be prepared.

Except that maybe the locals knew something I didn't. As I pedaled along, I saw evidence that Little Bridge residents were preparing for an all-out weather catastrophe. Along the main thoroughfare businesses were boarding up, literally hammering boards over their plate-glass display windows. The pharmacy had already pulled down its metal gates. Only a small handwritten sign on the door indicated that it was still open.

And once inside Frank's, I was in for a surprise: the shelves had the same barren look of shops in apocalyptic films and television shows after they'd been looted by survivors. Only this was real life.

"You're just in time," a familiar voice said, and I turned to see Lucy Hartwell, Drew's aunt and the owner of the Mermaid Café, waving a bag of chips at me. "Last one. You want it?"

I felt a sudden and overwhelming longing for the chips, though they hadn't been on my list. "Yes . . . unless you do."

"I've got plenty." She pointed down at her shopping cart. She did, indeed, have plenty. Seven, to be exact, of many varieties, including jalapeño and rippled. And over a dozen bottles of wine, as well.

She must have noticed my surprise, since she laughed and said, "I'm having a hurricane party tonight for everyone who isn't evacuating. I take it you're one of those, since I saw your name is still on the schedule for breakfast service tomorrow morning."

Unlike some restaurant owners I'd met, Lucy Hartwell was hands-on, paying attention to everything that went on at the café, from the workers' schedules to which of Little Bridge's many local fishermen was selling the freshest yellowtail.

Part of this was due to the fact that she was related to most of her employees—and roughly half of the island's permanent residents—by either blood or marriage; the other part was simply because of her personality. Born Lucia Paz (according to café gossip) to one of the island's most prominent Cuban families, Lucy had apparently had her pick of suitors in her day, but for unknown reasons had settled on Ed Hartwell. Since the two had been married for over thirty years, it seemed to have been a good choice.

"Uh," I said, surprised to hear the restaurant was still going to be open even though a Category 5 hurricane was bearing down on it. "Sure. I mean, no, I'm not evacuating." I said this more to convince myself than Mrs. Hartwell. The store seemed so deserted. How had this happened, and so quickly? "Aren't you?"

"Oh, no," Mrs. Hartwell said with a laugh. "Ed would never hear of it. The last time we evacuated, looters from Miami broke into the café and stole the cash register."

I gasped. "Really? That's terrible!"

"Oh, it wasn't so bad. There was nothing in it. But they took the meat slicer, too. Now, what would anyone want with an industrial meat slicer? I always wondered. Unless they had their own restaurant. But what are the chances of that? Well, I suppose they pawned it. But, in any case, Ed's refused to evacuate ever since, so he could keep an eye on the place. So, we're staying, and tonight we're having a hurricane party. And you're coming."

It was a statement, not a question.

"Um, I'd love to." This wasn't a lie. Although I wasn't exactly a social butterfly, part of me was dying to come. The Hartwells' home was legendary, one of Little Bridge's premier estates, and I'd never before been inside. "May I bring anything?"

"Nothing," she said tartly, "except yourself. As you can see, I have plenty. Everyone still in town is going to be there."

"Still in town?"

"Well, everyone with children is evacuating, of course," she said. "And well they should—it would be irresponsible of them to take the chance of staying and then having this thing turn out to be worse than what they're reporting."

My eyes widened. Worse than a Category 5? According to the messages my mother had left me—all seven of them—there was nothing worse than that.

"And of course," Mrs. Hartwell went on, "anyone who lives in a home that isn't built to code—to withstand at least Category Three winds and a storm surge of up to ten feet—ought to be getting out or at least heading for one of the local shelters now. It's simply unthinkable not to."

Then what was I doing?

"But do you think it's going to be okay?" I asked, because

if Lucy Hartwell said something was going to be okay, it most definitely was.

"Not at all." She threw her head back with a laugh. "Cuba will give us some protection, of course." This was something all locals said, I was beginning to notice, like a mantra. The high mountaintops of Cuba often interfered with hurricanes churning for the Florida Keys, slowing their intensity by one or two categories. "But we're definitely in for a devil of a ride."

I must have looked even more alarmed, since she let out a cackle and said, "Don't worry! Last time this happened was Wilhelmina, and that was ages ago. We only lost power for a week or so."

"I . . . remember," I said, though of course all I remembered about Wilhelmina was that the gourmet pizzas at our hotel in Miami had been amazing.

"Where do you live again?" Mrs. Hartwell asked. I noticed that her mobile phone, attached to her belt like a workman's tool, had begun to buzz, but she ignored it.

"Oh. In the Havana Plaza apartments, over on Washington."

She nodded, clearly knowing the place. "Good, solid construction . . . will definitely hold up to hurricane-force winds. But that area is only at eight feet above sea level, so it floods. If things get bad, you'd better come to my place, sooner rather than later. I'm right up the hill from you, so it shouldn't be a problem."

Again, it was a statement, not a question.

"Oh, no." I felt slightly horrified. Who went to their boss's house in a hurricane? Especially when their boss was

Ed Hartwell, who'd probably throw you out for using a cell phone. "Thanks, Mrs. H, but I wouldn't want to impose—"

"What imposition?" She looked genuinely baffled. "We have a generator, we're at twenty feet above sea level, and the house has already stood up to over two hundred years' worth of hurricanes. Ed's great-great-grandfather, a ship captain, built it. Now, those fellows knew how to build a house. They built them of Dade County pine. It's extinct now, because every single one of those trees was chopped up to build houses around here and up and down the Florida Keys—some of the strongest wood known to man. You can hardly get a nail through it, so it stands up to high winds. You'll stay with us. It will be fine."

I couldn't help feeling touched. I'd only worked for this woman for a few months. She hardly knew me!

And yet her generosity—and that of her otherwise sour-tempered husband—was legendary around the café. Angela had already told me that if I stayed at the job for six months, I'd be offered health benefits—with vision and dental.

"Not the best plan." Angela, recently divorced, had moved back home with her mother and was working her way toward a business administration degree at the local community college. "But the best plan around here that anyone is offering, and that includes jobs with the city. I may keep working at the café even after I get my degree."

Now Mrs. Hartwell was offering me a bed in her own house in the event of catastrophic flooding.

I wondered how this kind trait had entirely skipped her nephew, who—except for his generous tipping—wasn't known for his friendliness. Then again, his uncle wasn't exactly the pleasantest man in the world, either.

"Please," I said, holding up a palm to stop Mrs. Hartwell. "I really couldn't. I have a rescue cat, and he just had oral surgery—"

Lucy Hartwell made another face.

"Oh, never mind about that. We love animals. Do you have any idea how many strays Nevaeh has volunteered to foster from the shelter? A parrot, a pair of rabbits, and a tortoise. And don't even get me started on those three mangy mutts of Drew's. Your cat will be fine. We'll find a nice private room for you, and the two of you will be snug as bugs."

So her nephew would be riding out the hurricane at his uncle's house, too? Interesting.

Well, it made sense. On the news they'd emphasized that those living on or near the shore would be given first priority in hurricane shelters, as they'd be most at risk of Marilyn's dangerous tidal surge and wind. Drew Hartwell, with his half-finished beach house, would fall into that category.

But of course he wouldn't go to a shelter when he could stay in his ancestral mansion.

"I really couldn't," I said firmly. "I already have a place. A . . . a hotel room, in Coral Gables, with my roommate. She's a nurse and got evacuated there by the city."

Mrs. Hartwell raised her eyebrows. "And when are you going there?"

"As soon as the café closes for the storm," I said. "I didn't want to leave you short staffed. My roommate left me her car to drive up." This last part, at least, wasn't exactly a lie.

Mrs. Hartwell continued to look skeptical, but said, lifting her buzzing phone, "Well, all right. Stop by tonight around eight for the party. You know where I live, right?"

Everyone knew where the Hartwells lived, but Mrs. Hartwell went on as if she didn't know this. "Top of Flagler Hill, white house with the blue shutters. You can't miss it."

Of course not. Mrs. Hartwell's home was a gorgeous and stately mansion on the top of the highest point of the island, a hill referred to as "Flagler Hill," after the builder of South Florida's first (and only) railroad, Henry Flagler. The railroad had been destroyed in 1935 by one of the fiercest (though unnamed) hurricanes in American history and had never been reconstructed. Hundreds of lives were lost.

But that had been in the days before Doppler radar, advanced warning, and hurricane shelters.

"I'll be there, Mrs. H," I promised.

"Lucy," she corrected me as she finally answered her buzzing phone.

"Lucy." But it didn't sound right in my mouth. She was as much Mrs. Hartwell as her husband was Ed. I simply couldn't think of her any other way.

"Oh, hi, Joanne," Mrs. Hartwell said, pushing her cart along. I was forgotten, for the time being. "Yes, eight tonight. What can you bring? Nothing except yourself."

Even though Mrs. Hartwell—Lucy—had said not to bring anything to her party, I shopped with it in mind, selecting even more food than I'd planned to from what few selections remained on the shelves. Who knew? Maybe I'd be invited to a lot of hurricane parties over the next few days. I wanted to contribute my fair share.

That's how I ended up back home with an odd assortment of the suggested canned goods from Daniella's list in addition to Sonny's orange soda and Sour Patch Kids (he was embarrassingly grateful), plus a vast array of charcuterie (apparently not many hurricane shoppers were looking for chianti-flavored salami), plus gourmet crackers, cheeses, and spreads. I might die during Hurricane Marilyn, but I'd definitely go out in style.

Plus I'd snagged the alcohol that Daniella had suggested (vodka, not tequila, since I'd never had a head for tequila), as well as a few bottles of champagne and a great many cans of cat food for Gary—as many as could fit into my bike basket, plus dangle in canvas totes over my handlebars. I didn't want Gary to go hungry, and who knew how long the grocery store would remain open? Even as I was leaving, I saw the owner's sons stacking plywood outside, getting ready to board it up.

What did remain open, however, were most of Little Bridge's many bars. My friend and fellow Mermaid coworker Angela waved to me from the beachside seating area of one as I rode by.

"Girlfriend! See you at the Hartwells' tonight!" she shouted excitedly, a cocktail in her hand.

"Yes, you will!" I shouted back at her.

This hurricane thing, I thought as I motored home, just might be fun.

It's almost laughable how wrong I turned out to be.

CHAPTER SIX

> Listen to local radio, read local papers, and tune in to social media from official sources before, during, and after the storm for important information.

Nearly the entirety of the news coverage that night was devoted to the approaching storm. Marilyn had grown so large that the width of its cone of uncertainty encompassed the entire state of Florida, which meant that people wishing to evacuate its path had to leave the state completely. Sonny and his mother were not going to be much safer in Orlando than they'd have been in Little Bridge.

But with fuel growing scarcer, and freeways already jammed, escape was mostly an impossibility. Images were shown of long lines of cars at the few still open gas stations, and of grocery store shelves emptied of food and bottled water.

A few ubiquitous shots were thrown in of homes and businesses with their windows boarded up (*Go Away*

Marilyn was spray-painted on a few of the plywood barriers), and of course of the now emptied beaches from Key West to Miami. News journalists interviewed Florida residents (none from Little Bridge) who confessed to being a little nervous because there was nowhere they could go "to escape the wrath of this fierce storm" (the reporter's words, not theirs).

I'll admit it was hard to take any of this very seriously when just outside my door it was such a beautiful, balmy evening, the sky streaked with tie-dye washes of pink and blue and lavender as the sun slid beneath the sea. A mockingbird had recently taken up residency in the top branches of our building's frangipani, and he periodically burst into enthusiastic song, hoping to lure a mate, while somewhere nearby someone who'd yet to evacuate was barbecuing. I could smell the tantalizing scent of grilled meat every time I opened my front door.

But the constant pings of text messages from my phone kept me grounded, reminding me of the oncoming threat:

From Caleb:

They're closing the Little Bridge airport to commercial air traffic tomorrow morning at 8AM. I can still arrange for a plane to be there anytime before that if you change your mind. I know you think I don't care, Sabrina, but I do. We can still be friends, at least. Call me.

From my best friend and college roommate, Mira, who was spending the year abroad in Paris:

What is this I hear about you not evacuating Hurricane Marilyn and riding out the hurricane by yourself??? Have you lost your mind? I love you, but you're insane. You know my aunt lives in Tampa if you need a place to hunker down in an emergency. And she loves cats. Call me. Luv u.

From Dani:

You need to get here ASAP. My room is huge, with a full mini-bar AND almost all the guys from the firehouse in Islamorada are staying at the SAME HOTEL. One of them is buying me shots at the bar at this very moment. In fact, I think there's a fire right now. In my pants. Get in my car and get here SOON!!!

From my mother:

They're evacuating the dolphins from the Dolphinarium on Cayo Guillermo in Cuba. This same hurricane is headed straight toward you, and yet you're not leaving. You think it's safer for you than it is for the dolphins? Please, please, I'm begging you, let Caleb come get you.

I'll admit that this last message gave me pause. I wasn't sure what a dolphinarium was, but I was glad the sea life in it was going to be safe. What precautions was the Cuban government taking to make sure that the people who lived near the dolphinarium were safe as well?

I was looking this up—after having changed into the third of the outfits I was considering wearing to the party—

when there was a knock on my front door. I could see through the iron grillwork that covered the Spanish-style door viewer that it was my next-door neighbors Patrick and Bill. I opened the door to find them standing on my front step with a tray of vodka Jell-O shots.

"Hurricane Preparedness Response Team," Bill cried. "Blueberry or cherry?"

"You guys are crazy." I laughed and helped myself to one of the little plastic cups containing a blue vodka Jell-O shot. "Want to come in?"

"Oh, well, we would," Patrick said, "but someone looks like she's got somewhere fancy to go." The owner of Little Bridge's Seam and Fabric Shoppe, Patrick, eyed the black sundress sprigged with tiny yellow flowers that I'd only just finished lacing myself into.

Since Patrick also performed on weekends as the island's most popular drag queen, Lady Patricia, at one of the local bars, I put a lot of value on his fashion tips, so I looked down as I fingered the edge of my admittedly very short skirt.

"Do you think so?" I asked, uncertainly. "I'm only going to a hurricane party. I've never been to one before, so I didn't know what people wear to those. You don't think this is too much?"

"Not if your plan is to make every straight man there fall in love with you." Bill, Patrick's romantic partner of twenty years and the loan officer at Little Bridge State Bank, had leaned down and was trying to pry Gary off his foot. "Why is your cat so obsessed with me?"

"He does that to everyone. So do you think I should change?" I asked Patrick nervously. "Maybe shorts and a T-shirt would be more appropriate."

"Don't you change a thing." Patrick leaned over to smooth one of my pink curls from my forehead. "Those yellow flowers bring out the brown in your eyes. And no one on this island bothers to dress up anymore unless they're going to court. I've always considered that a crying shame. It's refreshing to see someone actually looking like a lady. Now tell us why you're still even here. I couldn't believe it when I saw your lights on behind the shutters. I'd have thought you'd have evacuated hours ago."

"I could say the same thing to you guys." Why wasn't I evacuating? What was wrong with me?

But the very idea of fleeing from this storm struck me as horribly wrong. Which was ridiculous, because only a few months ago, I'd run from my problems in New York without a second thought, barely considering where I was going, how long I was going to stay, or what I was going to do when I got there.

But then I'd arrived in Little Bridge, and suddenly I hadn't felt the urge to run anymore. I wasn't exactly sure where in the world I belonged, but at least I was done running . . . for now.

And despite what my mother said, I wasn't being stubborn—or maybe I *was* being stubborn, for what felt like the first time in my life. I was standing up for myself, which meant running toward something. I didn't know what, exactly . . . but maybe that's why I was still here.

And maybe that's why I couldn't go anywhere else . . . for now.

"Where are we going to go?" Bill helped himself to one of his own shots, expertly running a pinkie around the edge of the Jell-O to loosen it before gulping it down. "We'd have to drive to Georgia to get out of the path of this thing. And even then, who knows? That might not be far enough."

"Last time we evacked to a hotel in Tampa," Patrick explained. "We took the babies"—Patrick and Bill had three pugs they called their "babies"—"and all of my couture and stayed in a La Quinta and it cost us three thousand dollars in travel expenses, and in the end the damn storm came there, too."

"Oh dear," I said, sympathetically, trying to imagine Patrick, Bill, all of Pat's drag ensembles, plus the three pugs crammed into one room at a Tampa La Quinta. "But you can't exactly stay here, either, because I hear this place floods—"

"Oh, honey," Patrick said. "Don't you worry about that. We booked a suite at the Cascabel."

"The Cascabel?" I raised my eyebrows.

The Cascabel was one of Little Bridge's most expensive hotels . . . and also one of its only buildings that had been allowed to waive the two-story height restriction because it had been constructed way back in the 1920s, before such restrictions became standard. A gracious five-story hotel built in the Spanish tradition, it had since been upgraded to withstand Category 5 winds while also offering luxury amenities such as a rooftop spa and wine bar.

"We've got a suite on the fourth floor," Patrick went on. "We check in tomorrow morning. We've got it through the weekend. We're going to ride this thing out like true queens."

"We're taking our George Foreman grill," Bill, who loved to cook, informed me. "Because my uncle Rick just sent us a batch of Omaha steaks, and I'll be damned if we're going to let them sit here and spoil when the power goes out."

"But." I was confused. "You won't be able to grill on the balcony if there's a hurricane."

"No, we're going to grill them in the room. Because the Cascabel has a generator. So even if there's no power on the rest of the island due to the storm, we'll still be eating like civilized human beings."

"Oh." I tried to picture the two of them grilling Omaha steaks in a luxury hotel room during a hurricane. "I'm sure the Cascabel staff will be thrilled about that."

"Oh, it's going to be bougie as hell," Patrick assured me, "but fabulous. And you're going to be fabulous, too, because you'll be coming with us, of course."

"What?" I burst out laughing. "No, I'm not."

"Girl, yes, you are. We couldn't in good conscience enjoy our steaks knowing that you're here, possibly drowning in disgusting harbor water. Of course you're coming with us. We'll have them set up an extra cot in the suite. And you're bringing this bad boy." Patrick stooped down and gave Gary a scratch under the chin. Gary let out a small mew in protest since he hadn't finished marking their feet, but then allowed himself to be stroked, mostly because the area under his chin was his most sensitive spot, and any stroking there sent him into spasms of ecstasy, and Patrick knew it. "You know he gets along with the babies."

It was true that Gary did, indeed, get along with Patrick and Bill's three pugs.

"That is the nicest invitation." I watched as Gary fell over onto his back, showing his round white belly, all four paws up in a gesture of complete surrender. "I just might take you up on it."

"Oh, perfect!" Patrick straightened, and Gary promptly rolled back onto his feet and went after their toes again. "Well, we have to go finish delivering these." He indicated the Jell-O shots. "It's important to keep up people's spirits during these trying times."

"I understand," I said. "Thanks again."

When they were gone, I made sure Gary was well stocked with food and water, checked out my reflection one last time in the mirror to make sure Patrick was right about the dress, swallowed the Jell-O shot, then got on my bike. I'd decided it would be best to bike rather than take my scooter to Mrs. Hartwell's party since I knew I had to continue to conserve fuel. Plus, I would be consuming alcohol.

Fortunately I only lived directly down the hill from the Hartwells. As I pedaled by the boarded-up homes of my neighborhood, not a single car or pedestrian passed me. It was as if I lived in a ghost town. Over my head, fast-moving purple clouds were beginning to pile up, flashing brilliant fuchsia with heat lightning here and there behind the trees. The storm was still too far out to sea for this to be one of the "rain bands" the meteorologists kept warning us about, though the wind had picked up significantly.

After locking my bike to an ornamental streetlamp close to Mrs. Hartwell's house, I pulled the bottle of champagne I'd brought along as a house gift from the basket of my bike and climbed the long flight of white wooden steps to the Hartwells' wide porch. Fans swung lazily overhead as I pressed the old-fashioned brass buzzer bell beside the Victorian door and heard a corresponding ring inside the house—along with the steady rhythm of salsa music and loud conversation.

Nothing happened. No one had heard me. Behind me, far off in the distance, thunder rumbled. Maybe that hadn't been heat lightning after all. Maybe the meteorologists had been wrong, and the first of Marilyn's rain bands was coming sooner than they'd predicted.

There was a large window in the front door, but it was covered by a lace curtain, so I couldn't see what was behind it. I could, however, hear laughter. People were having a good time, despite the impending threat.

Encouraged, I laid my hand on the door handle, and let myself in.

I found myself in a long entrance hallway filled with dark-stained wood and an elaborate crystal chandelier. A strong scent of pine hit me. That must be the extinct wood the house was made of that Mrs. H had mentioned.

The home clearly hadn't been renovated much since the day it had been constructed by the original Captain Hartwell, but that's because it didn't need it—unless you were someone who was into modern décor, which I wasn't, necessarily.

The walls were wainscoted and wallpapered in traditionally nautical patterns and colors, pale blue with crisp white stripes or shells, the furniture heavy but comfortable looking, the original wood floors carpeted here and there with Persian throw rugs. Gold-framed portraits of ancient Hartwell ancestors lined the walls, the ship captains and their wives glaring down at me sternly in their dark frock coats and gowns, in which they must have been quite uncomfortable, considering the subtropical heat.

There was about as little Floridian as you could imagine in the Hartwells' home, except for a large parrot cage that I passed in the living room on my way toward the back of the house, from which I could hear the music. The parrot greeted me with a cheerful "Hello, Joe!" as I made my way past.

"Hello to you, too," I said.

The house was dark, thanks to all the windows being shuttered in anticipation of the storm . . .

. . . at least until I followed the cheerful flow of music and voices past the old-fashioned and ornate dining room, and then onto a wide, wraparound back deck, which opened onto a vast backyard and pool area, lit by tiki torches.

"Bree?" asked a deep, all too familiar voice.

CHAPTER SEVEN

Time: 8:10 P.M.
Temperature: 80°F
Wind Speed: 9 MPH
Wind Gust: 20 MPH
Precipitation: 0.0 in.

He'd changed out of the beat-up T-shirt he'd been wearing earlier in the day into a soft blue chambray button-down and a pair of chinos so faded they looked almost white.

"What are you doing here?" Drew Hartwell demanded.

This didn't seem like the most welcoming way to greet a guest, even one he hadn't been expecting, so I didn't think I could be blamed for bristling.

"Uh," I said, hoisting up the bottle of champagne I'd brought along. "It's a party? Your aunt invited me? I don't know. Are Fresh Waters not welcome, or something? Should I leave?"

He blinked those impossibly blue eyes like someone

who was just waking up from a particularly bad dream and shook his head.

"But," he said. It was difficult to hear him due to all the laughter and conversation coming from the people in the yard, and the salsa music playing merrily from the outdoor speakers above us. "I thought you were evacuating."

"No. I said I wasn't evacuating. Remember, we had a whole conversation about the frustrations of family?"

He shook his head again. His pupils weren't particularly dilated, so I didn't think he was high on anything.

But his eyebrows were constricted, and he definitely wasn't smiling. He seemed genuinely concerned.

"Have you even been listening to the weather reports?" he demanded. "Do you know how bad this storm is?"

"Uh, yeah," I said. "Do you?"

"I live here."

"Well, so do I."

"I've lived here my *whole life*. I know about hurricanes. And this isn't one anyone should mess around with."

"You mean like someone who lives on the beach?" I blinked up at him, feigning wide-eyed innocence. "The beach everyone is warning people to evacuate?"

It was at that exact moment that I was hit by a slim, sweet-smelling rocket that came racing toward me out of the darkness of the yard, wrapping a sweaty arm around my neck.

"You came!" Nevaeh planted a kiss on my cheek. "I knew it! I knew you'd come!"

"Oof," I said, as she crashed into me. "Of course I came.

What else was I going to do tonight? I'm surprised you're here. Didn't you have a hot date?"

Nevaeh's lack of hot dates (her aunt said she was too young to date and forbade her seeing any of the many young men who constantly hung around the café, thirsting for her) was a steady source of humor between us.

"No," Nevaeh said, pretending to pout. "But what about you?" She backed away, eyeing my dress. "You look so pretty! You could have had a date tonight if you wore this more often. Why haven't I ever seen you in this before?"

"Well, I thought about wearing it to mop the floors at the café. But then I decided it wasn't formal enough. Where can I put this?" I waved the bottle of champagne. Drew, I noticed, had drifted away, probably to whichever section of the party had been reserved for hot brooding bachelors who were building their own beach houses.

"I told you not to bring anything." Mrs. Hartwell was standing right behind her niece, looking stern.

"I'm glad she didn't listen to you!" Nevaeh eagerly snatched the bottle out of my hands.

"Not until you're twenty-one, young lady." Mrs. Hartwell took the bottle from her niece. "Very nice," she said, glancing at me with raised eyebrows after scrutinizing the label. "Hardly worth wasting on this bunch. I might have to hide this for my own personal use."

"Please do," I said. "It's for you."

Mrs. Hartwell snorted, looking embarrassed, and called to her husband, who was in a sunken part of the yard by the grill—or I should say multiple grills, with multiple men, all of whom were busily barbecuing by the light of numerous tiki torches.

"Ed," Mrs. Hartwell screeched. "Ed, Bree Beckham brought us some champagne!"

Unsurprisingly, since Ed Hartwell hardly ever spoke except to yell at someone, there was only a grunt in reply. It sounded approving, however.

"Well, let's go get this on ice," Mrs. Hartwell said, and began moving at the speed of light. "And get you a drink, too, of course."

She headed down the steps, into one of the biggest backyards I'd ever seen on the island—which, being only two miles by four miles, was in a constant and desperate battle to preserve green space.

The Hartwells had done a good job of conserving it. The yard was lush with native growth, mostly different varieties of palms, some of which towered as high as twenty feet overhead, forming a cooling canopy against the moody night sky. The air was thick with the fragrance of night-blooming jasmine, ylang-ylang, and grilling meats and vegetables. Exotic orchids in multiple colors, white, purple, yellow, and orange, grew from the trunks of some of the palms, the flowers swaying softly in the warm evening breeze.

Mrs. Hartwell placed my bottle of champagne in a silver bucket that held ice and a number of other bottles of wine, most of them open, that sat on an ornately carved Moroccan bench by the pool. Kidney shaped, and lushly landscaped so that it looked almost like a naturally occurring pond (only turquoise colored), the pool glowed iridescently in the darkness of the yard, a shimmering sapphire amid the bright ruby and topaz tiki torches.

At Mrs. Hartwell's urging, I helped myself to a plastic glass of white wine from one of the opened bottles while Nevaeh, who'd trailed behind us the entire time, stood beside me, chattering nonstop.

"And over here is where we're keeping the rabbits," she was saying, guiding me toward an area of the yard that was near what appeared to be one of the most picturesque potting sheds I'd ever seen, painted white with blue trim to match the house. "We volunteered to foster animals from the ASPCA during the storm. They always make sure to find foster homes for every pet in the shelter during a hurricane. They gave us two rabbits. What do you think? Aren't they just the cutest?"

After my vision had adjusted, I saw that the rabbits were comfortably snuggled into newly constructed wooden hutches, their pink and brown noses twitching away as they nibbled at a head of lettuce someone had dropped inside their pen. I agreed that they were, as Nevaeh had said, the cutest.

"We'll bring them inside when it starts to rain," Nevaeh prattled on. "I've made a pen in the laundry for them out of baby gates. I want to keep them forever—along with the parrot and the tortoise—but Uncle Ed says we have enough animals. I don't know why, we only have a couple of stray cats that come around because I feed them. They actually live under the church down the street. I know I'll change his mind. Oh my God, Katie!"

This was directed at a young girl who'd just arrived at the party, Nevaeh's best friend, Katie, who like Nevaeh was dressed in a halter top, short shorts, and some sort of silky robe. Like Nevaeh, she'd also flat-ironed her hair to a sheen. Both let out a delighted scream at the sight of each other.

Since Mrs. Hartwell had long since been snatched up by another partygoer, I drifted away as Katie and Nevaeh shrieked over the coincidence of their wardrobe selections, having noticed that Angela was standing beside a nearby table laden with chips, dips, and other party favorites.

"Hey, girlfriend," she said, when she saw me approaching, and gave me a welcoming hug. "Check out the spread."

When I turned to look at the impressive array of food—much of what had been in Mrs. Hartwell's shopping cart that afternoon, only now it was transformed into tantalizing trays of gooey nachos, simmering brisket, cool and spicy fish dip, truffle popcorn, strawberry trifle, and watermelon salad—Angela leaned over to whisper into my ear, "And check out what's behind us."

I turned to look. The Hartwells owned an outdoor pool table, around which seemed to have gathered most, if not all, of Little Bridge Island's most eligible bachelors (and bachelorettes). It would have been hard not to notice that one of the former was Drew, since he was currently breaking. Under the misty yellow glow of the party globes that someone had strung above the pool table, I could see that he'd pushed the sleeves of his chambray shirt up to his elbows, revealing his darkly tanned forearms. These flexed tautly as he leaned across the green felt to take a shot, as did his left butt cheek, clearly outlined by the thin fabric of those super-faded chinos.

Well, a girl could look, couldn't she? Even if she was most definitely not interested in buying, and was, in fact, off the market.

Except that Drew chose that exact moment to look up from beneath the chunk of dark hair that had fallen across his eyes, almost as if he'd felt the direction of my stare. That ice blue gaze met mine.

Crap.

I glanced quickly away, feeling myself blush.

"So how's the food?" I turned to ask Angela, taking a quick sip of wine. I wished I'd thought to put ice in my plastic cup, to cool my suddenly burning cheeks . . . and other places that happened to feel hot.

"The food?" Angela hadn't noticed the look Drew and I had exchanged, whatever it had been, thank God. "It's great. You should try the spinach dip. Oh, and the brisket is good, too."

"Great." My blush was deepening. Damn it! One of these days I was going to track down my biological mother and ask her if blushing ran in the family. Neither my mom nor my dad had ever blushed in their lives and had always teased me (good-naturedly) for doing so. "Is he looking over here?"

Confused, Angela glanced in Drew Hartwell's direction, from which I could hear nothing but the murmur of casual conversation and, for some reason, a whining dog.

"Is who looking over here? What are you—"

"Nothing. Good. Never mind."

Angela started to laugh. "Oh my God. You have got to be kidding me. Drew Hartwell?"

"No. Absolutely not. He just caught me looking at him, and I don't want him to think—"

"Oh, right. Because nothing could be further from the truth?"

"Exactly."

"Then why are you so dressed up?"

I knew it had been a mistake to listen to Patrick.

"It's just a dress," I said. "It's a party, so I wore a dress."

"A hurricane party." Angela shook her head in amusement. "No one dresses up for a hurricane party. Everyone's all sweaty from boarding up all day, so they just throw on whatever so they can get their drink on. Man, I should have known this was going to happen when you were outside this morning, talking to him for so long."

"I wasn't talking to him. I was talking to other people," I hastened to remind her. "On the phone. Nothing is going on between me and Drew Hartwell, I swear. You warned me to stay away from him, remember?"

"Yeah, like you've ever listened to me." Angela had a paper plate in her hand and was filling it with truffle popcorn. "I told you not to eat the lobster roll at Duffy's Clam Shack and you went straight out and tried it."

"It was featured on the Food Network!"

"That doesn't mean anything. You know, now that I've gotten to know you better, I've come to think that you and Hartwell might not be the worst thing that's ever happened. You actually have a lot in common."

"Oh, right." I sampled the spinach dip. It was delicious, like everything Lucy and Ed Hartwell made. "Name one thing."

"Well, you're both white."

I smirked. "Oh, well, everyone knows that guarantees happiness in a relationship."

She laughed. "And you can both be pretty sarcastic when you want to."

"That might be true, too, but again, not a guarantee of relationship success."

She grew more serious. "You do both like animals. You have that crazy cat, and Drew's got, what, like five dogs out there on the beach with him?"

"I heard it was only three."

She grinned at me. "Wow, you really *are* into him. You've been checking into his private life?"

"His aunt mentioned the dogs, that's all. And anyway, what about that truck of his? You're the one who told me—"

"Oh, forget about that. That was years ago. Before he left for New York. His truck has pretty much been parked in the same place for ages now."

"Which is?"

"His own driveway. And the Mermaid parking lot. And Home Depot, of course, where he buys all his—"

"Excuse me." A man's deep voice cut through our conversation. I turned to see Drew Hartwell standing beside me, holding a paper plate.

I felt my face heating up again, and it wasn't because of the sultriness of the evening air.

"Yes?" I asked, with concentrated primness. "May I help you with something?"

"My aunt's brisket." He pointed at something behind me. "You're blocking it."

"Oh." I hopped out of the way while Angela stifled a snort of laughter. "Sorry."

How much had he overheard? Any of it? All of it? He didn't appear at all discomfited, if that was the case. He was digging into his aunt's brisket like a starving man, piling it onto one of the rolls that had been provided to make sandwiches of the meat.

I should have known to run to a different section of the party when I saw Angela smiling mischievously beside me. But of course I didn't.

"So, Drew," she said conversationally, her laughter barely contained. "Is it true what I hear, that you're going to stay in your house on Sandy Point for the storm?"

"It's true." Drew was hesitating over the vast selection of homemade and commercial barbecue sauces for his brisket sandwich.

"That's a really bold choice, Drew," Angela said, still grinning. "They're warning everyone with places on the shoreline to head inland."

"I built my place to withstand two-hundred-and-fifty-mile-per-hour winds." Having made his selection, Drew now squirted barbecue sauce all over his brisket. "It's made of poured concrete and rebar, on forty-foot pilings to keep it above the storm surge. The place should be fine. And if not, it'll be good for me to be there to make any necessary repairs on-site as breaks happen."

I stared at him. "Are you insane? That's exactly what they're telling people *not* to do."

He'd taken a large bite of his sandwich. "You do realize," he said, as he chewed, "that there's nowhere on this island you can go that isn't coastal."

"Yes," I said. "But you can go inland. You don't have to stay on the beach—"

"What do you care?" Those bright eyes glittered at me a little too intensely. "Why is what I do during the hurricane so important to you?"

I took a sip of my wine to escape his smirk. "It's not. Trust me, whether you live or die makes no difference to me."

Drew grinned. "Now you're starting to sound more like a local, Fresh Water. So where are you hunkering down, if you're so intent on staying?"

I'm sorry to say that I flipped my hair. What was wrong with me? I wasn't even drunk, I'd only had one Jell-O shot and a few sips of wine. "Oh, I have a lot of options."

"Really?" He was still grinning. "Like where?"

"I invited her to stay with me," Angela said mildly, leaning over between us to scoop some spinach dip onto a corn chip. "But apparently, she got a better offer, since she said no."

I almost choked on the sip of wine I'd taken. This statement was a complete falsehood, and Angela knew it. What she'd actually said earlier that day back at the café was that she'd be staying at her mother's during the hurricane.

Mrs. Fairweather's home was a historic Spanish-style bungalow made of concrete and not situated in a flood zone, and so ideal for hunkering down during storms.

I was welcome to join them, Angela had said, but her brother's rottweilers would be there as well, and might not be too thrilled to see Gary.

I had not taken her invitation seriously.

"Um," I said. No way was I going to mention that Drew's own aunt had invited me to stay with her. That seemed like it would be walking into whatever mischievous trap Angela was setting for me. "Yes, well, Lady Patricia invited me to stay with her in a fourth-floor suite at the Cascabel—"

His grin vanished. "The Cascabel? You're not staying there, are you?"

"Well," I said, noting that his objection appeared to be over the hotel, not whom I was staying with. Lady Patricia was the most well-liked drag queen in Little Bridge, and everyone bought fabrics for their curtains and outdoor furniture at Patrick's fabric shop. "Well, yes, I thought I might. Pat says it's rated Cat Five, too—"

"The building itself, sure. But the lobby and stairwells flood every time there's even a minor rainstorm. Why doesn't anyone ever remember that?"

"Remember what?" Ed Hartwell was approaching with a platter still sizzling from the grill. He appeared to have almost every variety of barbecue possible, from burger patties to hot dogs to kebabs to portobello mushrooms.

"The Cascabel," Drew said. "What's the point of being safe from wind damage on a high floor when you can't exit in an emergency because there's three to six feet of floodwater on the first?"

"They have a generator," Angela pointed out.

"Sure, to power the rooms," Drew said. "Not enough juice to handle the hallways or lobby. And I wouldn't trust the electricals anyway under those conditions. Salt water will have flooded the elevator shafts, corroding the cables. So you're still going to have to walk up and down a dank, dark, smelly stairway every time you need to go out for anything—"

Who knows how long I would have been forced to stand there politely listening to these locals argue the pros and cons of riding out a hurricane at the Cascabel Hotel if the dog that had been whining up until that point hadn't suddenly let out a yelp of pain? All four of us swiveled our heads toward the sound.

"Oh, no," Angela said.

That's when I noticed for the first time that we had a hurricane-party crasher.

CHAPTER EIGHT

Avoid consuming alcoholic beverages before, during, and after the storm. Although seemingly refreshing, these can be dehydrating and impair judgment.

Rick was a Mermaid regular, though many of us who worked there wished he'd visit less. He never missed the lunch special, always ordering the same thing—half a Cuban sandwich and a cup of soup for $6.95—every day, but he augmented it with several Bloody Mermaids (Bloody Marys, only with a cocktail shrimp on a skewer).

Except that Rick's Bloody Mermaids were always doubles.

I'd have felt sorry for him if it weren't for one thing. Rumor had it that before the ravages of alcoholism had stolen them away, he'd once had a wife, kids, and a successful rental property business. I still saw faded Rick Chance Rentals signs on the sides of various bus stops around town, and Rick himself was usually stylishly dressed in an impeccable white button-down and khaki pants, and often informed me that he was waiting on a million-dollar property deal to go through (but somehow it never quite came to fruition).

But then there was Socks.

Socks was a scruffy but cute black and white dog (well, would have been black and white if he'd ever been given a bath. He was more black and gray) with one ear that stuck up, and another that seemed permanently to droop. Socks had somehow attached itself to Rick, out of all the people on Little Bridge.

Socks followed Rick Chance everywhere, including into the Mermaid, even though technically we allowed only service animals.

But I suppose in a way Socks did provide assistance to Rick, since the dog didn't approve of his owner's lifestyle, and often grew impatient sitting beneath whatever barstool Rick was haunting.

When this happened, Socks would whine to be taken for a walk, and Rick would be forced to pay up and leave. I'd see Rick weaving down the street to the next bar, Socks trotting proudly beside him, excited to have an owner at last.

However, occasionally when Socks whined to go, Rick had not finished his drink and did not feel like leaving.

And so instead he'd nudge Socks in the ribs with his foot—though not always gently enough to be called a nudge.

Rick had received plenty of warnings about his treatment of Socks from all of us, but especially from Ed Hartwell. Several times Rick had even been ordered to leave the Mermaid altogether and not come back until he was sober. Little Bridge Island offered plenty of services for anyone looking for help in this area, almost all of them free. There were several large and enthusiastic Alcoholics Anonymous groups, one of which met regularly at the long back table of the Mermaid, calling themselves Anchors Aweigh.

But Rick refused to admit that he had a problem, or that his treatment of his dog was wrong.

Since Rick was so pathetic, and Socks so cute, Mrs. Hartwell often overruled her husband's orders and allowed Rick back into the café, even when he was obviously inebriated, if only so that she could give both Socks and his owner the proper food and water that they needed to stay alive.

I hadn't noticed the man in the button-down shirt sitting on a high-topped chair over by the pool table until the dog on the patio tiles beneath him began to cry.

But as soon as this happened, all eyes were upon him, including Drew Hartwell's.

Drew had just lifted his beer to take a sip. Now he lowered it and said, in a voice so cold it could have chilled even this steamiest of summer nights, "Excuse me, but did you just kick that dog?"

From the droopiness of his eyelids and the unsteadiness with which he was perched on the stool, it looked as if Rick might have been consuming more than just beer.

"Me?" His weather-beaten face assumed an expression of overexaggerated astonishment. "Aw, no! Hell, no. No, sir, that wasn't me. I wouldn't kick a dog."

It was clear from both the demeanor of the dog and the accusing expressions on the faces of everyone in the nearby vicinity that Rick had, indeed, just kicked the dog.

But Drew hadn't seen it himself, so there was no way he could prove it. And no one was talking. Everyone in this crowd, it seemed, felt too sorry for Rick, probably remembering the wife and kids he'd abandoned (or, more likely, who had thrown him out of the house).

The salsa music playing from the speakers on the back porch seemed uncomfortably loud in the silence that followed, during which Drew stared at Socks's owner.

Ed Hartwell was the one to break the silence. "Rick," he said, in his deep voice, one that was generally hoarse from lack of use. "I've told you before not to mess with that dog."

Rick's own voice turned self-defensive. "Ed, you know me. I'd never kick no dog." When drunk—which was most of the time—Rick's grammar became erratic. He also developed a Southern twang, which was odd given that he claimed to be from Rhode Island. "I love dogs!"

Drew pointed straight in Rick Chance's face. "I think you did kick that dog," he said, in the same cold tone. "And if I catch you doing it again, I will lay you out."

Even though it was the warmest of tropical nights, with only the softest of breezes stirring the tops of the palm fronds, I felt a chill up my spine. Drew Hartwell wasn't kidding around. Small lines had appeared around the corners of his blue eyes that I'd never seen before, not even the day Leighanne had thrown her keys and saltshaker at him.

He was angry. If I'd been Rick, I'd have left the party immediately.

But Rick only laughed foolishly and took another slug from his beer bottle. "Well, no worries, cuzzy. That ain't goin' to happen because I ain't the type to kick no dog."

Drew lowered his arm and said in a voice dripping with disdain, "I am not your cousin."

Then he turned and walked back toward the pool table, since it was his turn once again to shoot.

I didn't realize until he was gone from my side that I'd been holding my breath during the entirety of the two men's exchange. It was only after Drew turned away that I exhaled, and oxygen began to circulate through my lungs again.

"Wow," I said softly.

Angela, beside me, took a long sip of her drink. "Yeah. That was intense."

"I'll say. Hasn't Drew ever met Rick before?"

Angela shrugged. "You mean from before he got the way he is now? Yeah, I'm sure. Everyone knew Rick when he was riding high. He had the biggest rental property business in town. But now? Drew's more of the breakfast crowd, remember? He's always gone before Rick gets in for lunch."

This made sense. The breakfast and lunch crowds rarely mingled.

"I need a refill after that drama," Angela said, holding up her empty cup. "How about you?"

My own cup was empty as well. I nodded and the two of us began to make our way toward the little grotto by the pool where Mrs. Hartwell was keeping the wine on ice—

At least, that's where we were headed before we heard it: another yelp of pain from Socks.

"Oh, no." Angela froze beside me. "Tell me he did not just—"

Before either of us could turn to see what was happening, we heard it: the sickening—and unmistakable—sound of bone crunching on bone. I spun just in time to see Rick crumpled on the Hartwells' pavers, clutching his face in apparent agony.

"Yeeee-ow," Rick wailed into his cupped hands. "Did you see that? Did y'all see that? Drew Hartwell hit me! He hit me in the face. Why'd you have to go and do that, Drew?"

Drew Hartwell stood a few feet away from the prone man, waving his right hand in the air. The knuckles seemed to be smarting.

"You know why I did that, Rick," he said, calmly.

"You can't say he didn't warn you, Rick." One of Drew's fellow pool players was setting up for his shot as if nothing had happened. "You had it coming."

"Get up, Rick," said another. "You're blocking the table."

Rick did not seem inclined to get up, however. Instead, he rolled around on the Hartwells' pavers, his fingers pressed to his face, while Socks worriedly tried to lick his face.

"My nose is probably broke," Rick cried. "You all saw it! Drew Hartwell broke my nose! I'm going to sue. I'm going to sue you, Drew Hartwell!"

"Please be my guest," Drew said politely, then walked over to the food table where there was a large ice cooler filled with beer and soda. He plunged his sore hand into it.

Ed gave his nephew an aggrieved look, then leaned down to help Rick to his feet. "Come on, Rick," he said. "Your nose ain't broke. But let's go get you some ice for it. And maybe some black coffee, too, I think."

"I don't want no ice." Rick yanked his arm from Ed's grip. "And I don't want coffee, neither. I want your boy arrested. Did you see what he did to me?"

"He didn't do anything to you that you haven't had coming for a long time, Rick, and you know it." Ed was speaking to Rick, but he was glaring at Drew. "Now come with me—"

But it was too late. Rick darted out of Ed's grasp, then disappeared from the pool table area into the darkest part of the yard, toward the rabbit hutches, still clutching his nose.

Socks, ever loyal to his master, would have followed if I hadn't reached down and grasped him by the collar to keep him where he was. The two of us had a certain rapport since I always gave him water and biscuits at the Mermaid whenever Mrs. Hartwell wasn't around to do it.

The dog only tried for a moment to break free, glancing nervously after his owner, whining softly, confused by my restraining him.

It wasn't that I didn't want Rick to have a pet. I just thought it might be better for him not to have a pet until he'd learned how to take better care of one.

"Shhh," I said to the dog, stroking his droopy ear to calm him. He was a mixed breed, a lot of border collie with a little bit of everything else. It would probably be easier to tell after he'd had a bath. "It's okay. Everything's going to be okay now. Sit, Socks. Stay."

"Someone should give that dog some water," Drew said testily, his right hand still soaking in the beer cooler.

"Do you think so?" Drew's aunt Lucy looked furious. I wasn't sure whether it was because her lovely party had been broken up by a fight or because her beloved nephew had been the one who'd thrown the first—and only—punch. "Do you think that might have been a better way to have handled the situation than to have knocked his owner's lights out?"

Drew had the grace to look a little sheepish. "Yeah." He lifted his hand from the cooler and examined his sore knuckles. "Well, I get a little hot under the collar when it comes to animal abuse."

"Oh, and the rest of us think it's just swell. But we somehow manage to restrain ourselves."

He stared at his aunt for a beat, as if he couldn't believe what she'd just said. I couldn't believe it, either. Frankly, I wished I'd been the one who'd punched Rick Chance. I was glad someone, at least, had finally done it . . . and I couldn't help a growing feeling of admiration for Drew Hartwell.

Admiration? For Drew Hartwell? No. This was not part of the plan. Not that there *was* a plan, exactly, but what there was did not include allowing myself to feel anything at all for Drew Hartwell. I was off men, I was man free, I was on a mancation . . . at least until I could figure out how I'd had the bad judgment to get involved with a guy like Caleb in the first place.

Fortunately Nevaeh appeared from nowhere, kneeling down to set a large bowl of fresh water in front of the dog, and divert me from my dark thoughts.

"Here you go, Socks," she cooed. "Don't pay any mind to those two, they're just fussing, like always."

Happily Socks, torn between the cool water and his beloved master, chose the water, and lowered his head to lap noisily, giving us all a welcome distraction.

"Poor baby." Mrs. Hartwell turned her attention away from the dog and toward her nephew. "He really was thirsty. I should have brought out some water sooner. Then maybe we wouldn't be in this mess."

"It's my mess, not ours, Lu," Drew said, his jaw set and his gaze gone flinty. "I'll take care of it."

"How?" Mrs. Hartwell demanded. "How are you going to take care of it? Where is that poor man supposed to go to get his nose looked at? The ER is closed. The walk-in clinic is boarded up because all of the doctors have left town, except for Dr. Schmidt, but he's a vet, and last I heard, he was at Martina Hernandez's hurricane party up on Stork Key. To get any sort of medical care, Rick'll have to go to Miami, but he's certainly in no shape to drive, even if he had a car, which he doesn't, because his wife took it away. Unless you care to drive him—"

"Uh, no, thanks."

"You need to think about your actions. You never think. You just—"

"Excuse me."

The click of pool balls, which had ratcheted up again once Rick had left the vicinity, stilled as a tall shadow fell across the patio. I could hardly believe it when I looked up to see the sheriff standing there—in full uniform, no less—with Rick Chance standing right behind him.

My eyes widening, I glanced from Rick to Drew, but the latter appeared unruffled, reaching down to take hold of Socks's collar, since the dog had given a delighted whine at the appearance of his owner and made a motion to rush to his side.

"Lucy." The sheriff gave a polite tip of his hat toward the older woman. "Ed. Sorry to interrupt."

"Oh, you know you're never interrupting, John." Mrs. Hartwell's face was lit with genuine pleasure. She didn't seem to have any idea what the presence of the sheriff meant. "We were wondering when you were going to drop by. I saved a plate of my brisket for you. I know how much you love it."

"Kind of you," John Hartwell said. "I was actually just on my way over."

He was tall, with Drew's dark hair and blue eyes, since like almost everyone else on the island he was related to Ed Hartwell, as well—though exactly how, I wasn't sure. I'd waited on him numerous times. He liked his coffee black and his eggs over easy. Like most of the Hartwells, he said little but tipped a lot.

"But I guess this isn't a social call anymore," he went on, "since I ran into Rick here, on my way in, and he says somebody hit him."

"Not somebody," Rick insisted. "Him!" Rick pointed at Drew. "Drew Hartwell hit me, and everyone here saw it!"

CHAPTER NINE

Do not count on aid from first responders during and immediately after the storm, as they will likely have evacuated with their families for their own safety.

Sheriff Hartwell looked around the yard, his cool blue eyes narrowed.

"That true?" he asked the party in general.

I held my breath. Authority figures—anyone in uniform—had always intimidated me.

But someone was going to have to come to Drew's defense. Rick had obviously had it coming. Who went around kicking poor, innocent animals anyway?

Except that it would be obstruction of justice (or perjury) if someone lied for Drew. I had been a miserable law student—in more ways than one—but even I knew that under the right circumstances, failing to report a crime—not to mention lying to the police—could get you slapped with criminal charges of your own.

Glancing at the faces of those around me, I recognized in each the same stony resolution I felt—to not get Drew in trouble for what he'd done, which had, after all, been the right thing.

But I saw also a hint of indecision . . . no one wanted to get themselves in trouble, either.

If there was anyone at the Hartwells' party who could fight off a perjury charge (or afford to make bail) without any trouble, it was me. I was Judge Justine's daughter, after all.

I guess that's what I was thinking as I found myself, against my better judgment, tentatively raising my hand and saying in a soft voice, "Uh, Sheriff?"

The tall man glanced over at me.

He wasn't the only one. I felt as if every gaze in the yard was boring into me. My cheeks flared red. What was I doing?

"Miss?" The sheriff obviously didn't recognize me outside of the café, without my Mermaid tee and nametag.

"Um," I said, lowering my hand. "I didn't see anyone hit Mr. Chance," I lied, in my politest tone. "But I did see Mr. Chance kick that dog."

As I pointed from Rick to Socks, a number of the heads around me began to nod, and I saw the expressions on them turn from shocked to knowing.

"Me, too." Angela, beside me, took a step forward. "I saw him kick that dog, too."

"He kicked him a couple of times," one of Drew's friends said. "*Hard,*" added another.

"He's always kicking that dog," claimed a third. "It's disgusting."

The sheriff glanced at Rick, his cool blue gaze narrowing. "Is that so?"

"Just a tap." Rick was beginning to back away from the glow of the party globes, into the shady darkness of the yard, far from the accusation of the stares he was receiving. "You know how dogs can be. And that ain't even my dog—"

"Really, Rick?" Drew was having to keep a tight hold on Socks's tattered collar, the dog was bucking so hard in his attempt to return to his master, since even abused dogs still love their owners. "You're claiming this isn't your dog?"

Rick shook his head vehemently. "I have never seen that dog before in my life."

Everyone in the yard let out a groan of protest.

I'd waited on Sheriff Hartwell enough times to know two things about him. One was that he was a single father, but didn't date—the same women who'd offered to fill Drew Hartwell's saltshaker had made similar offers to the sheriff, to no avail—and two was that he was a dog lover. He always stopped to pat the head of any dog he saw.

It didn't take him long to come to a decision about Rick.

"Come on," the sheriff said, taking Rick's arm.

"W-where are we going?" Rick's eyes were wide.

"You know where we're going." The sheriff's voice was surprisingly gentle as he dragged the smaller man from the shadows and back into the glow of the party lights. "Nowhere you haven't been before."

"But you can't arrest me!" Rick's voice rose to a pitch that bordered on the hysterical. "I didn't do nothing! *He*'s the one that did it." Rick pointed at Drew, who was observing the developments with an interested expression on his face. "He hit me!"

"He may have, Rick," the sheriff said, half dragging, half propelling the man through the crowd of partygoers, toward the Hartwells' back gate. "But no one here seems to be willing to stand up and say they saw it. What they *are* saying is that you kicked that dog. And that's animal cruelty, and subject to a seven-thousand-dollar bond in this county. Time you had a little cooldown."

"In *jail*?" Rick was furious. "There's a storm coming!"

"Safest place in town for you to ride it out. Jail's on high ground and rated Cat Five." The sheriff threw a last glance at Drew before he and his prisoner disappeared into the night. "You'll look after the dog?" It was a question the dog's owner hadn't thought to ask.

Drew nodded, tightening his grip on Socks's frayed collar. The dog was whining, anxious to follow the only owner it had known in recent months, even though that owner hadn't been a very good one.

"I got him," Drew said.

Why did I feel so turned on by the tone of cool authority in his voice? Or the way the sheriff nodded crisply and left, completely accepting that Drew Hartwell did, indeed, "have it," and that the situation with the dog would be handled?

There was something very wrong with me tonight. Maybe it was the alcohol (though I hadn't had very much of it).

Maybe it was how good Drew Hartwell looked in that shirt.

Maybe it was the coming storm.

Maybe it was that I hadn't felt admiration for a man in so long.

Whatever it was, I needed to get out of there before I did something I'd regret.

"Okay," I said, turning to Angela. "I'm done. See you tomorrow."

Angela looked shocked. "What? You just got here. You haven't even tried the brisket!"

"I'm sure it's delicious." I set my empty wineglass down on a nearby wrought-iron garden table. "But I'm working the breakfast shift tomorrow—"

"Uh, excuse me, but so am I."

"Great." I tried not to glance in Drew's direction, though I was aware he was the center of attention of most of the rest of the partygoers. They were congratulating Drew on his escape from prosecution for punching Rick, and petting Socks. Socks, at least, looked as if he was loving the attention. Drew, not so much.

"I'm just really beat," I said to a suspicious-looking Angela, who'd followed the direction of my gaze. "I'll see you tomorrow."

"Okay." Now Angela sounded dubious. "Well, you can write up the breakfast specials on all the chalkboards, then."

"Deal."

I air-kissed her good-bye, then hurried over to Mrs. Hartwell, whom I'd spied by the wine grotto, pouring herself a glass from the champagne bottle I'd brought.

"Oh, Bree," she said, smiling when she saw me approaching. "Have some of this, will you? You're the one who brought it—and also the one to whom we owe all our thanks."

I felt myself blushing for what felt like the millionth time that evening.

"No, thanks," I said. "And I didn't actually do anything—"

"You saved our boy from going to jail tonight." Mrs. Hartwell gazed toward Drew, who was still receiving pats on the back from her other party guests, while surreptitiously slipping bits of brisket to Socks, who appeared to be warming up to his new, much kinder master.

I glanced quickly away, mistrusting how the sight of him made my heart jump. When I got home, I was going to check online to see if dips in barometric pressure affected one's sex drive. Some people said that full moons did. Maybe there was some kind of similar phenomenon with approaching hurricanes.

I could think of no other reason for finding myself suddenly so attracted to Drew Hartwell.

"Not that I'm celebrating," Mrs. Hartwell went on, plunging the bottle back into the large silver wine chiller. "What happened just now was very sad. I feel terrible for Rick, and even worse for his poor wife and kids."

"Sure," I said. "I totally understand. But—"

"I know. I know what you're going to say. But he's had that coming to him for a while."

That was so completely not what I'd been going to say. All I wanted to do was leave, not get into a conversation about Rick Chance.

"And at least this way both he and that sweet dog will be safe for the storm," Mrs. Hartwell went on. "The sheriff will take good care of Rick, and Drew will take good care of that dog."

"Yes." This was the kookiest town I'd ever lived in in my life, and that was saying a lot, considering I'd lived in New York City. True, Little Bridge's kookiness was one of the things that had drawn me to it. But things seemed to be getting slightly out of control. Maybe it was time to move on. Too bad I was only figuring this out now, during a gas shortage just before a massive hurricane. "Well, I just wanted to say good night, and thank you so much for inviting me—"

Mrs. Hartwell nearly choked on the mouthful of champagne she'd just taken. "You're not leaving, are you?"

Nevaeh, who'd been sitting nearby with her friend Katie, taking sexy selfies together while eating strawberries, bounded over, echoing her great-aunt's concern. "Bree, you can't go!"

"Oh, yes," I said. "I'm afraid I have to. I had a lovely time, but I have the breakfast shift at the café tomorrow morning, so you know that means I have to be there before six—"

Mrs. Hartwell cut me off. "Oh, of course. But how did you get here?"

I pointed in the direction of the street. "On my bike," I said, wondering what that had to do with anything. "Thank you again for a great—"

"*Alone?*" Nevaeh exchanged horrified looks with her great-aunt. "She biked over here *alone?*"

"Well, of course," I said.

None of this was going the way I'd planned, which had been to say a polite thank-you to my hostess, go home, and snuggle with Gary in the safety of my apartment, where there were no darkly handsome brooding men saving cute dogs from abuse, and causing my heart—and other parts of me—to tingle uncomfortably. I had purposefully come to this island to be alone and figure out my next move. None of that had included becoming attracted to darkly handsome brooding men who were kind to dogs.

"I live really close by," I offered, "just over on Washington. I barely had anything to drink. It's very safe—"

"Of course it is, honey," Mrs. Hartwell said, patting me on my bare shoulder as she looked around distractedly. "Under *normal* circumstances. But these aren't normal circumstances. We're under a mandatory evacuation. There's hardly anyone left in town, and the ones who are here—well, let's just say that except for the ones at this party, most of them don't have good reasons to be here."

What was she talking about?

"*Looters,*" Nevaeh hissed at me, under her breath, apparently recognizing my confusion. "They come down from Miami, knowing there's a mandatory evacuation, wait for everybody to leave, then rob all the empty houses. And molest any girls they can."

I stared at her, belatedly remembering Mrs. Hartwell's story back in the grocery store about how someone during Wilhelmina had stolen the cash register and meat slicer from the Mermaid.

"Oh," I said. "Right. But I'm sure I'll be fine. I'm just going to hop on my bike and—"

"Let me get Drew to walk you home," Mrs. Hartwell said.

"What?" My eyes widened. "No—"

"Oh, it's no problem," Mrs. Hartwell said kindly. "*Drew!*"

CHAPTER TEN

Time: 10:18 P.M.
Temperature: 80°F
Wind Speed: 13 MPH
Wind Gust: 21 MPH
Precipitation: 0.0 in.

All the blood in my veins froze.

"What?" I said. "No. No, no, no, that is not at all necess—"

But it was too late. She was already calling across the festively lit yard to her nephew. "Drew? Oh, Drew!"

"No, really, Mrs. H." I was dying inside. "I'm perfectly fine—"

Even as I said the words, however, I could see Drew loping obediently toward his aunt, Socks the dog—who'd been won over by his new master completely with only a few pieces of brisket—trotting at his side.

"You rang?" Drew's expression was at once curious and sardonic as he stood before his aunt, taking in, no doubt, my burning cheeks.

"Bree has the breakfast shift at the café tomorrow and needs to leave now," Mrs. Hartwell said. "She rode her bike here, alone, and you know it isn't safe for any young girl to be out this time of year by herself." Young girl? Since when was twenty-five a young girl? "Could you walk her home?"

The last thing I wanted was to look into those eyes of Drew Hartwell's one more time.

But of course as soon as I raised my gaze to meet his, there they were: those bright blue irises, the same color as the water in Mrs. Hartwell's pool . . . and gleaming just about as brightly.

"Sure." Drew gave me one of his snarky half grins. "Guess I owe you one, anyway, right, Fresh Water?"

That grin. Oh God, that grin.

"Honestly," I said again. "I don't need—"

"Then that's decided." Lucy Hartwell gave a satisfied clap of her hands. "I'll see you tomorrow, Bree. Nevaeh, Katie, will you help me bring those dips inside? They've sat outside in the heat long enough, I think it's time they went into the AC of the dining room."

"Yes, ma'am." The girls rushed to help the older woman.

"Really," I said, striding after Drew as he headed for the back gate. "I don't need an escort home. Nothing's going to happen to me in Little Bridge Island, of all places."

"Hey." Drew held up both hands in a "What-do-you-want-from-me?" stance as both Socks and I followed him. "I do what Lu tells me to. I've learned better than not to follow her orders."

"And I appreciate that." We were in the front yard, which

was appreciably quieter—and darker—than the back, lit only by the front porch lamp and the glare from the decorative streetlights, streaming through the branches of the large gumbo-limbo trees that took up most of his aunt and uncle's lawn. The fragrance of night-blooming jasmine was heavy in the air. "But she's not here now, and I'm telling you, I'm fine."

"This your bike?"

Other party guests had chained their bicycles to streetlamps as well, but Drew zeroed in on mine.

"Why do you think that one's mine?" I asked. "Because it's purple?"

"That," he said, poking at the wicker basket, "and the plastic flowers. They're a nice touch."

"Yes, it's mine," I growled ungraciously, stooping to unlock it. "I happen to like flowers."

"I'm not saying anything against flowers." He watched as Socks sniffed his aunt's fence. It was a white picket, which the Little Bridge Island historic board had deemed was the only acceptable kind of fence for homeowners to install. "The bike just looks like something you'd own, that's all."

"What's that supposed to mean?" I snapped, certain he wasn't giving me a compliment.

"Nothing. It was simply an observation. What are you getting so hot under the collar for?"

"I don't need people making judgments about me based on my taste in bicycle colors." There is a segment of the population that feels that anything feminine—such as purple bicycles with flowered baskets, and perhaps even pink salt—is less worthy than more masculine things. I was positive he was a member of it. And this certainty was helping me to remember to dislike him, and thus push him away, despite his good looks, because good-looking men especially weren't to be trusted. "And I don't need you to walk me home. It's nice of your aunt to worry about me, but I'm perfectly capable of—"

"Look." Drew leaned forward to seize both handles of my bicycle. "I was not making judgments about you—"

"Weren't you?" I stuffed my bike chain into my basket. We were the only two people on the quiet, moonlit street, so my voice sounded especially loud. "My bike's the only purple one out here with flowers on the basket, and you knew it belonged to me? That wasn't a judgment?"

"I assumed it was yours because it's kind of girlie." He released the bike handles and threw his arms into the air, walking a few steps away in frustration. Socks, done sniffing the picket fence, trotted after him, thinking they were going somewhere. But then Drew turned back toward me, so Socks followed. "And you were the only person at that party wearing a kind of girlie dress. It seemed like a logical conclusion. So sue me. What is wrong with you?"

A part of me didn't want to respond. A part of me warned, *Just get on your bike and ride away, Bree.*

But another, stronger part of me just kept talking. This is another problem I have. Sometimes, I'm Sabrina, painfully shy. Other times, I'm Bree, who can't seem to shut up.

"The likelihood of my being attacked on my way home is so small that it's statistically insignificant," I informed him.

"You're aware that in the majority of sexual assaults against women, the victim knows her attacker?"

Drew stared at me, dumbfounded. "Are you saying that you think I—?"

"No," I said, instantly mortified. Why couldn't I listen to the part of me that was painfully shy, get on my bike, and ride away? But I couldn't. I was as welded to the spot as the streetlamp beside me. "Of course not. I'm just saying that it's highly unlikely I'm going to be assaulted by a stranger on my way home tonight, despite what your aunt may think. It's not really her fault. She, like so many others, has fallen victim to Mean World Syndrome, something I know a lot about because my mother makes her living off it."

His dark eyebrows furrowed. "Mean world syndrome? What—" He stopped and, as if only just registering what I'd said. "Your mother?"

"Yes, my mother. She's a judge. Judge Justine."

"Your mother is Judge Justine . . . *Justice with Judge Justine* from the radio?" His hands went to his dark hair, causing it to stand more riotously on end than usual. "But she's . . . famous."

"Yes." I stuck out my chin. I'd dug my grave. Now I had to lie in it. "Yes, she is. And not only from the radio. She also did that stint on—"

He said it along with me. "*Dancing with the Stars.*"

He stared at me, as if completely reevaluating who I was—and what to think of me.

I didn't blame him. I'd have been reevaluating me, too. All this time he'd thought me one person—Bree, the plucky, long-working, pink-haired waitress, living entirely on her own.

And now suddenly I'd morphed before his eyes into this other person, Sabrina Beckham, with a famous radio personality millionaire mother, one who was no doubt always there to help out financially . . . except of course he didn't know I was barely speaking to her, or that I'd come to this island in the first place to get away from her, because she, like my ex, had broken my heart.

I probably shouldn't have told him.

But I couldn't help feeling as if Drew Hartwell, of all people, deserved to know the truth. At least this way he'd stop thinking I was some dumb Fresh Water.

"So what is Judge Justine's daughter doing here, of all places?" Drew asked, finally, spreading his hands wide to indicate the whole of Little Bridge. "Working as a waitress in my aunt's diner?"

"It's a café," I reminded him, stiffly.

"Whatever."

"I'm . . . I'm taking a break to work through some things."

I saw his gaze narrow. "Drugs," he said, finally.

"I beg your pardon?"

"I'd be thinking drugs if I hadn't seen you every morning at eight A.M. for the past few months, all bright-eyed and bushy-tailed."

"See," I said, slamming the wedge heel of my sandal into my kickstand, then hopping onto my bike. The thought of him thinking about my tail—metaphorical or not—was unsettling. In a good or bad way, I couldn't tell. "That's exactly what I'm talking about. That kind of negativity—my mother's perfected it, all in order to engage her listeners. She uses fear—fear that the world is a much more dangerous place than it actually is, that if a girl takes a break for a while to work through some things, she must be on drugs, or that if she walks home at night by herself that she's going to get sexually assaulted—to convince others that the world is this dangerous and unforgiving place. But it isn't. Or at least, for the most part, it isn't. I mean, yes, bad things do happen. My dad died last year—but of cancer, not from being murdered, or anything. And—and, well, bad things have happened to me, too, but it was because of someone I knew, and thought I could trust. Bad things happen to everyone sometimes. That's just life. I don't believe the only safe thing to do now is stay home and put bars on my windows and invest my money in gold coins from the U.S. Treasury—"

"Hey," he said, gently. He'd taken a step forward and wrapped his fingers around my handlebars to keep me from riding off. "Bree. I'm sorry. I didn't mean that crack about you taking drugs. Obviously, you're the last person who would ever do drugs. You're way too uptight."

I rolled my eyes at him. "Thanks a lot."

"And a real addict would have gone to Miami. Or Key West. There are no drugs here in Little Bridge. At least, no hard stuff."

Frowning, I stared down at his fingers. In the misty light from the streetlamp, I could see that the knuckles were still raw from where they'd come in contact with Rick Chance's jaw.

The back of his hand was also lightly furred in dark hair, the same finely textured hair I'd seen when he'd lifted his shirt that morning, making a vee down his taut stomach before disappearing beneath the waistband of his shorts.

Just the reminder caused a tingle in a place I'd sworn to keep away from men for the foreseeable future.

And yet all I could think about was how those hands might feel on my bare skin.

"Let go of my bike," I said in a strangled voice, lifting my gaze to his.

"No. Look. I'm sorry about your father. I didn't know. I just . . . Bree—" His voice sounded as choked as my own.

Suddenly, one of those warm, calloused hands closed over my own. The second his skin touched mine, I felt something akin to an electric jolt course through my body.

Except it wasn't electricity. It was desire.

Oh, no. This couldn't be happening. I could not want Drew Hartwell. I could not.

Who knows what might have happened next if the street hadn't been abruptly lit up by a shaft of lightning so brilliant, it cast everything into stark white relief, bright as daylight. For a split second, I could see every smile line in his darkly tanned face, every threadbare patch on his faded blue shirt, every dark eyelash rimming those ocean blue eyes.

Then we were once again plunged into semidarkness, and thunder crashed so loudly that I started, ripping my hand from his and nearly dropping my bike in alarm.

"Wow," Drew said, looking up. The clouds overhead

were racing by at a noticeably more rapid pace, while the leaves of the gumbo-limbo trees had begun to tussle along with the palm fronds in the wind. "Something's on its way, all right. Must be one of the first—"

Feeder bands, is what he'd probably been about to say. They were the outermost rain bands of the hurricane, and the meteorologists had been telling us to expect them all day.

But another crack of thunder, so loud and long it seemed to reverberate in my chest, cut him off.

When it was finished rumbling, Drew glanced at his wrist. Like many islanders, he wore a heavy, water-resistant dive watch on an ancient-looking leather band.

"Right on time," he commented.

I looked up at the sky, and the dark clouds sliding across it, and felt relieved. Not only because now I had a perfect excuse to escape—him, and whatever that white-hot flash of yearning had been that had shot through me at his touch. I couldn't. I wasn't ready. Not for this. Yet.

"If you mean rain, I'm out of here," I said. "This dress is dry clean only. Good-bye."

I tugged on my bike to get him to release it, but he only held on tighter.

"Come on," he said. "Don't go. You did do me a solid tonight, so allow me to return the favor. I've got my truck here. Why don't you let me drive you home before it starts to pour?"

I burst out laughing.

"Just how much of a Fresh Water do you think I am,

anyway?" I asked, thinking of all of Angela's warnings about him—that pickup truck of his, never parked in front of the same woman's house twice. This was exactly the sort of offer a player like Drew Hartwell would make. "I'm not going anywhere with you. I'm going home, like I said. By myself."

I reached out to pluck his fingers from my handlebars, and this time, he did let go.

"See you later, Drew." I swung my bike around and began pedaling.

He let me go. But not without trying to get the last word.

"Phone my aunt when you get home, so she knows you got there safely," he called after me.

I waved—without looking back—to indicate that I'd heard.

I was grateful my back was to him, though, so he couldn't see through the thin material of my dress how hard my heart was hammering.

CHAPTER ELEVEN

Emergency Disaster Survival Kit Basics—Home

First aid kit
Prescription medicines
Painkillers
Mosquito repellant
Watertight, easy-to-carry container to store essential documents such as cash and family records (birth certificates, proof of occupancy, important phone numbers in case your cell phone becomes inoperable, insurance documents, passports, bank and credit account numbers, etc.)

I reached home just before the heavens burst. I thought about poor Mrs. Hartwell's party, and hoped they'd managed to save the brisket.

I texted Angela to tell her I'd made it home all right (I hadn't seen another soul on the street), and asked her to let Mrs. Hartwell know, as well.

Angela texted back that she would, and also let me know that it was a shame I'd left the party early: after the rain started, everyone had moved inside to the dining room, where they'd pushed back the furniture and begun dancing to "Rock You Like a Hurricane" and other storm-related hits.

I figured I could live with the disappointment.

Gary was waiting for me just inside the door, as always. I don't know how he always knew exactly when it was me coming through the courtyard gate, but somehow, he did, and managed to race from his usual perch at the end of my bed to the front door before I even managed to turn the key.

"Hey, big boy," I said to him, as he launched a purring assault on my feet. "How have you been? What have you been up to while I was gone?"

The answer was: licked his food bowl clean, dragged every toy from his basket to the middle of the living room, and generally acted like a well-adjusted, well-loved cat.

After I was done texting Angela, I opened another can of food for him (chicken, his favorite, though I had to shred it a little with a fork before serving due to his lack of teeth), while listening to the eleven o'clock update from the storm hunters, which had just come on over the news.

No change in Hurricane Marilyn's strength or direction, let alone the urgency in the voices of the meteorologists. Anyone in its path was doomed.

I should have known my mother would have been watching the same forecast. My phone rang, and the words *Judge Justine* flashed across the screen. I'd never been able to list her as *Mom* in my contacts. She'd always been Judge Justine.

I felt guilty because it had been so long since I'd last talked to her, and the forecasts were so frightening. She had to be going out of her mind.

"Things can't get worse, right, big boy?" I asked Gary, whose only reply was a satisfied grunt. He was chowing down on his chicken medley as if he hadn't eaten in days, when in fact it had been only a couple of hours.

I pressed *Call*.

"Hi, Mom," I said.

"So you finally picked up," rasped the voice enjoyed by millions of daily listeners. "You'd better be on your way out of there!"

"I'm not, Mom." I slipped off my wedges and hauled a can of sparkling water from the fridge. This was going to be a long conversation. "I'm sure Caleb told you I'm staying put."

"Sabrina." How did she manage to inject so much disappointment into so few syllables? "Why? Why on earth would you do something so foolish? That's not how your father and I raised you. Have you even seen what they're saying on the news?"

"Yeah, I have, Mom." I unclipped my bra, slipping it out from beneath my dress and letting it drop to the floor before settling down on the couch. "And I'm going to be fine. Lots of people here aren't evacuating."

"Oh," she said, in her loftiest Judge Justine tone. "And have those people been through Category Five hurricanes before?"

"Mom." I cracked open my soda. "Give it a rest."

"I just don't understand it," she said. "Explain it to me, Sabrina. A very nice man—a man who wanted to marry you, by the way. That's right, Caleb told me—offers to come rescue you from a Category Five hurricane in his private jet, and you tell him no?"

"He's not that nice of a man." I lifted the remote and changed the channel on the TV. But it was no good. Daniella and I had only basic cable, and storm coverage was on every station except PBS and the ones dedicated to sports and home shopping. And on PBS they were having a fund-raising drive.

"Why are you still blaming Caleb for Kyle's actions?" Mom demanded.

"I don't blame Caleb for Kyle's actions. I blame Caleb for continuing to be friends with Kyle after I told him what Kyle did."

"In my day," Mom said, ignoring this, "we would have called what Kyle did a bad date."

I rolled my eyes. She'd said this before.

"I know, Mom," I said. "There are only two things wrong with that. One, I wasn't dating Kyle. I was dating Caleb. And two, if that's what they used to call a bad date in your day, I shudder to think what they'd call assault."

"Oh, Sabrina," my mother said, exhaling gustily into the phone. "What happened to you wasn't sexual assault. If you talked to some of the women who call into my show, they could tell you about sexual assault."

"I'm sure they could." I'd had to learn patience over the years in order to be able to deal with some of the things that came out of my mother's mouth. "I feel very badly for them. Do you make sure to tell them that the best thing for them to do is invest in gold, like it says during all the commercials on your show?"

Mom's patience with me, on the other hand, was running out. I could tell by the clipped tone in her voice.

"That is neither here nor there," she said. "And you know most of my audience don't have so much as a savings account, let alone a 401(k). They could do worse than investing in a few gold coins."

"Okay," I said, as Gary, done with his evening meal, leaped onto the couch and came purring into my lap, ready for his nightly ear scratching. "Well, it's been fun chatting with you, but I have to go to bed now. I'm working the breakfast shift tomorrow."

"It's not too late, you know," my mother said in desperation, just before I moved to hang up. "If you won't accept a ride from Caleb, I can still send a plane myself."

"Mom, the airport here is closed."

"To commercial traffic. But I talked to your uncle Steen"—her entertainment lawyer, and not my real uncle; my parents had no siblings—"and he says he knows one of the executives with NetJets, and they can have a jet fly down there to pick you up tomorrow morning, as a personal favor."

"Mom." The rain outside had stopped. I could no longer hear it beating on the metal shutters. All I could hear was Gary's loud, staccato purring as he lay on me, his paws gently kneading my belly. He was blissfully unaware of the tension I was feeling. He wanted only for my fingers to continue stroking his furry gray ears. "That's really nice of Uncle Steen. But I told you: I'm not leaving."

My mother sighed again into the phone. "Well, you'll call me when you change your mind. God willing it won't be too late."

I grinned. This was such a Judge Justine kind of statement.

"God willing," I said. "Good night, Mom."

"Good night, Sabrina. Remember, I love you."

This was a new thing. We'd never been the sort of family that said "I love you." Not that we hadn't loved one another, we'd just never said it out loud . . . not until after Dad had died, and I'd found out that my mother and I weren't actually related—not by blood, anyway.

"There just never seemed to be a good time to mention it," Mom had said when I'd asked why she'd never told me about how I'd been conceived. "You were always such a serious, anxious little kid. I didn't want to stress you out more than was necessary."

So it was better for me to find out the truth in my twenties, from a commercial DNA testing kit, purchased by one of my best friends as a joke to cheer me up?

"I love you, too, Mom," I said now, meaning it, and hung up.

I looked at Gary, snuggled up on my stomach, still furiously kneading my belly with his paws.

"I love you, too, little man," I said, cupping his sweet face with my hands. "I love you more than anything in the whole wide world. And I promise to take the best, best care of you, and protect you since you can't protect yourself."

Gary responded by purring harder, then flexing his front claws and sinking them through the material of my dress.

"Ow, Jesus!" I cried, and rolled him onto the floor, where he meowed plaintively, not understanding why his petting session had come to such an abrupt end.

But that was often the way with males. It took some of them longer than others to learn not to play too rough.

CHAPTER TWELVE

Time: 5:17 A.M.
Temperature: 80°F
Wind Speed: 19 MPH
Wind Gust: 35 MPH
Precipitation: 0.6 in.

Emergency Disaster Survival Kit Basics—Home

Gasoline
Propane
Coolers
Gloves
Garbage bags
Battery-charged radio
Batteries
Flashlights
Tools such as utility knife, machete, power drill, chain saw

By dawn the next morning, the wind had picked up noticeably. It was still warm—it was always warm on Little Bridge Island—but the bamboo that Lydia had planted outside our bedroom windows for privacy was beginning to beat against the shutters, as rhythmically as drums.

When I stepped out to get the paper—Daniella insisted on getting home delivery of *The Gazette*, Little Bridge's local paper, and I never complained, because every morning over my coffee I liked reading about which of my customers at the café had been busted for DUI—I could see that some of the pink and white blossoms on the frangipani had been sent skittering across the courtyard, piling up against our front door, where they lay like inert ballerinas, their tutus deflated.

The mockingbird was still on his usual perch in the treetop, however, singing his heart out, hoping to attract a mate. So things couldn't be that bad.

The staff of the newspaper had decided to go for a less than subtle approach with their morning headline: "GET OUT!" screamed the front page, with a photo of motorists lined up along the highway out of Little Bridge.

The morning news shows weren't any less emphatic. Basically, anyone in the path of Marilyn was still on a road to their demise. There was little to no news from Cuba, over which the slow-moving storm had just passed. All power and communication from there had been lost. The eye of the storm would soon be chugging its way across the Florida Straits on a direct course for the U.S.

We were, as my mother had assured me, all going to die.

I let Gary out to perform his morning ablutions (they

included chewing on the few blades of grass that grew beneath the frangipani, and then rolling in the dirt), then let him back inside, gave him his antibiotics for his now toothless gums, fed him, and headed out to the café. I took my bike instead of the scooter since I still wanted to save on gas, and also because they'd said on the news that there would be rain bands on and off all day.

As I pedaled across the quiet, sleepy town, I marveled once again at how many homes had been boarded up, seemingly overnight. I didn't spot a single one with bare glass showing.

Until I got to the café, that is. There, the boarding process was only just under way. And the person in charge of it was someone I recognized only too well. Someone who wasn't wearing a shirt.

"Hi," Drew Hartwell said in a flat voice as I hopped off my bike.

"It's good to see you, too."

I pushed down my kickstand with my heel and snaked my lock between my bike frame and the rack, keeping my back toward him. His truck, I noted, was the only vehicle in the parking lot this early. Not even Ed was at work yet.

Drew didn't reply, merely lifted his drill and sent another bit through the metal grid that secured the shutters he was using to cover the café's large windows.

"How's Socks?" I asked, still keeping my gaze pointedly averted from his shirtless chest.

"You mean Bob."

Now I had to glance at him, because I was confused. "No. I mean Rick's dog, Socks."

"He's my dog now," Drew said, "and I've renamed him Bob. He went through a really bad time, but he's got a new life now, so I figured he should have a new name to go along with it."

I was a little startled by this, more by how similar it felt to my own life than anything else. I'd dyed my hair pink and started calling myself Bree, not Sabrina, to represent my new life in Little Bridge . . . or at least, my new life in Little Bridge for now.

It made sense to me that a dog who'd gone through a bad time ought to have a new name, as well, as long as he wasn't too attached to his old one. Gary had been found as a stray on the streets by volunteers for the animal shelter. They'd decided to call him Gary, and the name seemed to fit him. I hadn't even considered changing it, since he came cheerfully when called.

But why not change an abused dog's name to something different to represent his new, better life?

"Well," I said. The man really did look great without a shirt on. There was no denying it. "That's good. As long as he's happy."

"He seemed very happy," Drew said, "when I left him this morning. He'd taken over my bed with all my other dogs. I'll be lucky to get it back, I guess." He drilled another screw.

Well. This told me something else about Drew Hartwell. He let his dogs sleep in his bed.

Not that this was a bad thing. I let my cat sleep in my bed.

But Gary was only one cat. Drew now had four dogs. It seemed as if things were getting fairly crowded in Drew Hartwell's bed.

Wait. Why was I even thinking of Drew Hartwell's bed? I was on a mancation. I wasn't even supposed to be interested in that kind of stuff. I was only supposed to be working and painting and enjoying a healthy Little Bridge lifestyle. Get it together, Bree!

My conversation with Drew Hartwell seemingly at an end thanks to the scream of his drill, I opened up the café and went to work writing the specials on the chalkboards, as I'd promised Angela I would, minding my own business and paying no attention whatsoever to the extremely good-looking shirtless man putting up the shutters outside the place.

At least, that's what I told myself. Truthfully, I might have slipped him a glance or two. I definitely overpoured more than a few cups of coffee as I watched him bend over to pick up more screws, and once I accidentally gave the mayor over easy instead of sunny-side-up eggs.

By the eight A.M. hurricane update—when the place was as packed as I'd ever seen it—Drew had mercifully finished shuttering everything except the front door. We had to hang a handwritten sign (*Come on in! We're open!*) so people would know there was life inside (although the lights were on, and there was cold AC blowing). This was a relief, not only because he put his shirt back on, but also because I could once again concentrate on my work.

Still, the eight o'clock update was grim. Reports had finally begun to roll in from Cuba. A ten-foot storm surge had taken nine lives so far. The storm was now only two hundred miles away and though winds had dropped to "only" Category 2 level (as Lucy Hartwell had predicted, the mountains of Cuba had taken a lot of energy out of the storm), forecasters expected Marilyn to gather strength over the warm waters between Cuba and the Keys, then hit coastal Florida with "possibly unprecedented strength, causing imminent death."

Many of the old-timers, upon hearing this, lifted their beers (it was never too early for beer at the Mermaid) in a toast. "To our imminent deaths!"

But this turned out not to be as humorous as they thought when it was reported that, even though the storm hadn't yet arrived, there'd already been a death in Little Bridge attributed to Marilyn.

"You guys, I was already called to the scene of an accident out on Highway One," Ryan Martinez, one of the sheriff's deputies, came in to breakfast to announce. "An evacuee, in a panic to leave town before the rains hit, had a stress-induced heart attack at the wheel, then drove his vehicle straight into the mangroves. He drowned before emergency personnel could get to him."

"More people die evacuating from hurricanes than from the actual hurricanes themselves," Ed informed us gravely.

"True." His shuttering complete, Drew had come inside to enjoy his usual (Spanish omelet, only he'd added a side of real bacon, most likely since he'd expended so many calories lifting the heavy metal panels). "But don't most deaths occur in the aftermath of storms, from flooding?"

"Yes," Ryan said. "But that's not going to happen here. The sheriff's got me and the other guys helping him set up cots over at the high school as a shelter of last resort for anyone who hasn't been able to evacuate and feels they might be in danger. High school's on high ground and built to withstand Cat Five winds. I think we're gonna have quite a crowd in there."

I was listening closely. "What about pets?" I asked. "Will you take people with pets?"

"Of course. Me and my girlfriend are going to hunker down there with this fine lady for the duration."

At the words "this fine lady," Ryan softly tapped the lowest rung of the stool he was sitting on, and his canine partner—a beautiful and sweet-natured German shepherd who'd been dozing peacefully at his feet—alertly lifted her head and gave her long, fringed tail a wag.

The dog's sweet nature was deceptive, however. I'd once seen her lock hold of the wrist of a diner fleeing without paying his bill and refuse to release it until Ryan gave her the command.

"We were going to spend this weekend in Orlando at my cousin's wedding," Ryan went on, "but duty calls. This'll be more fun, anyway."

"Only a cop would consider a hurricane more fun than a wedding," Angela whispered to me in passing, rolling her eyes, and we both laughed.

As the day wore on, the crowd at the café began to

thin out, even the island's hardiest charter boat captains beginning to take the order to evacuate seriously. Everyone began going home to make sure their houses and boats were secured against the expected 130-mile-an-hour winds.

By one o'clock, the place was empty—save for a few of the regular afternoon barflies—and dark, thanks to the shutters and the fact that the sky had become so gray and overcast. Thunder rumbled in the distance—though there was no visible lightning—and the wind was stronger than ever, thirty miles per hour, with gusts of up to fifty, according to the Weather Channel.

"Anyone left in the Florida Keys," a reporter stationed in Key West cheerfully said into his microphone as wind and surf buffeted him, "must surely have a death wish."

"Go on home," Ed said to me and Angela gruffly, switching off both TVs. "I'm gonna close up early today. I'll pay you through the rest of your shift, though."

Angela and I eyed each other uncertainly. Although Ed and his wife happily paid their employees' insurance, they had never, in all the time I'd known them, let us off early with pay.

"Are . . . are you sure, Ed?" Angela asked.

He'd grunted, giving the counter a swipe with his favorite striped dish towel. "No sense staying open for the lunch and dinner shifts today when it's just gonna be dead like this." He'd already kicked out the barflies, who'd shuffled amiably off to Ron's Place, a bar up the street that had never, in anyone's memory, closed due to weather. "No one'll be comin' in anyways once it starts rainin'."

With Angela hurrying off to her mother's and no other hurricane parties to go to, I had nothing else to do, so I took Ed up on his offer, pedaling home to feed Gary, have lunch, and make sure all of my belongings were sitting at least a foot off the floor in the event of flooding.

At least, that's what my plan was until I finally got to my place after battling the wind—which I expected to be much more oppressive than it was, but at this stage was more like riding against the stream of a blow dryer set on cool—and opened the heavy wooden gate to the courtyard to wheel my bike inside . . . and froze.

The frangipani tree that for the entire time I'd lived there had provided shade and, at least part of the year, beauty and fragrance from its blossoms, was gone.

Well, not gone, exactly, but completely uprooted and lying on its side, as if someone had chopped it down, leaving pink blossoms scattered everywhere.

But no one had chopped it down. Its root-ball was facing the gate, leaving a deep, gaping hole in the courtyard floor, while its distressingly broken branches were pressed up obscenely against the doors and windows (fortunately shuttered) to both my apartment as well as Lydia and Sonny's and Patrick and Bill's, as if crying, "Let me in! Let me in!"

But thankfully, none of us had been home at the time it had blown over. At least, I didn't think so. Except for the wind, which continued to lazily sweep the frangipani blossoms back and forth across the tiles, the courtyard was completely still. The mockingbird that for so long had perched atop the tree and sung its little heart out was gone.

Most of the birds on the island, in fact, seemed to be gone. I could hear no birdsong. Clearly, they sensed something instinctively that I did not.

"Crap," I said aloud. Because I could see no way in which I was going to be able to carve a path through those twisted roots and broken branches—some of them oozing a sticky white liquid—back into my apartment. Not without the aid of a saw. Or possibly a bulldozer. I was locked out of my place until help, in some form, arrived.

Which was bad—really, really bad—because Gary was in there. Sweet, helpless Gary.

I whipped out my cell phone, snapped a shot of the fallen tree, and sent the photo along with a few urgent texts to both my landlady and to Patrick and Bill, then stood there and . . . waited.

What else could I do? I didn't have any tools, or access to any, and it didn't seem like the kind of thing to call 911 over when what few emergency personnel we had left on the island were already so stressed with real emergencies. Over and over on the Weather Channel they'd shown clips of the governor saying that anyone who chose not to evacuate was taking their life into their own hands, and not to expect rescue from emergency services, who were evacuating themselves or were already overloaded with real emergencies (which this was not . . . yet).

But of course, this would be a real emergency soon—to me, anyway—if I couldn't get in to save Gary.

And what about Patrick and Bill? It didn't look as if they were home—surely if they were they'd have heard the tree fall and be trying to open their door.

But what about Sonny's guinea pigs?

When no one texted me back in ten minutes I knew what I had to do, even though I really didn't want to.

I didn't bother texting him, because Ed was so anti–cell phones. Instead I called him at his home, on his landline. The Hartwells were some of the few people I knew who still had one.

He answered on the second ring. "This is Ed."

"Hi, Ed," I said, trying not to sound as desperate as I felt. "It's me, Bree. I'm really sorry to bother you, but a tree—a really big tree—has fallen across the courtyard of my apartment building and is blocking my door, and the doors to some of my neighbors. I think a wind gust must have blown it over. Anyway, I can't get in, and my cat is inside, and I think—"

Ed's voice was sharp with interest. I'd forgotten how much he loved any kind of crisis, especially if it allowed him to use large tools. "A big tree, you say? How big?"

I eyed the tree. How was I supposed to know how big the tree was? I was no arborist. "Really big. Twenty feet, maybe?"

He sounded disappointed. "That's not so big."

"Well, it looks like it just flopped over, roots and all—"

Ed sounded more interested. "Root rot. Probably from all the rain last night. Okay, you stay put, we'll be right over. Where are you again?"

I thanked him and gave him the address. It wasn't until I hung up that I realized what he'd said . . . *we'll* be right over.

We who?

And sure enough, less than five minutes later, Ed Hartwell arrived in a battered red pickup that I recognized as belonging to his nephew . . . with that same nephew driving.

No. Oh, no.

I tried not to notice how enticingly male Drew looked as he swung from the truck, his white linen shirt half-unbuttoned due to the oppressive heat, revealing illicit glimpses of that taut brown stomach and chest.

I especially tried not to notice as he grabbed one of the biggest chain saws I'd ever seen out of the back of his truck. I told myself not to pay attention to how naturally he held it, or how good he looked with it. I mean, a chain saw? Since when was I attracted to men who carried chain saws?

"I don't know how it happened," I babbled as the two men walked over. "The tree was fine this morning when I left. And then when I walked in a little while ago after work, it was like this—"

I gestured at the tree. Drew whistled appreciatively at its size.

"Definitely root rot." Ed, inspecting the damage, sounded more excited than I'd ever heard him. "Rains last night must've soaked it, and these wind gusts we've been having pushed the whole thing right over. Some of 'em have gotten up to fifty miles per hour, which isn't that much comparatively, but for a tree with roots like this—" He touched one of the branches, which snapped off in his hand but oozed an unctuous liquid. He shook his head. "This tree is sick. It got too big for the space it was planted in. Not enough permeable surface for its roots to absorb moisture and grow. Even if we pushed it back in, it would just fall over again in the next big windstorm. Tree commission should never have allowed it to be planted here in the first place."

Yes. Little Bridge Island had a tree commission. No one was allowed to cut down, plant, or trim a tree without its permission. The "Cheers and Jeers" section of the *Gazette* was often devoted exclusively to savage personal attacks on citizens who'd done a hack job on their trees.

"Lucky you weren't inside," Drew commented laconically to me.

"Yes," I said, keeping my gaze carefully averted from his open shirtfront. "But my cat is inside. Apartment B, right there, with all those branches pressed up against the door? Oh, and my landlady's son's guinea pigs are in A. Someone is supposed to be coming over to take care of them, but I don't know how he's going to—"

"Easy."

Then Drew pulled the chain on his saw, and it started right up—so loud that I flung my hands over my ears.

"Do you have to—?"

Grinning, he began to hack away at the branches blocking access to my front door.

"You want to see your cat again, right?" he shouted over the din. "Then the answer is yes, I have to."

I glared at him. I would have liked to present a calmer, cooler, more collected self in the crisis, but I wasn't used to people starting chain saws right next to me. Especially people who looked like he did, with his muscles gleaming with sweat, and his five o'clock shadow darkening his jawline.

Things got even worse a few seconds later, when he took his shirt off. Apparently, the heat and humidity simply became too much for him.

"Here," he said, distractedly handing the limp, damp garment to me. "Mind finding a place for that?"

It wouldn't have mattered if I did mind, I thought as I took the shirt between a thumb and forefinger. I needed to play nice with him, since he was the one with the chain saw. And not just for myself. Though I'd heard back from Patrick and Bill that they and their dogs were safe—they had already checked in to the hotel—Sonny's mother had sent a frantic text in response to my voice mail:

No gas. Staying w/friends in Vero Beach. Cousin Sean says he will look after the piggies if you can have tree removed. So sorry, save all bills for me! Much luv, Lydia

So it was up to me to save Gary as well as R2-D2 and C-3PO.

Well, me and this half-naked, hard-muscled guy in my courtyard.

"There," Drew said, in a satisfied tone, switching off the saw. He'd made short work of the frangipani, clipping away the branches blocking all the doors in what seemed like seconds. "That should work for now. Anything else I can do for you, Fresh Water?"

Was there anything else he could do for me? Was he serious?

I blinked at him as he stood there, holding the heavy chain saw, his tanned, well-muscled arms and chest glistening with even more sweat than before, which was odd because the sky was really quite overcast.

Why, yes. Yes, actually, there was quite a lot he could do for me. He could run that razor-stubbled mouth of his all down my—

God, what was wrong with me?

"No," I said quickly, shaking myself. "No, no, thanks. Thanks so much, both of you, for helping me." All of my attention had been so focused on shirtless Drew, I'd practically forgotten that Ed was still standing there, too. "I'm so grateful. I'm sure you want to get going—" Please, please get going. "Unless . . ."

Was I being rude? What was the correct protocol when a shirtless man and his uncle came to your house and removed a bunch of tree limbs with a chain saw so you could get inside it?

"Could I, er, get you a drink first? I think I might have some beer in my—"

Before the words were fully out of my mouth, Drew was already setting down the chain saw. Then he took his shirt from my hand, threw it over his shoulder, and strode toward my front door. "Sure. Beer would be great."

This was not the outcome I'd been expecting.

"I gotta go," Ed was saying as he looked down at his cell phone—on which, it turned out, he did know how to both send and receive texts. "Lu needs me to pick up more of that smoked barbecue sauce at Frank's while they're still open. I guess she just likes me wasting gas when there's a shortage."

Drew tossed him a glance. "You're wasting my gas because you're in my truck, Ed."

Ed waved at him dismissively. "I'll be right back. I'll pick up more beer, too, if they have any left."

I watched in some dismay as he left. *Don't,* I wanted to cry. *Please don't leave me alone with your hot shirtless nephew.*

Especially as the sky was looking more and more overcast, thunder rumbling more often, and the wind getting stronger . . . strong enough that it was picking up all the blossoms that had shaken loose from the branches of the frangipani tree and was sending them spiraling around the courtyard in a desperately sad ballet.

But of course I couldn't tell him not to go. So instead, my fingers unaccountably shaky, I merely undid the locks and led Drew Hartwell into the cool air-conditioning of my apartment.

"Sorry about the mess," I babbled. "My roommate's out of town so I haven't been bothering to clean up after myself—"

Gary rocketed toward us like a furry gray missile, giving me an indignant meow for having been gone so long, then buried his head against Drew's work-booted feet.

"Whoa," Drew said, looking down.

"Oh, that's Gary." I noticed my bra from last night lying on the floor, swiftly lifted it, and stuffed it between the sofa cushions before he noticed. "He does that to everyone. I got him from the shelter, he'd been there for years. They don't know what happened to him before that, they think he was abandoned and lived on the streets for a while. All his teeth rotted out, so I had to have them removed." I was babbling, but I couldn't help it. Drew Hartwell was in my apartment. "He's attention starved."

"I can tell." Drew stooped to rub Gary's head with an outstretched index finger. "Hey, there, Gary," he said, as Gary purred, contorting himself in absolute ecstasy around Drew's foot. "You're a good boy."

"I'll . . . I'll just get you a beer."

I hurried into the kitchen, trying not to freak out over the fact that Drew Hartwell—*Drew Hartwell*—was in my apartment, shirtless, being nice to my cat.

"Thanks," I heard Drew say, from the living room. "And then you better start getting your stuff together. Yours and whatever you need for Gary, here."

I popped back out from the kitchen, two cold bottles of

beer in my hands, not sure I'd heard him correctly. "I'm sorry, what?"

"Your stuff," Drew said pleasantly, reaching out to take one of the bottles from me. "You should start getting some stuff together. Because I'm taking you back home with me."

CHAPTER THIRTEEN

Time: 1:36 P.M.
Temperature: 84°F
Wind Speed: 24 MPH
Wind Gust: 44 MPH
Precipitation: 0.3 in.

He tugged on the beer, since I still hadn't released it.

"For the hurricane?" He raised his dark eyebrows. "My aunt Lucy said she told you. You obviously can't stay here."

"What?" I released the bottle but continued to stare up at him in shock. "Yes, I can. Of course I can stay here. You cleared the tree out of the way. Why can't I stay here?"

"The tree's just the beginning of your problems." Drew twisted the cap off his beer. "The storm hasn't even started yet and you already almost got trapped in here. Imagine what will happen when the rain and storm surge come. This apartment building is in the flood zone. Why do you think all of your neighbors have left?"

I looked past him, through the partially open door,

where Gary had sneaked out into the courtyard and was cautiously sniffing at the fallen limbs of his former shade tree. "Okay," I said. "I can see your point. But I don't need to stay with your aunt. I told you I have a place to stay, over at the Cascabel, with—"

"I thought we went through this already." Drew shook his head in disbelief. "You're not staying at that hotel. Despite what people say, it isn't safe. You want to take your cat somewhere that isn't safe?"

That stung. "No. Of course not."

"Then go get your stuff. I'm taking you to my aunt's house." He swigged from the beer. "And hurry up. I want to get back to my place and let the dogs out for a run before the next rain band hits."

God. Was there ever anyone bossier in all of human existence—except for my mother, of course?

What made it worse was that he was right. Mrs. Hartwell's offer seemed like a much more sensible choice than sharing a room with Patrick and Bill and their three dogs and George Foreman grill at the hotel, or even hunkering down at the high school, which I'd also been considering. And I had long ago given up on the idea of driving up to Coral Gables to stay with Daniella, given the gasoline situation.

So I went into my bedroom and quickly began throwing things into an overnight bag . . . at least until I heard Drew call curiously from the living room, "Hey, who did all these paintings?"

My heart sank. Suddenly I remembered something else

I'd done the night before, something besides leave my bra draped across the middle of the living room floor.

"Uh, no one." My cheeks flushed with embarrassment as I darted from the bedroom, hoping to mitigate whatever damage was already done.

But it was too late. I'd forgotten that last night, after talking to my mother, I'd taken out every painting I'd done since arriving in Little Bridge, and laid them out in a half-sentimental, half-proud display across the coffee table, as if to remind myself that my stay on the island hadn't been a total waste of time.

Now Drew Hartwell was standing over the coffee table, looking down at them—twenty-four in all, twenty-five if you included the one I hadn't finished—with his beer forgotten in one hand, a professorial air about him . . . if professors ever went around in half-open linen shirts, cargo shorts, and Timberlands.

Noticing I was hesitating in the entranceway, he glanced at me with those too bright blue eyes.

"*No one?*" he asked. "*No one* painted two dozen little cloudscapes and left them in your living room?"

"Okay, fine." I was still flushing. "I painted them. It's . . . it's a hobby."

He whistled, looking back down at the watercolors. "Impressive work for a hobby. You're pretty good."

My pride felt pricked. *Pretty good?*

Because I knew they were better than *pretty good*. Or at least, better than average. I'd always loved painting, and because I'd loved it, I'd practiced. All the time. Practicing makes most people good at anything, whether they have a natural talent for it or not.

And I had natural talent. That's what every art teacher I'd ever had had told me.

"Thanks," I said, keeping my pride in check. "I like to paint. I don't know about the subject matter . . . clouds. It's a little clichéd. But painting them relaxes me."

"You did this one by the dock." He pointed at one of the paintings that showed a little more foreground than the others. None of them were larger than six by four inches, but in some I managed to work in a little seascape in addition to sky. "The dock outside the café?"

"Yes." I was still embarrassed. I'd wanted to be an art major in college, but my mother especially had discouraged it. "How will you possibly be able to support yourself with an art degree?" she'd asked. "What kind of job will you be able to get, after college?"

She'd been right, of course. So I'd majored in history, since it was a degree everyone said would help you excel in law school.

Not true in my case.

"Anything with a sky-to-ocean view is popular with tourists," Drew said, still looking down at my watercolors. "And these are small enough to fit into a carry-on suitcase. You could easily sell these around here. For a lot."

"Thanks," I said again, and this time I wasn't just being polite. "But I kind of want to hang on to them. I liked . . . making them."

"I understand."

And for the first time, I thought he actually might. After all, he was a carpenter. He restored historic homes and was making one for himself. He loved making things with his hands, just like I did.

"You didn't inherit this kind of talent from Judge Justine," he said, nodding toward the paintings. "Unless there's something about her I really don't know. Was your dad artistic?"

Remembering my dad, and how he'd made sure that we showed up on the dock—the same dock from which I'd made most of these paintings—to watch the sunset every night when we were in Little Bridge, I felt myself becoming emotional.

"No." I ducked my head, so he wouldn't see that my eyes had suddenly filled with tears. "Neither of my parents was artistic."

My egg donor mother, though. She'd included a few drawing samples in her application—along with multiple photos, making it easy to see that it was from her I'd inherited my small frame, blond hair, and brown eyes—no doubt in order to make it stand out to a discriminating couple like my parents.

It had worked.

I wasn't about to tell any of this to Drew Hartwell, however.

"I better finish getting my stuff together before Ed gets back," I said, instead.

"Oh." Drew glanced down at his enormous dive watch. "Yeah. Sure."

What did one pack for a hurricane? I wondered. I still had Daniella's list, of course, but it no longer seemed to apply since I'd be staying in someone else's house. The Hartwells probably had more emergency candles and batteries than they needed.

Still, it wouldn't hurt to bring my own. Everyone in a crisis needs to pull their own weight.

So in addition to the candles and batteries, I threw the chips and charcuterie I'd bought at Frank's Food Emporium into a canvas shopping tote, as well.

Drew stood in the kitchen doorway, watching me curiously, his half-finished beer in one hand.

"What are you bringing all that for?"

"I'm not a charity case," I said, as I added the bottle of vodka, as well. "I don't expect your family to feed me."

He said nothing more until I pulled something out of the vegetable crisper.

"Is that a cheese ball?"

"Yes. So what?"

He took a last swig from his beer. "So, nothing. I just haven't seen one of those in a long time."

"They didn't have much left by the time I got to the store," I said, hoping my hair hid my flaming cheeks as I slipped the cheese ball into the tote. "But who cares? People like a good cheese ball."

"Well, some people."

"What is that even supposed to mean?" I snapped. "Is that some sort of classist statement about cheese?"

"Whoa," he said, backing slowly away from the kitchen. "What is your problem?"

I shook my head and stomped away from him, into my bedroom. I didn't have time for him or his judgmental opinions about cheese. I needed to get back to my list. I couldn't forget Gary's antibiotics and canned food. I didn't know how long hurricanes lasted, but I brought a ten-day supply, just in case.

But what about clothes? Packing for a hurricane evacuation wasn't like packing for a weekend in the Hamptons. Even though I was going to be staying in the home of an excellent hostess (who was also my boss), I doubted there were going to be any dinner parties, so no need for sundresses. I distractedly threw some shorts, T-shirts, lounge pants, underwear, toiletries, a rain jacket, and a pair of running shoes into an overnight bag.

Then, grabbing Gary's cat carrier, I went out into the living room and pronounced myself ready to go.

Drew eyed the flashlight sticking out of the tote bag. "You don't need that."

"I intend to pull my own weight," I said, stubbornly.

But he'd already taken the bag from me and was going through it, looking in disbelief at the lavender-scented candle I'd bought.

"My aunt and uncle have a whole-house generator powered by a thousand-gallon propane tank that's buried under their front yard. That's enough for them to run every electric device in their home for a week, if they needed to."

He held up the candle. "So what good is this thing going to do?"

I snatched the candle out of his hand and stuffed it back into the tote. "Lavender is a little-known mosquito repellant," I said. "Everyone is going to want my candle when mosquitoes start bothering us."

"You're not going to be bothered by a lot of mosquitoes when you're sitting inside in the air-conditioning, thanks to the generator, Fresh Water. How about instead of that," he said, pointing at the candle, "you bring those." He pointed at my paintings. "If it floods in here, you're going to lose them."

I looked at my cloud paintings, still sitting on the coffee table. It pained me to admit he was right about something.

"Fine," I said with reluctance. "I'll bring both."

"That's not what I—"

But it was too late. I was already stacking the paintings in another tote bag I'd grabbed from the kitchen, along with my painting supplies (I kept them in a small tackle box I'd bought at the marine hardware store).

It was only then that I felt ready to face the daunting task of getting Gary into his carrier.

Gary was, truly, the sweetest and most affectionate of cats, which was why I'd felt so lucky as opposed to aggrieved that the animal shelter had allowed me to adopt him, despite his costing me a small fortune in medical bills.

But the one area in which he could have used some improvement was his attitude toward his carrier. He hated it.

So the minute he laid eyes on it, Gary turned tail and

tried to run out the open front door for the relative safety of the courtyard, despite the rising wind and increasingly loud thunder.

Drew, however, caught him and swung him into the air.

"Hey, there," he said, cradling Gary in his arms like he was a large, furry baby. "Where do you think you're going, buddy? You're coming with us. That's the only place you're going."

Gary didn't exactly purr, but he didn't try to flay Drew alive with his claws, either (Gary had learned over the past week and a half that biting didn't work anymore, since he had no teeth). He seemed to accept his fate, lying limply in Drew's arms, giving me a reproachful look that seemed to ask, *Really? You're letting this happen? Fine.*

It took me a second or two to open the door to the carrier. That's because, upon seeing Drew Hartwell standing there with my cat in his arms, my heart had stuttered.

But whose heart wouldn't have skipped a beat at the sight of a big, handsome man holding a cute, furry cat in his arms—even if that cat happened to have no teeth?

Gary had begun vocalizing in an irritable way—his claws still sheathed—to show he was unhappy with the situation when Drew looked up and caught me staring at him.

"What?" he asked, still cradling the cat. "Am I doing this wrong? Should I put him down? I'm more of a dog than a cat person, but I like cats, too."

"No," I said, glad for the excuse to look away. I did not need my heartstrings pulled in his direction right now. I stepped forward and took Gary from his arms, taking care to pay no attention to the way he smelled—deliciously, of clean, male sweat and frangipani—or his body heat, which was tantalizingly warm. "It's all good."

Gary put up only a token fight as I stuffed him into the carrier. It was as if he, like the birds, sensed something bad was coming, and he'd better not stand in its way. Or more likely he sensed that I was in no mood for his nonsense.

"There," I said, when I'd latched the cat in safely. "All set."

As if on cue, a car horn sounded outside. Ed was back with Drew's pickup.

Drew took a last look around the living room. "You sure you have everything?"

I glanced around, then remembered. "The starter!"

I scampered to grab it from the fridge. Thank God I'd remembered or Daniella would have been crushed. That sourdough starter had been in her family for years. Every holiday, she made tons of loaves, which she shipped off to various members of her family, who worshipped her for making bread that tasted just like Grandma's.

Drew eyed the clear container in my hands distrustfully. "Should I even ask?"

"It's probably better that you don't."

He sighed. "Fine. Let's go."

CHAPTER FOURTEEN

Emergency Disaster Survival Kit Basics—Pets

Pet carrier and leash
Pet medications/travel documents
Pet food (7–10 day supply)
Cat litter and box
Current photos of pet in case you are separated
Pet bed and toys

The room into which Mrs. Hartwell ushered me was lovely.

"I'm sorry it isn't a bedroom," she said, apologetically. "But all of our guest rooms are upstairs, and a central room on the first floor is the safest place to be during a storm, especially one that could generate tornadoes."

"Oh, no, this is . . . fine." I could hardly believe what I was seeing. "Thank you so much, Mrs. H."

The first-floor library—with its own set of French doors that I could close off from the rest of the house for privacy, as well as to keep Gary from wandering—had originally been the home's morning room, where the first Mrs. Hartwell (whose husband, Captain Hartwell, had built the house in 1855) had probably sat and answered her correspondence every day after breakfast.

And why wouldn't she want to? Where the walls weren't covered in ornately scrolled white bookcases, double stacked with books, they were stenciled—not papered, because that would have been unheard of in South Florida in 1855—in cornflower blue overlaid with gold fleur-de-lis. The room smelled tantalizingly of pine and old books.

I felt like an elegant lady just being in the room. Gary seemed to realize that he, too, was moving up in the world, since he quickly made himself at home on the air mattress Ed had inflated for me on the floor, though I noticed that he was eyeing one of the antique love seats, with its temptingly puffy pink silk cushion.

All the information about the first Mrs. Hartwell was given to me by Nevaeh as I unpacked Gary's things and set up a litter box for him, deep in a far corner of the room. There was a portrait of the first Mrs. Hartwell hanging over the antique scroll-top desk, and she looked like a handsome but unhappy woman, wearing heavy mourning clothes.

"All of her four children," Nevaeh informed me, "died of yellow fever before the age of ten. They said she died of a broken heart soon after."

"Oh," I said. "My."

"But no worries. Her husband went to the convent school and found a new girl to marry. They had eleven children, all of whom lived and went on to produce their own kids, and then those kids had kids, and then those kids had kids, one of whom was my uncle Ed!"

This was one of the strangest local history lessons I'd ever received, but I attempted to roll with it.

"Wow," I said. "Neat."

"We're going to have so much fun while you're here," Nevaeh assured me, as if thunder wasn't rolling ominously beyond the lace curtains of my room's single window (shuttered, so I could see nothing of the view). "We can do each other's nails!"

This did not sound fun to me at all, given that I kept my nails clipped as short as possible to avoid nervously biting them.

But I politely refrained from saying so, since Nevaeh was my hostess by proxy.

"Sure," I said. "Maybe later, though. I need to make sure Gary gets settled in."

"Oh, of course," Nevaeh said, though she gave me an odd look, since anyone could see Gary was currently contentedly cleaning himself, as at home as if he'd always lived there. This was a far cry from my apartment, and an even further step up from the animal shelter where he'd spent so many years. Gary clearly thought he'd won the feline lottery.

"I have to go put this in the refrigerator," I said, showing Nevaeh the container holding Daniella's yeast starter. "It's my roommate's, and it's super important to her that it stays cold at all times."

"Uh, sure."

Nevaeh glanced nervously toward the kitchen. I soon realized why. I could hear raised voices coming from there—one belonging to Drew. It appeared he was getting yelled at for something by his aunt and uncle.

Was this more drama about what had happened last night at the party with Rick Chance? And was it wrong that I felt as if I needed to get in there to watch? Not to defend him, of course—I was quite sure Drew Hartwell didn't need my help. But I felt a natural curiosity about what was going on.

"Well." I got up from the floor and grabbed the handles to the tote bag containing all the foodstuffs I'd brought along. "Do you mind?" Nevaeh looked as if she did mind, so I added, "I brought a cheese ball, too, you know. Maybe you'd like some?"

Nevaeh finally stood up but looked confused. "What's a cheese ball?"

"You don't know what a cheese ball is? Let me show you."

Closing the library doors to keep Gary from roaming—I knew both the parrot and the rabbits would be temptations he might find too hard to resist—I followed Nevaeh toward the kitchen.

The Hartwells' fifty-six-inch flat-screen television—so fun but so out of place in such a historic home—was on in the living room. We had to pass it to get to the kitchen. It was tuned, obviously, to the Weather Channel.

"Things are looking grim here in Key West, Cynthia," a reporter was saying into the camera as he stood, in all-weather gear, on a pier beneath a leaden sky. "And the first bands of the storm are only hours, if not minutes, away. We can only wonder what it will be like when they finally arrive."

Behind him, tourists who'd neglected to evacuate stood wearing shorts and T-shirts, holding cans of beer, and making rude gestures into the camera.

"Idiots," Nevaeh said, shaking her head. "And those stupid reporters aren't even brave enough to come here to Little Bridge, where the storm is actually heading."

I raised my eyebrows. She was right. The feed was bouncing among news journalists stationed all over South Florida—Key West, Miami, Naples, and back—but not a single one was in Little Bridge.

"Maybe," I ventured, "it's because they consider this island too small to be of interest."

"That's not it." Nevaeh's tone was bitter. "It's because they know if they stay here, they'll be trapped. Or die."

I glanced at her in surprise, about to ask if she believed this, too, when there was a knock on the front door.

"Oh, Katie!" she cried, in a completely different voice. "Katie's here, yay!"

She turned and went skipping for the door without another word, leaving me, feeling a little stunned, to make the rest of the journey to the kitchen solo.

Mrs. Hartwell was standing in front of the stove—a very old-looking six-burner, on which multiple pans were sizzling. I could smell the tantalizing scent of frying onion and garlic.

But she wasn't looking at what it was that she was cooking.

All her attention was focused on her nephew, whose strong, muscular back was pressed up against the refrigerator, his arms folded across his chest and his head bowed low enough that his dark hair fell across his face, obscuring it from view.

He'd managed to find a new shirt somewhere and had even buttoned it up properly and washed his hands. But he was still wearing the Timberlands with cargo shorts, a look I could only imagine Caleb sporting on Halloween when dressed as some sort of celebrity contractor from a fixer-upper show on cable television.

"Haven't you been listening to a word of what they've been saying on the news, Drew?" Mrs. Hartwell was demanding. "This isn't some run-of-the-mill tropical depression! It's a full-fledged hurricane—the strongest one that's come close to this island in years. And you still intend to weather it out in your new house on the beach?"

"Lu." Drew sounded tired. "I told you. I built that house to withstand a storm this big."

"Fine." She waved a wooden soup spoon. "That's great. But why do you have to be *in* it while the storm is going on?"

"Because." I caught a brief glimpse of one of those preternaturally bright blue eyes as he lifted his head. "I've got to be there to fix things on the fly in case something goes wrong."

"Oh, things will go wrong, all right." Mrs. Hartwell turned back to her onions and garlic and gave them a vicious stir. "Do you remember how Sandy Point looked after Wilhelmina? That's what it's going to be like with this one, but maybe ten times worse."

"Now, Lu." Ed was standing by the pantry door, unloading the barbecue sauce and beer he'd bought at Frank's. "What the boy is saying makes sense. Lotta people want to be in their own homes so they can make repairs when storms like this hit—"

"Or so they can be swept away," Mrs. Hartwell said, angrily turning down the heat on her onions, "in the ten-foot tidal surge they're expecting. That sounds stupid to me. Do you think that sounds stupid?"

I noticed with a start that she was pointing the wooden soup spoon in my direction.

"Me?" I nearly dropped my tote bag. "Oh . . . I really don't think my opinion matters either way."

"Yes, it does. Tell him." Mrs. Hartwell turned off the heat on her onions and folded her own arms across her chest, mimicking her nephew's stance exactly. "Tell him he should stay here with us, where it's safe."

I blinked in surprise. Why was she putting this on me? I was a virtual stranger here.

"Um," I said. "I really don't think I—"

"Oh, don't be ridiculous. He'll stay if you ask him to." Mrs. Hartwell went on. "You're a pretty girl, and he likes you."

"Lu." Drew's warning was so low, it was practically a growl.

"Well, it's true." Aunt Lu uncrossed her arms to lay down her soup spoon and wipe her hands on a kitchen towel, though I couldn't see that she'd dirtied them in any way. "I haven't seen you this way about a woman since before Leighanne. Lord knew you never liked her much, she just followed you here from—"

"Do you have room in your fridge for this?" I interrupted hastily, holding up Daniella's container of starter.

I did it more for my own sake than Drew's, since I knew everything Mrs. Hartwell was saying was untrue, and I couldn't let her embarrass me—or her nephew—a second longer. If Drew Hartwell was interested in me, it was only because I was the only girl on the island with whom he hadn't yet had sex.

And sex was the last thing I was interested in, at least for the time being. Or so I told myself.

From the look on Drew's face, the feeling appeared to be mutual.

"Uh," Mrs. Hartwell said, glancing from the plastic container in my hands to my face. "Yes, I suppose so. Ed, move out some of that beer so she can put that in the fridge, will you?"

Ed looked dismayed. "But, Lu—"

"There's plenty of beer in there already. Put what you've got there in the fridge out back in the shed."

"But it'll be raining! You want me to have to go outside to get beer in the—"

"Ed!"

Ed moved some of his beer, and I found a nice dark place in the bottom of the Hartwells' fridge for the starter. I also managed to squeeze in my cheese ball.

"Now," I said, straightening. "If you'll excuse me, I just have to run back to my place really quick to get my scooter. If that area actually does flood, I can't leave it parked there."

"I'll drop you off." Drew pulled the keys to his pickup from one of his many pockets.

Mrs. Hartwell looked stricken. "But you can't leave! I'm making your favorite—*ropa vieja*."

Drew looked heavenward before taking me by the arm and physically steering me from the kitchen. "Let's go."

"But you'll be back?" I heard his aunt cry, as he hustled me down the hall. "You're not going to drive back out to the beach, are you, Drew? Except to get those dogs of yours?"

He called back to her in Spanish—a language I never learned properly because I took French in school, though I'd picked up a few phrases around my dad's clients and the café—and the next thing I knew, we'd brushed past Nevaeh and her friend Katie, doing their nails on the living room couch, and burst out the front door.

"Good God," he said, as soon as we were headed toward his red pickup, parked in his aunt and uncle's driveway. "Thanks for that."

I had no idea what he was talking about. "For what?"

"For giving me an excuse to get out of there. You saved me. Again."

"How did I do that?"

"With that excuse about having to go get your scooter."

"It wasn't an excuse." I eyed him as he unlocked the driver's-side door to the pickup. "I paid good money for that scooter." Used, but it had still taken a sizable chunk out of my savings. "I don't want it to get ruined."

"Well, good timing, anyway." He'd climbed behind the

wheel, and now he leaned over to unlock the passenger-side door. "You saved my ass."

"I assure you," I said, climbing into the truck, which smelled as pungently as ever of wet dog, "that your ass is the last thing I was thinking of." This was a lie. I was finding myself thinking about his ass—and other parts of him—more and more often, and it was disconcerting. "Why are you so mean to your aunt, anyway?"

"Mean to her?" He looked startled. "How am I mean to her?"

"All she wants is to have her friends and family safe around her during the storm, and you can't even do her that simple favor?" I pulled at my seat belt. It had given me trouble my first time in the truck and was doing so again.

He lifted both hands in a so-sue-me gesture. "Since when can't a guy stay in his own house—that he built himself, by the way—during a storm?"

"The storm of the century. That's what they're calling it."

"They say that for every storm. It's what the media is paid to do, hype things up. It's how they get ratings. I would have thought you of all people would know that, with your mother."

"Yes, but in the case of a hurricane they're probably right." I glared at him. "Wow, it must be so great to be Drew Hartwell, king of Little Bridge Island, who can do whatever he wants without regard to anyone or anything else."

"Whoa." He'd turned on the engine, but now he turned it off, and we sat in the driveway with thunder rumbling overhead, and the rain probably—most likely—coming at any moment, which meant I'd get soaked on my ride back on my scooter. "Hold on a minute. Just what the hell are you talking about?"

"Well, your aunt and uncle raised you, didn't they? And yet you don't seem to feel that you owe them even the slightest—"

"Whoa, whoa, whoa, *whoa*. My aunt and uncle did not raise me. They're very nice people, and they are raising my niece, for which I am very grateful, since my sister is a bit of a mess at the moment, and Nevaeh's dad took off basically the second she was born. But I had a pair of very kind, supportive parents until a few years ago, when a semi going the wrong way down Highway One took them both out."

I blinked at him, surprised. I'd never heard this.

"And yes, Lucy and Ed have been great ever since," he went on. "But I was twenty-five at the time. I did not need surrogate parents then, or now."

I sat for a moment in silence, staring straight ahead as a single fat drop of rain plunked down on the hood of the pickup. Then I said, "Well. I'm sorry about your parents. And your sister. That's awful. In different ways, of course, but still . . . awful."

"Thanks. But who are you, anyway," he demanded suddenly, "to talk about how I treat my relatives? Aren't you the one whose own family offered to send a private plane to get you out of here before the storm, then turned the invitation down?"

I whipped my head around to glare at him. "So you were listening to my private phone call after all?"

"How could I not? You were practically yelling. It was kind of hard not to hear."

"You know what." I grabbed for the door handle. "I don't need a ride to my place. I'll walk."

"Oh, no." He flipped a switch, and the door lock snapped into place. I was trapped. "You're not getting out of this that easily. You can't judge me for doing the exact same thing you're doing."

"Actually I can, because you're not doing the exact same thing I'm doing. I'm riding out a hurricane safely, at your aunt's house on the highest point on the island. You're doing it recklessly, in a house that's not even finished, on a beach."

"Honey, I've got news for you," he said, turning on the motor again, then revving it. "If you think there's anywhere safe on this island to ride out what's heading toward us, you're crazy." As I gaped at him, he added, with a wicked grin, "You really should have listened to your mother."

CHAPTER FIFTEEN

Time: 2:53 P.M.
Temperature: 79°F
Wind Speed: 37 MPH
Wind Gust: 55 MPH
Precipitation: 1.2 in.

He was right. I should have listened to my mother.

But not about fleeing ahead of the hurricane that was heading my way. She'd once told me to look out for guys like Drew Hartwell . . . well, not *him*, exactly, but "artistic types."

And what else could you call a carpenter who not only restored old homes and furniture but had built his own, on one of the most hurricane-prone beaches in the world?

Doctors, lawyers, financiers, any kind of business owner . . . fine with Mom. But pursuing a relationship with an artistic guy was almost as bad, to her, as pursuing an art career yourself.

Not that I was pursuing a relationship with Drew Hartwell. I was merely stuck in a truck with him.

Even worse, it had begun to rain in earnest. Large, leaden drops fell like bullets on the pickup.

"Great," I said, staring sullenly at the boarded-up windows of the houses we drove by. There was absolutely no one else on the street. The entire town might as well have been deserted.

"What?"

"Nothing. Except that now I have to ride my scooter back in the rain."

He glanced at me. "Didn't you bring your raincoat?"

"No, I did not bring my raincoat. You rushed me out of there so fast, I didn't have time to grab it."

"This is a hurricane, Fresh Water," he said, sounding amused. "You're supposed to always have—"

"Well, I don't!"

He slammed on the brakes. We were in front of my apartment building. Since I'd been unable to get my seat belt buckled back in the Hartwells' driveway, I would have gone sailing into the dashboard if he hadn't thrust out a strong arm to stop me.

"Thanks," I said, uncomfortably aware of how hard the muscles and bones of his arm felt against the softness of my breasts. Uncomfortable, of course, because I liked it.

He, however, didn't seem to notice. His arm moved past me.

"Stay here," he said, as he fumbled for something in the glove compartment.

"Why?" I was confused. What he'd been fumbling for

turned out to be a clear plastic rain poncho, which he unfolded, then tugged over himself. "Where are you going?"

"I'm going to go get your scooter," he said, turning those too bright blue eyes on me as the rain suddenly came pouring down in buckets all around us. "I'll throw it in the back of the truck."

Then, before I could say a word in reply, he stepped out into the silver, streaming rain, slamming the door behind him.

"What?" I watched as he strode toward my scooter, the only such vehicle sitting forlornly in my building's parking space meant for motorized bikes. "Wait. You can't— What are you—?"

I flung open the passenger door and was met by a flash of lightning, followed quickly by a clap of thunder.

I didn't care.

Nor did I care about the hard, stinging rain that quickly soaked my T-shirt and shorts, or the leaves that were being flung about by the wind and slapped against my legs, arms, and face. All I cared about was not allowing Drew Hartwell to do anything nice for me, because then I'd owe him something.

"Wait," I cried, rushing up to him as he expertly rolled my scooter off its kickstand. "You don't have to do this. I was only kidding. I'm happy to ride—"

His classy clear plastic rain poncho had a hood, but the wind was so strong it had blown it back, so his dark hair was already plastered to his head. "Get back in the truck."

"But I—"

Another flash of lightning, followed by another crash of thunder, this one much louder than the last. I felt it reverberate in my chest. Being outside in this weather was probably not a good idea.

Riding a scooter in it was probably an even worse one.

"Get back in the truck," he roared.

I wouldn't, however. I hurriedly opened the back of the truck and rearranged the oddities I found there so my scooter would fit—the fishing coolers, toolboxes, shrimp boots, and other assorted paraphernalia of Drew Hartwell's life, including, for some reason, several folding lawn chairs and, of course, the chain saw.

Then I helped him lift the bike into the bed of the truck, even though he kept roaring at me to stop, that he could handle it.

But I knew how much that thing weighed. Even though it was a small scooter—barely street legal in some states at 50cc, and so not requiring a motorcycle license to drive—it took both our efforts to haul it onto the truck.

He was seething by the time we both climbed damply back into our seats.

"I thought I told you to stay in the truck," he said.

"Well, I thought I told you that I could handle it on my own."

"You were going to try to ride that thing, in this?" He gestured at the rain that was now pummeling the windshield in sheets. We could barely see three feet in front of us. The high winds were sending leaves, including whole branches, sailing across the street. I thought I saw some of the frangipani blossoms sail by, even though we were parked beyond the high walls that surrounded the courtyard to my apartment building.

"I would have been fine," I insisted, "if you'd have let me grab my rain gear. I've ridden in worse weather than this."

This was a lie. I'd never seen weather this bad.

And I hated riding in the rain on my scooter. I didn't like how slick the yellow lines of the road felt under my wheels. I was no road warrior.

Drew shook his head. He'd evidently seen through my lie. "Now do you see why I said to always bring your raincoat?"

"Well, you could have loaned me yours, and then all of this would have been avoided. I'd be back at your aunt's by now, and you'd be on your way back to your beach house to fulfill your death wish."

He gave me a sour look as I struggled to buckle my seat belt.

"Look," he said. "You know how you feel about those cloud paintings of yours? That's how I feel about my house. I can't just leave it. I'd like to, but I can't. I've worked too hard on it, and I love it."

I didn't feel like it would be a good idea to remind him that my paintings were one of the last things I'd thought to pack. He seemed to have a slightly idealized notion of me as an artist.

I would have liked to live up to this vision, but I knew the truth: I'd been more worried about Gary than I had about my art.

Instead of replying, I fumbled once again with the seat belt. "Is this thing broken, or what?" I mumbled.

Looking irritated, he leaned over to help. "It's not broken. You just have to—"

The second his fingers brushed mine, I felt the same jolt shoot through me that I'd felt the night before, when his fingers had closed over mine on the bicycle handle.

Only this time, there was no bike between us, and our mouths were just inches apart. I could feel the heat coming off his body through his damp clothes, heard his breath quicken as our hands touched, and when I looked up, I could see that his gaze was on mine.

There was no question: whatever strange chemical attraction I felt was going on between us, he felt it, too.

It made absolutely no sense. But it also seemed 100 percent right to close the slight distance between our lips by lifting my head and pressing my mouth to his.

The second our lips met, it was like lightning striking all over again. Only this time the lightning was inside the truck—or more specifically, my shorts. I wasn't sure what I'd been doing with my life instead of kissing Drew Hartwell. It had definitely been time wasted. This, *this* was what I'd been meant to be doing, because it was making every nerve ending, every fiber in my body feel alive. My toes were curling inside my sneakers. I wanted to straddle him right there behind the wheel.

And he wasn't exactly urging me not to. His tongue had launched a pretty thorough exploration of the inside of my mouth while both his big, calloused hands cupped my breasts through my soaked T-shirt and bra. With the rain pouring down in torrents around us, we were steaming up the windows of the truck. But I didn't care, because who was going to walk by to see us?

It was only when he started leaning me back against the pickup's bench seat and was skillfully peeling off my shirt while murmuring, "Let's go to my place," that I suddenly remembered where we were . . . in Drew Hartwell's truck.

That's when I sat up . . . so abruptly that I almost head-butted him. "*What?*"

He sat up, too, after tugging on his cargo shorts to better accommodate his burgeoning erection—which I'd felt, long and rock hard against my thigh. "I said let's go to my place. I hate making love in cars. I'm too tall. And your place is about to flood—"

"Your place on the *beach*? Are you insane?"

"I already told you, it's built to withstand hurricane force—"

What was I doing? This was so not part of how I was supposed to be living my life right now. I was not supposed to be making out with guys—even insanely hot ones—in trucks. I was supposed to be getting my shit together, not doing . . . well, whatever this was.

I yanked my shirt back into place. "I'm not spending the hurricane with you on the beach, Drew. All of my stuff is at your aunt's house. My cat is—"

"I like your cat. We can go get your cat."

"So he can die, too? No, thank you."

"No one is going to die."

"You don't know that!"

"Of course I don't know that. But you could just as easily die crossing the street and being hit by a bus any day of the week—"

"Can we just agree that one's chances of dying in a hurricane are statistically higher if you stay in a house on the beach than if you stay in a house farther inland?"

"I'll agree that it depends on the house."

"Oh my God." I turned to wipe away some of the steam on the passenger-side window so I could look out at the rain. The crotch of my panties, the only part of me that had been dry, was now just as soaked as the rest of me. "Just drop me back off at your aunt's."

"Okay, fine. But I'm not staying there. You are a very attractive woman and I want to be with you in the worst way, but not if it means spending this hurricane at my auntie's house eating her lemon pudding cake."

I sent him a withering glance. "Don't get ahead of yourself. It was only a kiss."

"Only a kiss?" He leaned forward to turn on the engine. "I think we both know that was a little more than a kiss, Fresh Water."

"Where I come from, that was a standard greeting," I said, glad that the cold air blowing on me from the air-conditioning in the dashboard could be my excuse if he noticed that my nipples were rock hard.

"Oh, so you put your tongue in the mouths of all the guys who help you with your seat belt?"

"Basically."

"Fresh Water, I lived in New York for three years and I never saw anyone kiss their cabbie for helping them with their seat belt."

"Well, you probably didn't travel in the right circles."

"Oh, okay. Whatever you say."

We drove the rest of the way in silence, which was a mercy, since I didn't feel like talking. What had I been thinking, kissing him like that? Now I'd started something I really didn't need, much less want or have time for. He was Drew Hartwell, the last guy on the island any girl who'd sworn off men should be messing with.

And he wasn't even my type . . . if I had a type, which I wasn't sure I did. But if I did, it wouldn't be him. He was too sarcastic, and he often seemed to struggle to wear an actual shirt, and he drove a pickup truck—worse, a pickup truck that stank of wet dog fur and that he seemed often to have left parked overnight in front of multiple women's homes.

There were signs of Drew's beloved four-legged pack everywhere, from abandoned leashes to chew toys littering the truck's floor to dog hair carpeting just about every available surface. Since I was so damp, a lot of the fur was sticking to me.

But I figured most of it would wash off in the rain once we got back to Drew's aunt and uncle's house and I helped him haul my scooter off the truck bed.

Except that when we started to pull into the driveway, I saw a figure waiting for us on the front porch. He was barely recognizable due to all the rain and the fact that he was dressed in full all-weather gear.

But it was most definitely Drew's uncle Ed.

"Oh, no," I said. "He's not—"

"Come on." Drew was grinning a little devilishly. "You knew he'd be waiting. He loves this stuff."

Of course I knew that.

But did that make it right when, a moment later, Ed, a man in his sixties, had leaped into the high wind and rain and was signaling for his nephew to back the pickup into the driveway?

Drew put down his window and called, across the sheets of rain, "I got it. I'll put it in reverse."

"Don't put it in reverse," Ed cried. "Just back it up."

Drew turned toward me, his eyes bright, his mouth opening to make some smart-ass remark about his uncle's malapropism, but I held up a hand to stop him.

"Stop. I heard it."

"Now do you see why I might find riding out a hurricane in my own house preferable to doing it with these lunatics I'm related to?"

I refused to rise to his bait. "I think your family is adorable, and you're lucky to have them."

"Of course you'd think that." Drew sighed as he expertly backed his truck into the driveway. "You're a Fresh Water. You, like all the other tourists, think we were put on this island for you to gawk at and take photos of for your social media accounts."

My frustration level at bursting point—for multiple

reasons—I snapped, "I'm not a tourist. I've been here for three months—not to mention having spent a lot of time here as a child. And though I know that's hardly any time to you, I think it's fair to say I've gotten to know this island, and both you and your family, fairly well. So what I think is that you're lucky to have such sweet relatives who love and support you so much, no matter how stupidly you behave."

He threw a foot on the brake, his dark eyebrows raised in surprise as he gawked at me.

"Stupid?"

"What else would you call your plan to go to the beach for a hurricane?"

Instead of replying, he simply narrowed his eyes at me, threw on the parking brake, then got out of the truck, giving me a curt "Stay here" before slamming the door.

Of course I didn't listen. I wasn't going to let two men half drown themselves on my behalf.

I instantly regretted it. The wind had risen again, whipping leaves and palm fronds and of course the rain in all directions . . . but mostly, it seemed, at us. Both Drew and his uncle curtly told me to go inside, and this time, considering the fact that I was wearing no protection at all from the weather, I obeyed, though I only went as far as the front porch so I could watch as the two of them struggled with my scooter.

It was as I was doing this that Mrs. Hartwell came out of the house with a dry beach towel, warm from the dryer.

"Here you go, hon," she said, draping the towel around my cold, wet shoulders. "You should go inside and take a nice warm shower while you still can. Sometimes the aqueduct authority turns the water off out of an abundance of caution if it floods and they can't control the water quality or pressure."

This was something I wished I'd known before deciding not to evacuate. The *water* could be turned off?

"Thanks." I wrapped the towel around me. The warm terry cloth felt delicious. "But I'm all right. I just feel so bad that they're doing all this work for me—"

"Oh, they love it." Mrs. Hartwell peered affectionately through the rain at the two men she loved most in her life. "Anything involving machines. And if there's a pretty girl in distress they can help, that's just icing on the cake."

I clutched the towel around my shoulders more tightly, feeling even more uncomfortable. "Thanks. But that's just it. I wasn't really in distress. I could have ridden it back over here." It wouldn't have been fun, but I could have done it. Probably.

She patted me kindly on the shoulder. "Of course you could have. But some people are better suited to some jobs than others. That's just the way things are. Which reminds me, after you get showered and changed and have maybe had a little bit of a rest, I could use your help in the kitchen."

"Okay. Sure. I'd be happy to."

I threw a final glance at Drew. He was wheeling my scooter through the rain toward a safe parking spot out of the gales, near the side of the house, his clear plastic poncho flapping in the wind.

I felt a sudden lurch deep inside my gut. *You're making a terrible mistake,* a voice inside me seemed to be screaming.

What? Where did that come from?

And a mistake about what? Staying in Little Bridge for the hurricane? Or staying at the Hartwells'?

Or letting myself get involved with Drew Hartwell?

If it was the latter, why was I feeling such a powerful urge to run back out into the rain, throw my arms around his neck, and beg him not to get back inside that truck?

I didn't know. None of it made any sense.

So I ignored the feeling and followed his aunt inside the house.

Except I couldn't shake the feeling that this was the biggest mistake of all.

CHAPTER SIXTEEN

Emergency Disaster Survival Kit Basics—Personal

Hand sanitizer or disinfectant wipes
Travel-size beauty products
Toilet paper, paper towels, garbage bags
Dental care and vision products
Blankets, sheets, pillow
Clothing, no-rinse detergent

I didn't know what had happened until I emerged from the bathroom after spending a long time under the hot water, washing the smell of gasoline and Drew Hartwell's dogs from my body. That's when I heard the cry.

"He's not coming back!"

I rushed into the kitchen just in time to see Mrs. Hartwell press a hand to her mouth as she gazed down at the screen of her cell phone.

My heart sank. I knew exactly whom she was talking about, but for propriety's sake, I had to pretend that I didn't.

"Who's not coming back, Mrs. H?" I asked.

"Drew. He just wrote." She held up her phone so I could see the text she'd just received, although it was difficult to read, since her fingers were trembling a little. She wasn't a woman who wore her heart on a sleeve but it was clear she was upset. "He says the roads by the beach are already so bad, he doesn't think he can get back here safely, so he's going to wait out the storm with his dogs at that ridiculous house of his. He's not coming back here. He's not coming back!"

I patted her on the back as comfortingly as I could. I realized that what Drew had said to his aunt in Spanish before we'd left to pick up my bike must have been an assurance that he'd be back to hunker down for the storm with her.

Of course he'd been lying. He'd never had any intention of spending the storm anywhere but his beach house. But, like a typical male, he'd been too cowardly to tell his aunt so to her face.

"Now, Lu." Ed had come in from the dining room and was as matter-of-fact about his nephew's reckless choice as he was about everything else. "The boy will be fine."

"He won't." Mrs. Hartwell sounded as close to tears as I'd ever heard her. "He's going to die out there."

"Unlikely. He's got a boat. Worse comes to worst, he'll get himself and those dogs of his into it and ride out the storm there."

Understandably, this did not seem to comfort the anxious woman.

"He's got nothing! No generator, no landline, no satellite phone—"

"He's got his wits." Ed walked over to the counter to check on the *ropa vieja* his wife was cooking for dinner, the ingredients for which had all gone into a slow cooker. The smell that emanated from it when Ed lifted the lid was so appetizing, my mouth almost watered. "Mmm, now that's going to be delicious, Lu."

His wife ignored this compliment. "He's going to die."

"He's been through lots of these storms before, Aunt Lucy," Nevaeh said. She'd come into the kitchen as well to see what all the fuss was about, and now she wrapped a comforting arm around her aunt's waist. "He'll know just what to do. Uncle Drew always does."

Well, I wouldn't go that far. Maybe he knew just what to do when it came to construction and hauling motorbikes.

When it came to matters of the heart, however, not so much.

Then again, I was no champ in that department, either.

It was just then that it happened: a flash of lightning so strong—accompanied by a boom of thunder at the same time, indicating that a storm cell was directly over us—that the lights flickered, then went out.

Nevaeh and Katie screamed as if their throats were being slit. The parrot, in the living room, joined them.

"No worries, no worries." Ed puttered toward the counter, where a powerful-looking flashlight sat. It was still daytime, but the thick clouds overhead coupled with the tightly closed shutter over every window had made the house as dark inside as if it were dusk. "I had the propane in the generator topped off this morning, so we should be—"

There was a groaning sound—like a powerful boat engine starting up—and suddenly the lights flickered on again. That sound—the groaning—had apparently been the sound of the Hartwells' generator springing to life, as it was programmed to do the minute the city's electric grid failed. Fueled by the thousand-gallon propane tank Drew had mentioned, the Hartwell house was now being powered by its generator.

"Oh, thank God," I heard Nevaeh cry. She'd run into the living room to check on the television. "But the cable's completely out!"

"Yep." Ed didn't look particularly surprised. "Can't believe it lasted as long as it did."

The island's cable television service was the source of most of the jeers in the "Cheers and Jeers" section of the newspaper. It seemed to go out weekly, even when the weather was fair, and when it was foul, forget about it. Satellite dish service was worse, because any amount of rain, even up the island chain, could knock it out. Many of my customers could predict when rain was on its way based solely on the amount of pixilation on their television screens.

Nevaeh, her face pale, came back into the kitchen, waving her cell phone in the air.

"The Internet isn't working!"

Mrs. Hartwell managed a smile. "I'm sure you girls can live without the Internet for a few days."

"A few *days*?" Katie looked as panic stricken as if someone had suggested she live without oxygen.

"You do know that some of us lived almost our entire lives without the Internet?" Mrs. Hartwell seemed amused. "I managed to graduate from high school and college without ever using it once."

Nevaeh's eyes widened. "How did you even have a social life, let alone do homework?"

"It was called the library." Mrs. Hartwell didn't look so amused anymore. "And we used something called a telephone to contact one another. You know, if you girls are bored, I've got a cake that needs fixing."

Nevaeh smiled apologetically at her great-aunt. "Sorry, Aunt Lu. Of course we'll come help you. Katie, come on, let's go wash our hands."

Katie followed her friend, her gaze never wavering from her phone screen. "You know, Nevaeh, there's still cell service. I just got a text from Madison."

Once the two girls had left the room, I smiled at Mrs. Hartwell, who was gazing after her great-niece with a look of half-concern, half-adoration.

"Are Katie's parents worried about her being out in this weather?" I asked. Wind was sucking at the wooden shutters that covered the living room windows, causing them to creak. The walls of the house itself seemed to be swaying slightly—but Mrs. H had warned me this would happen. The house had been built to do this.

"The sheriff? Oh, no." Mrs. Hartwell waved a hand dismissively. "He asked if she could stay here. She didn't want to stay with him over at the high school. And who can blame her, with her dad working, and her best friend and cousin here?"

It dawned on me, slowly, that Katie was a Hartwell, too—Sheriff Hartwell's daughter. Was everyone in this town related, by blood or marriage, to the Hartwells?

"Wasn't there something here in the kitchen you wanted my help with?" I asked brightly. Not that I actually felt like helping. I felt like screaming, like Mrs. H had done when she'd received Drew's text.

But since they'd been so gracious as to house me, it seemed like the least I could do.

And a project seemed like a good way to keep my mind off what was happening outside.

"Oh. Yes, actually. If you wouldn't mind . . ."

Which was how I found myself, a half hour later, standing at the kitchen counter, using a hand mixer to stir up a batch of what Drew's aunt called "hurricane dip."

"It's so addictive," she explained to me. "You really can't have it in the house anytime except during a hurricane. Otherwise you'd be eating it all day long."

I believed her . . . and also knew why this wouldn't be the best thing, at least for anyone who cared about their health, since the sole ingredients for "hurricane dip" were mayonnaise, sour cream, and cream cheese, along with "about half a bottle" of barbecue sauce.

My job was to mix all of these ingredients together until they were a light orange color, making sure there were no lumps—difficult to do, considering the cream cheese.

I tried not to ask myself why mixing together a lot of heart-attack-inducing ingredients seemed to be the job for which Drew's aunt felt I was most suited. I did have other skills beyond food preparation . . .

But none that would be particularly useful under these circumstances. Law school didn't exactly prepare one for a hurricane, at least not a literal one. All of that cerebral stuff was as handy in this situation as my mom deemed art to be.

The only bright spot that I could see about my being pigeonholed into the role of resident dip maker was that Nevaeh and Katie had it a lot worse. They were being forced to make the lemon pudding cake of which Drew had spoken so disparagingly, and which involved a package of yellow cake mix combined with—what else?—a package of lemon pudding.

Although, as long as you were a fan of lemon (which I was), how bad could it be?

"That looks done," Mrs. Hartwell said, peering into the bowl I was holding. "Let's try it and see."

She plunged a chip—the "ruffled kind" were the best for this particular dip, she'd informed me—into the contents of the bowl and then brought the chip and dip to her mouth and chewed thoughtfully.

"Mmmm." She closed her eyes, something I'd noticed she did often while eating. "Perfection."

"Really?"

I wasn't sure how anything made up of so many different condiments could be any good, so I grabbed a chip and tasted it, too.

I was surprised by the tangy flavor explosion in my mouth. "Oh my God."

Mrs. Hartwell grinned at me. "You see? That's why we can only have it around during hurricanes. Otherwise we'd all be the size of trucks. Well, I already am." She patted her pleasantly curved belly. "But I don't need to be getting any bigger, or I'd have to go to Miami to buy all new clothes." There was no place to buy clothes in Little Bridge, except expensive boutiques that no locals could afford, and a Kmart on the outskirts of town. "Throw some plastic wrap on that and put it in the fridge so it can set, and then go rest up awhile. You deserve it."

"We should eat soon," Ed announced, wandering back into the kitchen. "The real heavy stuff is going to start coming down in an hour or so."

His wife nodded and began filling a pot of water. I looked at him questioningly. "How do you know when the heavy stuff is going to get here? The cable is out, and there's no Internet."

He sent me a withering glance, then held up a small metal box. "Radio. Ever heard of it before?"

"Oh. Of course." I flushed with embarrassment, remembering I hadn't told him who my mother was.

But it seemed better not to, for a variety of reasons. Not everyone was a fan of Judge Justine. I didn't know how Ed and Lucy Hartwell would feel about her.

"What kind of radio do you have?" I asked.

Ed, excited to show off his gadget, set his battery-operated shortwave radio on the counter and turned up the volume so I could appreciate the sound quality.

"Oh, Ed, no," Mrs. Hartwell exclaimed as she rinsed the rice. "I don't want to hear those two idiots. We were having such a nice peaceful time—"

I have no idea how anyone could describe this situation as peaceful, given how powerfully the wind outside was blowing. The shutters on the windows were all shaking, and the special pine the house was made of, despite its reputation for being so strong, was doing a bit of creaking as well.

But this apparently did not alarm the Hartwells at all.

"They aren't idiots." Ed sounded offended. "They are professional radio journalists who are risking their lives to stay on the air over there at the airport after everyone else has evacuated in order to bring us the weather—"

Aunt Lu snorted. "Risking their lives! They're in a bomb shelter. The only way they'll be risking their lives is if their broadcasting antenna blows down and one of them is stupid enough to go outside to try to repair it, which I wouldn't be surprised to—"

"Shhhh." Ed turned up the volume of his radio.

The voices of two men filled the kitchen.

"We've just clocked a wind gust of a hundred and eleven miles an hour," one of the men—who later identified himself as Wayne the Toad Licker—said. "That definitely puts us at a Cat Three."

"It does, Wayne," said his cohost, whose call sign I subsequently learned was Fred the Head. "But do we want to depend on mere technical instruments? Wouldn't we get a more accurate reading if you went out there and . . . you know?"

"No, Fred. I won't do it."

"You swore on the Conch Republic flag that you would!"

"Fred, I'm not a masochist. I'm not going out there."

"Ladies and gentlemen of Little Bridge, if you're just tuning in and wondering what my esteemed colleague and I are discussing, it's the fact that Wayne lost a bet, and as the loser he is supposed to go out into the parking lot of our station here and attempt to measure the winds of Hurricane Marilyn by spitting into them. And yet here he is, reneging on our—"

"Oh, for pity's sake," Mrs. Hartwell burst out. "This is the silliest, most revolting thing I've ever heard. Turn it off."

Ed only turned up the volume. "Now, Lu," he said gravely. "These gentlemen are providing a valuable service to the community. Everyone who's listening is having their mind kept off the storm, which is what we all need right now." He glanced at me. "Wouldn't you say so?"

I didn't want to get into the middle of my employers' marital squabble. Besides which, I was beginning to worry. The airport was less than a mile from Sandy Point Beach, where Drew was building his house. If the winds there were already up to Category 3 strength and the eye of the storm wasn't even on us, was it remotely safe for him to be there? It didn't seem like it.

"I mean, they seem dumb," I said of Fred the Head and Wayne the Toad Licker. "But entertaining."

"And informative." Ed took a small notebook and pen from his shirtfront pocket and began jotting something down. "So, if it's seven o'clock now, and the winds are already at over a hundred miles per hour, that means the eye should pass over at around—"

Mrs. Hartwell snapped, "Oh, for pity's sake, Ed. I don't want to hear it! Our nephew could be dying out there and you're standing there estimating exactly what time it's going to happen!"

Ed shrugged, still calculating. "I'm sorry, but it's better to be prepared for these things."

"Girls!" Mrs. Hartwell spun around and called to the teenagers. "Girls, come help set the table. We're going to eat dinner soon. Although to be honest," she turned to say to me, "I don't think I could eat a bite, I'm so worried. You?"

"Um." I suddenly thought of something. "Hold on a minute. I think I have just the thing."

CHAPTER SEVENTEEN

Time: 7:18 P.M.
Temperature: 77°F
Wind Speed: 65 MPH
Wind Gust: 115 MPH
Precipitation: 3.3 in.

"Oh, how thoughtful. I haven't seen one of those in years. The girls will love it."

That's what Mrs. Hartwell said when I dug out my cheese ball and offered to serve it as an appetizer, since I thought it might cheer her up.

It did. Neither Nevaeh nor Katie had ever seen such a thing before, and after obediently setting the massive dining room table, as Mrs. Hartwell had asked, with her best silverware and china, they dug into the unfamiliar treat, gushing over it as enthusiastically as if I'd made it myself.

"This is the best thing I've ever eaten," Nevaeh declared, shoveling port wine cheese spread into her mouth.

"Me, too!" Katie had bits of cracker stuck in her braces.

"Lu never lets me eat this stuff," Ed said, slicing off about a third of the cheese ball for himself. "She says it's bad for my cholesterol. Hey, where's the hurricane dip?"

"Coming," Mrs. Hartwell called from the kitchen, where she was warming tortillas for the *ropa vieja*. "Is anyone saving any of that cheese for me?"

I appreciated the brave show Drew's aunt was putting on. I appreciated it so much that, before clearing the tray to make room for dinner, I snapped a quick photo of what was left of the demolished cheese ball and sent it to Drew Hartwell, along with the message "See what you're missing?"

Since I knew both his aunt and uncle had tried to call and text him and received no reply, I didn't expect a reply, either.

So I was surprised when, just as we were sitting down to dinner, I saw a text bubble appear beneath my message to him . . . three animated dots, indicating he was writing back.

Indicating that, at least for now, he was alive.

I had looked up excitedly to share this fact with the rest of the table when Mrs. Hartwell, her tone brisk but polite, said, "No cell phones at the table, please."

"But—"

"That's the rule!" Nevaeh smirked. "We don't have different rules for guests. No cell phones at the table."

Guiltily, I dropped my phone in my lap and tried to ignore Nevaeh's and Katie's giggles . . . as well as the strange sense of disappointment I felt, realizing it would be a while before I'd be able to check for Drew's reply.

What did I care, anyway?

Unbidden, a memory of how Drew had looked, gently cradling Gary in his arms, came back to me.

And then an entirely different memory—how he'd looked earlier that day outside my apartment door, shirtless.

Anything else I can do for you, Fresh Water?

Oh my God. Maybe I *did* like him. Maybe I more than liked him. Why else was I so worried about him?

No. No, it wasn't possible.

But then why else was I shoveling the food Mrs. Hartwell had so lovingly prepared into my mouth so quickly? I hardly tasted it.

And then why else did I excuse myself to go to the bathroom while everyone else was midway through their meal, only so I could check my phone to see what he'd written back to me?

And then why else did I feel such a crushing sense of disappointment in the bathroom when I saw that the text bubbles had disappeared, and that Drew hadn't written back after all? In fact, I'd received no messages at all, not even from my mother, which was odd, considering she'd been texting me approximately once an hour. All that was written on my screen was . . .

"No service!" Nevaeh's voice was a panic-filled shriek.

The wind was gusting more strongly than ever. On the radio—which Ed had insisted on keeping on throughout our meal—Wayne and Fred said their anemometer had broken, torn off by one of the gusts, so they now had no way of measuring how strong the winds were, aside from spitting.

"No service!" Nevaeh cried again dramatically. "I'm going to die!"

"You're not going to die." Dinner was over, and Mrs. Hartwell was calmly cutting slices of lemon pudding cake for dessert. "Go and get your bedding from upstairs. You and Katie are sleeping down here in the living room on the pullout couch, remember?"

"What's the point?" Nevaeh accepted her slice of cake with an air of defeatism. "Without cable, we can't even watch TV."

"You can watch DVDs," Mrs. Hartwell said. "You've still never seen the last season of that *Sex and the City* you like so much."

Nevaeh brightened. "Oh, yeah. Do you want to watch that with us, Bree?"

I had just taken a bite of the slice of lemon pudding cake. I suppose it tasted good, but I was so worried about Drew, I could have been eating sand and not known the difference.

"I've already seen it," I said. "But after I help your aunt out with the dishes, I could join you guys for a little while, if you want."

Nevaeh looked at me like I was crazy. "Uncle Ed does the dishes."

Ed was too absorbed in his radio show to confirm this, but when I glanced at Mrs. Hartwell, she nodded. "On nights when I cook, Ed does the dishes. When he cooks, I do the dishes. That's how we've managed to stay married for so long without killing each other."

"Oh." I smiled at her. "That makes sense."

Relieved of dish duty, I went to check on Gary. He was curled up on the pink-silk-cushioned chair in the library, looking as if that was where he'd been sleeping his entire life.

He let out a pink, toothless yawn when he saw me, then stretched luxuriously, letting out a self-satisfied meow.

"No," I said firmly, and removed him from the chair before his claws could snag the undoubtedly expensive antique cushion, depositing him on the air mattress.

Gary let out a little grunt of discontent—he clearly considered the air mattress unworthy of a cat of his breeding and intelligence—but eventually curled into a ball and went back to sleep.

Before joining the girls, I stopped by the window in the front door. Pushing back the lace curtain, I peered out. I could see very little because the power was out everywhere except the house in which I stood. The entire street had been plunged into the thickest, darkest night I'd ever seen.

But because of the light streaming from the hallway behind me, I could see a few things . . . and those things were disturbing. Rain was streaming diagonally, blown sideways by the wind. Leaves and branches were tossed across the front yard like confetti, some of them quite large. Beyond the picket fence, out in the street, a four-foot-tall trash can went sailing by, tossed by the wind as lightly as if it were a child's beach pail.

The noise of the storm was disturbing as well. It sounded exactly as people always seemed to describe hurricanes on news footage—like a freight train, roaring relentlessly past, only never seeming to end.

But then there were the mysterious explosions. Pop. Pop. *Bang.* When I'd asked Ed earlier what these sounds were, he said they could be anything—coconuts flying through the air and hitting houses or cars. Trees falling. Transformers exploding. Literally anything. That's why it was important during hurricanes to keep windows shuttered, tree limbs trimmed, and people out of cars on which trees could topple.

Even farther away was another sound—a roaring, like a crowd in an enormous stadium, cheering on their favorite team or rock idol. That sound, Ed informed me, was the sea. We were fortunate that the storm had hit while the moon was waning, and at low tide. Otherwise, the surge would be much worse. As it was, businesses and homes close to the shoreline could expect to flood . . . including the Mermaid Café, which Ed and some of the busboys had sandbagged late in the afternoon, when it looked like Little Bridge was going to take a direct hit.

How was Drew faring in such high winds, so close to the sea, in all this darkness? He wasn't tucked up safe, high on top of a hill, in a comfortable mansion, with a generator providing power for air-conditioning and DVD-watching, with pink-cushioned love seats and warm, delicious food.

Was he all right? What about poor Socks?

I found myself uttering up a little prayer as I stared out into all that storm-tossed darkness. Please take care of him, I prayed. Please take care of that stupid, stubborn, silly man. And his dogs, too.

And then I hastily amended the prayer to include all the

people I knew in Little Bridge, lest anyone get the idea that I cared more about Drew than, say, Angela. Because that of course was not true.

"Bree!" Nevaeh called from the pullout couch in the living room. "You're missing it!"

I dragged myself away from the window and joined the girls, though my head—and heart—were elsewhere.

CHAPTER EIGHTEEN

Landlines and satellite phones can be a valuable resource when power and cell towers fail. It can help to invest in one or more of these if you live in a hurricane-prone area.

I woke to the ringing of my phone.

But that was impossible. When I'd gone to sleep the night before, there'd been no cell service.

Maybe service had been restored overnight. Why not? The storm was clearly over. The walls were no longer creaking, and I could see sunlight peeping in through the slats of the shutters over the library window.

I rolled over on the air mattress—disturbing Gary, who'd been curled up comfortably in his customary position against my legs—and grabbed my cell, squinting at it in the morning light.

But no. The screen was black. And my cell wasn't ringing. Something else very near me was.

I sat up, looked around, and realized that the source of

the ringing was an old-fashioned telephone sitting on a pedestal table beside the pink-cushioned chair. I hadn't noticed it before, although beside the phone was, of all things, an old-fashioned answering machine, like Rachel and Monica had had on the television show *Friends*.

A moment later the answering machine switched on, and I heard Lucy Hartwell's cheerful voice say, "Hello, you've reached the Hartwells! We can't come to the phone right now, but if you leave your name, number, and a message, we'll get right ba—"

I heard a click, and then evidently the line was picked up on an extension in another part of the house.

"Hello?" Lucy Hartwell asked.

"Hello? Lucy?" A woman's voice came on over the machine.

"Oh, Joanne!" Mrs. Hartwell sounded excited to hear from her friend. "Are you all right?"

"Oh, we're fine, fine. No damage at all, except we lost a few trees. You?"

"Same here. That was quite a storm last night, though, wasn't it?"

"Oh, terrible, just terrible. Though not as bad as they were saying it was going to be."

"Oh, nowhere near." Joanne and Mrs. Hartwell seemed to have no idea that their voices were being recorded, or that I could hear every word they were saying.

"Though my sister Gail called from Chicago. She says on the news, they're reporting that Little Bridge has been wiped off the face of the map."

"No!"

"Oh, of course. But not based on any actual reporting, since they never bothered to send any journalists here, before or after the storm. So how would they even know?"

Mrs. Hartwell's tone was indignant. "Fake news. Was there even any flooding?"

"Well, the lobby of the Cascabel. But it always floods. How is the Mermaid?"

"Ed went down to check on it at first light. Sandbags kept the water out."

"Well, that's a relief!"

"Yes. What about Sandy Point?" Mrs. Hartwell's voice was elaborately casual. "Any news?"

"No, sorry, hon." Joanne's tone was gentle. "No one can get near it—the roads are too bad. But have you heard about the bridge?"

"Which bridge?"

"The one from the island to the highway to the mainland. Gone."

"No!"

"They're saying a yacht from the Little Bridge Yacht Club got loose from its moorings and floated free and struck the pilings in just the right place."

"Oh, for pity's sake!"

"No one is going to be able to get on or off the island, possibly for weeks, depending on how long it takes them to shore it up. Which means everyone who evacuated is stuck wherever they are."

"Those poor souls!"

"Anyway, would it be all right if I dropped off some of Carl's insulin to keep in your fridge? We have it in a cooler for now, but who knows how long we'll be able to keep getting ice."

"Oh, of course, Joanne. Come over anytime. And we've got plenty of hot food and cold beer."

"Lu, you're an angel. See you soon."

The two women hung up. I looked at Gary, who was happily kneading my thigh. *Wow*, I mouthed.

I grabbed some fresh clothes and jumped into the shower, bathing and dressing in record time. Then I followed the smell of coffee into the kitchen, where I found Mrs. Hartwell whisking what looked like the contents of an entire carton of eggs in a red plastic bowl.

"Good morning," she said cheerfully. She, like me, was wearing shorts and a T-shirt, only her T-shirt was overlarge whereas mine was slightly too small. Both, however, had Mermaid Café written on them. "Did you sleep all right?"

"I did, thank you so much." It seemed incredible to me that anyone could sleep through a hurricane, but the monotonous roar of the wind and pounding rain—or maybe the extremely low barometric pressure—had eventually knocked me out. I'd slept as soundly as a baby. "Would you like some help with that?"

"I've got bread toasting. You can help butter them when they pop up. There's coffee in the machine, just grab a cup from the shelf there and press the silver button. The girls aren't up yet, but when they are I'll have them set the table."

"Great." I didn't want to say that I'd overheard her phone call, but I wanted to ask for more details about the storm damage. I also wanted to know if she'd heard from Drew. I tried for a general "So, have you heard anything about . . . the storm?"

"Well, it's not as bad around here as they were saying it was going to be." She set down her bowl to add salt and pepper to it. "Mostly wind damage, no flooding except for where you'd expect it. But I understand that farther up the Keys, it's quite a disaster. And the bridge that connects us to the highway to the mainland is out."

I widened my eyes, feigning surprise. "No!"

"Yes. And it could be for quite a while. So anyone who evacuated won't be able to get back for a bit."

"That's terrible." I couldn't help myself. I had to ask: "And have you heard from your nephew?"

Mrs. Hartwell's cheerful smile wavered only slightly. "Not yet. And since he doesn't have a landline, and cell service is still out, we can't call. But I'm sure he'll show up here soon."

I tried to keep my tone light, to match hers. "And you can't drive over there and check?"

It was the wrong thing to say. The smile collapsed. "Haven't you looked outside?"

Of course I hadn't. I'd seen the sun shining through the shutters and assumed all was well—except for the bridge, of course.

Mrs. Hartwell, seeing my puzzled expression, took me by the elbow and steered me from the kitchen, down the hallway, through the dining room, past the sleeping girls in the living room, past my own room, and to the front door.

"Look," she said, and threw the door open.

I gasped. I couldn't help it.

The Hartwells' beautifully landscaped front yard was gone.

Oh, it was still there, of course. But instead of the neat brick path leading up to the wide, airy front porch, I saw nothing but leaves and branches and refuse—actual trash, people's garbage that had probably been ripped from the trash can I'd seen blowing around, a pizza box here, a cat food can there—carpeting the entire front lawn.

The street was worse. There an actual tree had fallen across the width of the road, taking a power line down with it. Neighbors had gathered in the street to stare at it, many of them holding coffee mugs that I recognized as being the same pattern as the one I held. They'd come from the Hartwells' home. While I'd been sleeping, Mrs. Hartwell had been busy serving coffee to her neighbors, none of whom had electricity to power their own coffeemakers.

These same neighbors turned when they heard Mrs. Hartwell open her front door now and waved at us. Mrs. Hartwell waved back, but distractedly.

"Ed can't get to the beach to check on Drew," she told me. "The roads are like this all around the neighborhood. Thank goodness no one was hurt—on this side of the island, anyway. No one's house was damaged, either—well, except for Beverly's; she forgot to board up in the back, so she got a tree branch through her kitchen windows. But she's a snowbird who won't even be down again until November, so there's plenty of time to clean up her place before she gets here. But it could be days until they get the streets clear enough for anyone to be able to get out to Drew—"

I stood staring at the mess in the front yard. It was so horrible. The palm trees had fared better than the gumbo-limbo—it had lost whole limbs. The palms had only been stripped of their fronds. All of it was going to take months, potentially years, to return to its former leafy glory.

Then I noticed my scooter. It was sitting exactly where Drew had left it. It was coated now in leaves and mud, but otherwise it was untouched by the storm.

I was already formulating a plan inside my head, but I didn't dare mention it out loud, because I wasn't sure I had the courage to carry it out.

"I'm sure Drew's fine," I said to Mrs. Hartwell, as we both went back inside the mercifully air-conditioned house. Outside, the post-storm heat was so oppressive, my shirt had begun sticking to my skin almost immediately. If Drew was still alive—and that was a big *if*—he had to be miserable. "Maybe the storm wasn't so bad out on the water."

Mrs. Hartwell looked at me as if I'd said maybe the sky isn't blue.

"Of course it was," she said. "I've already heard they lost most of the boats over in the marina."

That was it, I decided. I was going to go through with my plan, crazy as it seemed.

"Where's Ed?" I asked.

Mrs. Hartwell waved a hand toward the back of the house. "In the backyard. But don't waste your breath talking to him—he's in a foul mood."

I went anyway. Ed was usually in a foul mood at work, so I was used to this.

I got as far as the back porch before I saw that this time, however, he had good reason to feel ill-tempered.

The Hartwells' beautiful backyard, in which they'd held such a memorable hurricane party only the other night, was unrecognizable. Their glimmering blue jewel of a swimming pool? Gone. In its place was a swamp, a hot, steamy, disgusting mud bath filled to overflowing with palm fronds and other vegetable debris. Most of the rest of the trees in the yard had lost limbs or were down entirely, the lovely footpaths lost under layers of foliage. The ylang-ylang blossoms, which had given off such a beautiful scent the night of the party, now sat rotting on the ground in the burning sun, giving off a sickly sweet smell of decay.

In the center of the yard, next to the pool, stood Ed, holding a long-poled net as he attempted to shovel as much of the muck from his pool as he could, a little at a time, though it appeared to me to be a futile effort. It was never going to be the same as it was before.

"Oh, Ed," I said, once I'd made my way gingerly across the

storm wreckage to his side. I saw flashes of purple, then orange, then yellow beneath my sneakered feet. The orchids—the beautiful orchids that had been growing from the trunks of the royal palms. The blossoms had been ripped from their stems by the wind, whirled through the air, and then thrown, bruised and battered, to the ground. "I'm so sorry."

"What are you sorry for?" he demanded crossly. "It'll clean up."

It never would. Or maybe it would, but it would take weeks. Months. Maybe years.

"Sure," I said. "Okay."

"Instead of being sorry," he said testily, "you could go grab a net and help."

It was so hot and swampy, I could hear mosquitoes buzzing in my ears. Drew had been wrong about my lavender candle. The candle would have been very useful right about now.

"Okay," I said, though I had no intention of helping with the pool. I had other plans. "Maybe after breakfast. Ed, do you have any extra gas?"

"What do you mean, do I have any extra gas? Of course I've got extra gas. What do you want with it?"

"I want to use it to top off my scooter."

"So you can go where? There's nowhere to go. Everything's closed, including the bridge. Didn't you hear? No one can get in or out of here."

"Come on, Ed, I'm not trying to leave Little Bridge. Why do you have to be so nosy? I just have places to go, okay?"

"Have you seen it out there?" He pointed in the direction

of the street. "There're trees and power lines down all over the place."

"I know that, Ed. A car couldn't make the drive. But a scooter could. That's why it's called a scooter. It scoots around hazards like that." I had no idea if this was true, but it sounded good.

"And I do know what a downed power line looks like," I continued. "So I'll avoid them."

Ed looked at me long and hard. He hadn't shaved that morning, which was unusual for Ed, and showed the agitated state of his emotions. Ed always arrived at the Mermaid each morning freshly shaved and wearing a neatly pressed Mermaid Café T-shirt, in jeans, never shorts, out of respect for his position as owner, despite the heat outside or in the kitchen.

Today he was wearing shorts. It was shocking to see how pale the skin of his legs was, compared to his well-tanned arms and neck.

"Well, I'm not going to give you gas for that," he said, finally. "That'd be like giving you gas to kill yourself. And later on I'm gonna need your help. I hafta go down to the café and open it up and start feeding folks there. There's gonna be a lotta hungry people who stayed and didn't prepare properly, and it's gonna be our responsibility to take care of them. Can't count on FEMA to do it. Might take days until they get here, if at all. And I gotta start getting rid of food before it rots. Don't have a generator over at the Mermaid. That's probably something I shoulda done, instead of investing in one here."

His gaze flicked in the direction of the house's generator,

which I could hear grinding away over by the pool table (which had miraculously remained intact; it was too heavy to have been blown over by the wind, though the cover was gone, the green felt now sodden and covered in leaves and other storm debris).

"Sure," I said. "I'll be happy to come back and help you with that. Just as soon as I've found your nephew."

CHAPTER NINETEEN

Never venture outside after a storm until local authorities have deemed it safe. Hidden hazards such as damaged electrical equipment can cause life-threatening injuries.

Ed Hartwell threw back the door to his toolshed—the one next to which he'd built the rabbit hutch—and revealed he'd filled almost the entire thing with red plastic canisters of gasoline.

"Wow," I said, eyeing them. "I'm really glad I didn't know about this during the storm."

He didn't understand why I found the idea of one hundred gallons of fuel sitting in a wood shed during hundred-mile wind gusts upsetting.

"Why?" He grabbed one of the five-gallon canisters. "It's totally safe. Unless somebody came out here and smoked."

The problem was, people had been out there smoking during the hurricane party. The canisters had to have been there then, and Ed had never said a word.

I thought it better not to mention this. What was done was done.

After cleaning the leaves and mud off my motorbike, then topping it off with fuel, Ed had a few pieces of parting advice for me.

"Anyone waves to you, don't stop," he said. "No matter how desperate they look for help. They're probably only after your bike."

"Jeez, Ed," I said. "This is Little Bridge, not *The Walking Dead*. Do you really think that's going to happen?"

"It might," he said. "That's why, just in case, you might want to bring this along."

He rolled up a pants leg and revealed that he wore an ankle holster. Tucked inside was a snub-nosed .22.

I recoiled at the sight of it.

"Ed. No. No way."

Of course I'd heard the rumors that Ed Hartwell walked around armed. For what other reason, Angela often argued, would a sixty-five-year-old man in reasonably good health wear a fanny pack, if not to hold a small pistol? His wallet, keys, and cell phone weren't in it. We could clearly see the outlines of those things in the back pockets of his jeans.

We knew that ever since Wilhelmina, when the Mermaid's cash register and meat slicer had been looted, Ed had begun keeping a pistol strapped beneath the counter, near the pie window display.

I'd been told, however, that he'd never had occasion to

use it, due to the frequency with which members of law enforcement dined at the Mermaid.

But now I had incontrovertible proof that Angela was right: Ed was packing heat, only not in his "bum bag," as the British tourists we frequently served referred to fanny packs, but in an ankle holster.

"Ed," I said. "I'm literally only going across town. I do not need a gun."

"Do you know how to fire one?" he asked, ignoring me.

The funny thing was, I did. You did not grow up the daughter of Judge Justine and a Manhattan defense attorney without, at some point, being taken to a gun range and offered target lessons by one of their well-meaning if dodgy clients. My dad, in particular, had defended some fairly reprehensible individuals—old-school mafiosos, dirty politicians, Russian mobsters, hired killers.

But that didn't mean I hadn't enjoyed the lessons. Especially the part where everyone had praised me for turning out to be an excellent shot. Something about my hand-eye coordination.

"Of course I do," I said. "But, Ed, who's going to try to steal my scooter? The bridge is out. The only people on the island right now are locals. And you can't honestly tell me that you think someone who lives here would—"

"Just take it with you." Ed shoved the pistol at me. "You never know. Someone could come here on a boat or a plane to—"

"—steal my used, ten-year-old scooter?"

"Just take it. You're a pretty young woman. It'd make me feel a lot better about letting you do this if you had a way to defend yourself. The piece is already loaded. Safety's here—"

"I know where the safety is, Ed."

I took the gun from him before he could flash it around some more. There were plenty of people walking around on the street, happy not to be cooped up in their homes now that the storm was over.

I shoved the gun into my backpack, into which I'd also packed a few bottles of water and a warm, foil-wrapped Cuban breakfast sandwich that Mrs. Hartwell had insisted on making for Drew when she'd heard where I was headed.

"Please bring him back to me," she'd whispered, tears in her eyes—the whisper was because Katie was on the landline, talking to her dad, and Mrs. Hartwell didn't want to disturb her. The tears were because she was so moved by my offer to go find Drew.

"Don't worry, I will," I'd assured her. I hadn't wanted to voice my fears about what I was really going to find once I got out to Sandy Point, which was nothing but rubble.

Katie came in just at that moment, looking perturbed.

"What's the matter, honey?" Mrs. H asked. "Is your dad all right?"

"Oh, he's fine." Katie lifted a piece of toast and nibbled on it absently. "Everyone over at the high school made it through the storm okay. The jail, too. But I guess things are pretty bad over by the bridge. There's already a traffic jam on the other side, locals trying to get back to their homes. Only they can't because there's no safe way through. Dad's there now, dealing with them. He wants me to call my mom in Miami and let her know I'm okay."

"Well," said Mrs. Hartwell, "you should. I'm sure she's worried sick about you. You know they're saying on the news that Little Bridge was destroyed in the storm."

"I know," Katie said. "It's just that I don't feel like talking to my mom. She's such a—"

Mrs. Hartwell gasped. "Katie!"

I knew how Katie felt, though. I probably should have used the Hartwells' landline to call my own mother and let her know I was all right. But like Katie, I didn't want to, either. There was something weirdly restful and almost comforting about being cut off from the rest of the world, without cell service, Internet, and television . . .

Well, except the part about not knowing whether Drew Hartwell was dead or alive.

But I intended to remedy that.

I was familiar with the drive out to Sandy Point because it was one of the prettiest beaches on the island, so I often visited it on my days off from work, sometimes even going there to paint. A state park, there weren't any hotels or commercial businesses out there, only a few private homes on land that had been purchased before the government had stepped in and declared the beach a national treasure, so the shoreline still had a pristine quality to it. There weren't any tiki huts or trucks selling snow cones or renting

Jet Skis or sun umbrellas, so tourists generally avoided the area.

Although who knew what that mile of white, palm tree–dotted sand looked like now? The closer I got to the shore, the more difficult the roads leading to it became to navigate. What was normally a fifteen-minute scooter ride took over an hour, because I kept having to back down a street once I'd started up it, due to fallen trees or power lines I couldn't get by, even on a motorbike.

But one thing I did not encounter were any hostile predators, despite Ed's predictions. In fact, I met the opposite. Thoughtful locals who lived in the area had already generously marked places where electric lines were down or hanging low, tying brightly colored bandannas or even plastic bags around the wires so anyone passing by wouldn't run over or into them.

I saw plenty of people out with their own personal chain saws, getting to work on fallen trees before city crews even had a chance to assemble. I recognized many of them from the Mermaid. All of them waved and called out as I rode by, happy to see a familiar face.

"When are you guys opening back up?" a few wanted to know.

"Later this afternoon," I called out.

This information was met with enormous smiles and cries of "Great, we'll be there!"

Ed was going to get plenty of takers for the food he was hoping to give away before it spoiled.

My heart grew heavier the closer I got to the beach, however. I'd seen virtually no damage to any of the homes I'd passed traveling through town, aside from a few missing roof shingles or carports.

But the first home I saw upon turning down Sandy Point Drive—a beautiful, three-story modern structure that I happened to know belonged to a wealthy real estate developer who'd hosted several charity benefits catered by the Mermaid—had been ripped from its foundation by either the wind or storm surge or both. It lay several yards into the surf, collapsed onto itself.

It had the sad, vacant look of a home that had been deserted—I knew the owner was a "snowbird" who resided up north during the summer months—but I still offered up a silent prayer that no one had been in the house during the storm.

Beyond it the road was virtually unrecognizable as such, there was so much sand, seaweed, and other debris thrown across it. My tires skidded unsteadily on the uneven surface.

The house next door to the one that had collapsed had lost part of its roof. The back deck was completely missing from the next house, torn savagely away and tossed who-knows-where by the waves.

And then—boom!—there it was, right in front of me: the Atlantic Ocean. Normally, the sea around Little Bridge was an eye-achingly bright turquoise blue, with streaks of paler and darker blue within it.

Not today. Today, I could see that the storm had changed not only the ocean's color—it was a dark, metallic gray-blue because of all the sand and sea grass that had been churned up from the bottom—but its surface as well. Instead of the smooth, almost glasslike body of water in which I could usually see the reflections of the puffy white clouds overhead, I found myself staring at raw, white-capped waves lapping at the hulls of overturned, half-sunken boats that had escaped their moorings, and pieces of floating jetty.

It would be impossible to navigate waters like this, not unless you were in a navy vessel. There were too many hidden underwater hazards that might damage or destroy a boat's propellers or hull.

The sea wasn't all that had been transformed by the storm. The landscape of the beach in front of me had been reshaped as well. The sand that had once been pure, powder white was now caked dark with seaweed and other flotsam, smashed stone crab traps and brightly colored fishing buoys. The gorgeous palm trees that had once loaned the beach such a tropical air had been completely stripped of their fronds by the high winds, and now resembled spindly toothpicks, pressing up out of the sand like misshapen candles on a mottled birthday cake.

The only consolation for the destruction that I could see was that the birds had returned in droves. There were seabirds everywhere, gulls, cormorants, herons, frigates, pelicans, and even osprey, picking through the debris on the beach for whatever tasty snacks they could find inside the rotting algae.

Halfway up the beach, however, was a piece of wreckage from the storm that the birds had no interest in: a large yacht, which had washed up and was resting on its side in the middle of the road, like a sixty-foot seal taking a quick nap in the baking sun.

The boat wasn't the only thing on the road that shouldn't have been there. I had to drive around a refrigerator, someone's Jet Ski, a kid's tricycle, and multiple pieces of deck furniture.

As I navigated my scooter closer to the address Mrs. Hartwell had given me as Drew's—42 Sandy Point Drive—and around thicker and thicker piles of sand and seaweed, I tried taking deep breaths to control my wildly erratic thumping heart. He wouldn't be here, I told myself. He couldn't. He'd have found shelter somewhere else on the island—the high school, maybe. It wasn't that far from here.

Because only a fool would have stayed on this side of the island. Sandy Point was all but destroyed, and any living thing that had remained here—where the eye of the storm had clearly passed over—would have been destroyed along with it.

Drew must have been able to see that, and had fled, along with his dogs, in advance of the worst of Marilyn's winds.

And yet suddenly, there it was, looming up in front of me. Number 42, exactly as he'd described it: a single-story building of poured concrete, painted white, standing tall on forty-foot pilings, which kept the home atop them not only well out of the storm surge, but also steady against hurricane-force winds since the pilings were sunk deep into the sand.

Cement steps led up to a whitewashed deck that encircled

the entire house, providing a 360-degree view of the island and beach. From my vantage point on the road, I could see that Drew had installed sliding glass doors to every room. He must have used impact-resistant glass, because none of these appeared to have been shattered.

Some of them, though, seemed to have been thrown open, possibly to let in the ocean breeze . . .

. . . unless they'd been sucked open by the hurricane-force winds. Long, filmy white curtains streamed out through the openings and fluttered in the strong ocean breeze.

There was no sign of Drew's pickup truck, but when I switched off the scooter's engine, I could hear—very faintly, over the rumble of the waves and the howl of the wind—the sound of dogs barking.

No. No way. Was I imagining this? I had to be.

Removing my helmet and setting it on the scooter's seat, I picked my way across the seaweed-strewn beach, heading toward the house's stairs, my heart hammering harder than ever. He couldn't possibly be there, I told myself. Or if he was, I was going to find him dead. Probably the storm had sucked open those sliding doors, then hurled a piece of driftwood inside, knocking him in the head, killing him instantly.

And if that's what had happened, how was I going to tell his aunt? I wondered as I began to climb the stairs, which were slippery from the muck and grime the storm surge had left behind. Drew being dead would break her heart.

The farther I climbed, the harder the wind from the sea whipped around me, and the louder and more insistent the barking seemed to become. Where was that barking even coming from? With the wind, it was hard to tell. It seemed to be coming from everywhere and nowhere all at once.

Then, just as I reached the top of the steps, the wind whipped my hair directly into my eyes. I couldn't see a thing, but as I fought to scrape back the wayward strands, I heard a different sound. A man's voice.

An all-too-familiar voice.

"Fresh Water!"

CHAPTER TWENTY

Risks of electrocution, drowning, and other physical threats can accompany hurricanes.

As soon as I'd finally managed to scoop my hair from my eyes, I saw something I'd become sure I'd never see again: Drew Hartwell's handsome, unshaven face smiling down at me.

"What are you doing here?" he asked—not accusingly, but curiously, as if I were a bird that had tumbled down from the sky and landed at his feet.

"I . . . I . . ."

I don't know what came over me.

Maybe it was how good he looked, dressed as always in a half-buttoned linen shirt, blown open by the strong ocean breeze, and a pair of cargo shorts, slung obscenely low on his slim hips.

Maybe it was my certainty that I was going to find him dead, and he was so very much alive.

Maybe it was that smile . . . that smile that revealed all

his white, even teeth, and caused my heart to somersault inside my chest.

Whatever the reason, instead of replying, I found myself flinging my arms around his neck, pressing my body against his, and kissing him full on the mouth.

"Whoa," he said in surprise, his lips moving against mine. "What—"

But it seemed to be a pleasant surprise, since his hands went quickly to my waist, then tugged me closer, crushing my breasts against his hard bare chest. I could feel the metal rivets of the fly of his shorts against my belly, since my T-shirt had hiked up.

Then his lips stopped moving to form words, but instead started moving to kiss me back. He tasted pleasantly of mint toothpaste, but when his tongue joined his lips in their gentle exploration, I tasted something else more flavor forward, and realized it was coffee.

Who knows how long we would have stood there kissing like that, with my arms around his neck and his around my waist, and a hot white heat rising from deep inside me, if something cold and wet hadn't pressed up against my thigh. I pulled away with a gasp.

"Goddammit, Bob," Drew snarled down at the large black Labrador retriever that was panting up at me, his pink tongue lolling. "Leave her alone."

The dog wagged his black fringed tail happily, looking entirely unapologetic. Behind him was another, smaller dog, a scruffy terrier mix also wagging its tail and smiling up at me. A third dog, some sort of beagle mix, stood behind Drew, while a fourth came trotting around the corner of the wraparound deck, one black ear tipped forward alertly, while the other drooped in a manner I found oddly familiar . . .

"Socks?" I could hardly believe what I was seeing. The bedraggled border collie mix had been transformed. His once dingy black-and-gray coat gleamed a lustrous black and white. He trotted with confidence with every step, his tail wagging joyously as he bounded over to greet me, and while one of his ears still drooped, the one that always perked up alertly seemed more alert than ever.

"It's Bob now," Drew said, leaning down to give the dog an affectionate scratch beneath the droopy ear. "Remember? I told you I changed it. New life, new name."

I pointed at the black Lab, who had jealously inserted his head beneath Drew's hand, eager for his own caresses. "But you called that one Bob."

Drew automatically transferred his hand to the Lab's head. "He's Bob, too. They're all named Bob."

I had begun scratching the head of the beagle mix, who'd placed its paws on my thigh, looking up at me with those big brown liquid eyes all beagles have.

"You can't name all your dogs Bob," I said, with a disbelieving laugh.

"Yes, I can." He looked perfectly serious. "And you never answered my question. What are you doing here?"

I stared at him like he was crazy. "I came to make sure you're okay. Do you even know what's going on out there?

The bridge to the mainland is washed out and no one can get on or off the island. Your aunt and uncle are worried sick about you."

There was a knowing glint in his electric blue eyes. "Really? My aunt and uncle were the *only* ones worried about me?"

I pretended not to understand what he meant, tugging my backpack away from the scruffy terrier mix, who was taking a pointed interest in it, most likely due to the egg, ham, and cheese sandwich inside. "Well, your niece, too."

"Ah," he said. "You rode all the way out here because my family is worried about me? It has nothing to do with your personal feelings toward me? Which I have to say you're making pretty obvious by all these kisses you keep laying on me."

I could feel myself blushing, but fortunately, it was windy enough that I knew my cheeks were hidden by my hair, which was blowing around all over the place.

"I . . . I . . . was just relieved that I wasn't going to have to go back to your aunt's house and tell her that you're dead. That kiss, that . . . that's just the way we greet people in New York when we're relieved they haven't been killed in a natural disaster."

"Oh, I see." He was grinning from ear to ear, looking so self-satisfied I began to wonder myself why I'd bothered to go to all the trouble of finding him. I'd forgotten how annoying he could be. "I should have stayed in New York longer, since I think I missed some of the more interesting local traditions there."

Hoping to change the subject, I opened my backpack and extracted the sandwich Mrs. Hartwell had made for him, still warm in its wrapping. "Here, this is from your aunt Lucy."

He peeled back the foil, sniffed, then nodded appreciatively. "God bless that woman. I think this calls for a beer. You want one?"

"No, I do not want a beer. Are you insane? It isn't even noon."

"There's a tradition Little Bridge natives follow after natural disasters. It's called 'It's never too early for beer.' I think you'll grow to like it as much as I like your native traditions."

He didn't wait for my reply. He turned and walked into the house, the dogs trotting excitedly behind him, obviously accustomed to getting a treat (or a dropped piece of sandwich) when he headed toward the kitchen.

I had no choice but to follow. Well, I could have made the long journey back down the stairs and across the beach to my scooter, but I was curious to see what the inside of the great Drew Hartwell's famous beach house looked like.

And now that he'd mentioned it, a beer did sound kind of good.

I wasn't disappointed by the interior of his home. It was like him, uncluttered and expansive. Because of the sliding glass doors, almost everywhere you looked you saw either the bright blue of the sky or the deeper, grayish-blue of the sea. Almost all of the sliding doors had been flung open to allow the ocean breeze to flow in.

I understood now why he didn't have air-conditioning.

He didn't need it. If Leighanne had left because of the lack of AC, she'd been a fool.

The walls were all as white inside as they were outside. The floor plan was open concept, one main large room that was a kitchen, living, and dining room combined, with a hallway leading off to what I assumed was the master. He owned very little furniture, only a leather sectional and a large wood-and-glass dining table that I was guessing he'd made himself. It wasn't much of a guess, since the tools he'd used to make it were scattered all over the table itself and even the darkly stained wooden floor, against which the dogs' claws went skittering as they ran to be close by when he opened the huge stainless steel refrigerator for the beers.

And when he said, "Bob, sit," all four of the dogs sat obediently, even Socks, watching him as he opened two bottles of Corona.

"Wait," I said. "They're all really named Bob?"

"Dogs are pack animals," he said with a shrug as he handed me my beer. "They don't need individual names. They do everything as a group anyway. I'm their alpha. They do what I tell them."

I took a swig from the bottle. It had managed to stay pretty cold, despite the lack of power to the fridge.

"Well," I said. "I think that's terrible. Everyone, even animals, needs their own individual name."

"Socks seem okay to you?"

I looked at the border collie and had to admit he appeared brighter eyed and happier than I'd ever seen him, and not only because Drew was tossing him a dog treat from a jar he kept on the black granite counter by the fridge.

"Well, yes. But—"

"Then who cares? Let's talk some more about that kiss. What other traditions do New Yorkers—"

"Let's talk about what happened here last night."

"Oh, yeah." He winced at the memory as he was biting into the sandwich his aunt had prepared for him. "That. Well, as you probably recall, after I dropped off your scooter at the house, I drove back here."

"Yes . . ."

"And that's when the weather started getting a little dicey. Do you want a bite of this?" He held the sandwich toward me.

I shook my head. "It's all yours. Where's your truck?"

"I didn't want it to get flooded out in the storm surge, so I parked it over by the high school, then hoofed it back here to be with the dogs."

This was the stupidest thing I'd ever heard . . . aside from naming all your dogs Bob.

"Did it not occur to you to take the dogs with you and stay at the high school? It's a storm shelter."

He shook his head. "Couldn't do that. The high school's a shelter of last resort for people who really need it."

"Yes. And?"

"So I didn't really need it. The dogs and I would have been taking away valuable space and resources from those in need."

I nearly lost it. Standing in the middle of his bright, airy home, the sun and sea shining all around me, I flung both arms above my head and cried, "Drew, did you hear me when I told you what's going on around here? The bridge to the mainland is washed out. Half your neighbors' houses are gone! Someone's refrigerator is in the middle of your street! Along with a boat!"

He chewed calmly on his sandwich then said, after swallowing, "Yeah, but my house is fine."

"But you didn't know it was going to be!"

"Yeah, I did. I built it. And look at it. It did great."

The problem was, I couldn't deny it. It *had* done great. Except for the sand and seaweed flung up against it, which could be hosed off, it hadn't received a single scratch.

I couldn't let him win the argument, however. My assignment had been to bring him back to his aunt.

"Well, you can't possibly be planning on staying here," I said. "You don't even have power."

"What do I need power for?"

"Oh, I don't know. Cooking food for human sustenance?"

He crooked a darkly tanned index finger at me. "Come hither, little girl."

Trying not to show how sexy I found the gesture—or how disappointed I felt when it turned out he was only leading me through the nearest open sliding glass doors, and not toward his bedroom—not that I'd have let anything happen if he had been leading me to his bedroom . . . probably—I followed him.

"Here." He pointed his beer bottle toward a massive outdoor grill, on which was sitting an enamelware percolator.

"Satisfied that my daily needs are being met without electrical power?"

I stepped closer to the grill and saw that there was also a frying pan sitting on it, on which I glimpsed the remains of egg whites.

"You already had eggs this morning?" I asked in disbelief. "And yet you ate your aunt's breakfast sandwich, too?"

"Hey," he said, patting his flat belly. "Don't you know calories don't count when you're going through hurricane recovery?"

I set down my beer and turned away from the grill—and him—in disgust. "Well, I guess you and the Bobs are doing just fine out here. Since you don't need my help after all, I should probably go."

"Whoa." He lunged for my arm, grasping it above my elbow just as I was about to head back to the steps. "I didn't say that. I mean, it's not like I've got Internet or TV. And the Bobs are fun, but they aren't great conversationalists. I could use some company."

"Too bad you didn't put in a generator when you were building this place," I said, prying his fingers off, one by one.

"Oh, I did. I built a nice tall concrete pad for it and everything, to keep it out of the surge. It just hasn't been connected yet."

"Well, don't worry. I know a guy with the power company. I'm sure he'll have the electricity back on for you soon, and you can return to playing video games or whatever it is you like to do out here by yourself."

He looked as wounded as if I'd said he liked to sit around

and watch porn. "Video games? Did you even look around in there? I do not even own— And who do you know who works at the power company? I thought you only just moved here."

"Three months ago, as I've told you repeatedly." I liked that he seemed a little jealous. "And I know Sean Petrovich."

"Sean?" His brow furrowed. "Sean Petrovich? If you think he's coming to anyone's rescue on his big white power truck, you're going to be sadly disappointed. I ran into Sean last night on the street while I was heading over to the high school and he and his girlfriend—ha, bet you didn't know he had one of those, did you?—were heading out of town like bats out of hell. I've never seen anybody so scared—"

"Wait." I held up a hand to stop the flow of his words. "Sean Petrovich, the nephew of my landlady, Lydia Petrovich?"

"Yeah, that's the one." He must have recognized something more than mere curiosity in my face, since he asked, "Why?"

"You're sure?"

"Of course I'm sure. I've known him since we were both kids. Played on the same ball team as Nevaeh's dad in high school, but he wasn't anywhere near as good. Only one who didn't know he was never going to go pro was him."

I felt a cold chill growing over me, despite the warmth of the wind blowing in from the sea.

"I asked him where the hell he thought he was going," Drew went on, "since the people who work for the power company get paid double overtime to stay here through the storm to help the town get back online after, and he said screw that, no amount of money was worth dying for, and that he and his girl were headed for Tampa. Which I doubt they even made it to, because that storm was already hitting here when they—"

"But that's terrible!"

He frowned, misunderstanding me. "Well, I mean, they might have made it. Probably, if the guy had any sense, he pulled over into a hotel when the winds got really bad—"

"No, not about that." I couldn't believe it. "Sean was supposed to be taking care of my landlady's son's guinea pigs. Did he have them with him?"

Drew stared at me. "Did he have what with him?"

"The guinea pigs. Was there a guinea pig cage in the car with him?"

He shook his head. "How would I know? It was pouring rain at the time. I didn't exactly stick my face in his window and take an inventory of everything he had in the car. But Sean drives a Camaro. I don't think there'd be room for anything in that car except for him and his girlfriend. Well, and Sean's pit bull, Pookie, who could barely fit in the—"

The chill I'd been feeling turned into outright dread.

"Damn it." I turned and headed for the stairs, and this time, I moved so fast, there was no way Drew could catch me. "Sorry, but I have to go."

CHAPTER TWENTY-ONE

Time: 9:08 A.M.
Temperature: 87°F
Wind Speed: 15 MPH
Wind Gust: 35 MPH
Precipitation: 0.0 in.

"Hey! Bree!"

He managed to catch me anyway. Well, the dogs did, thinking we were playing some kind of game. They tore after me, barking enthusiastically, and one of them—the beagle—thrust itself in front of me, blocking my path, so my choice was to either stop or trip over him and fall the rest of the way down the steps.

"What?" I turned and demanded ungraciously of my host.

Drew was taking the steps two at a time to reach me. "Where the hell are you going?"

"Back to my apartment building. My landlady evacuated, and she told me Sean was going to stop by and look in on her son's guinea pigs. But Sean evacuated, too. So could you please get your dogs off me?"

The beagle was standing on the step below me, barking at me. I'd had no idea that beagles could bark so loudly. It was wearing a pink collar, which indicated to me it might be a girl, and was a small dog. But she sounded like one of the cruise ships in the harbor, blowing its horn to warn passengers that it was leaving, so they'd better hurry up with their souvenir purchasing and get back onboard.

"I'm sure the guinea pigs are fine," Drew said, ignoring my request about the dogs. The black Lab had his cold nose thrust against my crotch, excited about the game he thought we were playing. "It's not like they have to be walked. And there's a water bottle in their cage, right? So no chance of dehydration this soon."

"Have you forgotten?" I gave the black Lab's large, bullet-shaped head a gentle shove. It did no good. His nose went right back to where it had been before. "My apartment building's in the same part of the island as the Cascabel Hotel. And the lobby of the Cascabel Hotel flooded."

To his credit, Drew didn't say anything like, "Well, they're only guinea pigs." He understood—I could tell by the sudden tightening of the skin around his eyes. Sonny's pets were living things, and they were as loved as any other family member.

"Give me a minute to grab my gear," he said. He turned and started back up the steps.

Confused, I demanded, "Wait. Why?"

He paused and looked back. "Because I'm coming with you."

Now a different kind of chill went over my body. "No. No, that really isn't necessary—"

"Are you kidding? Bree, do you even have a key to your landlady's apartment?"

I hadn't thought about this. "Well, no. But—"

"Then how do you plan to get in?"

"I don't know. Through a window, or something."

"Aren't all the windows boarded up?"

I felt ridiculous. But I also felt an equally strong—and very urgent—desire not to be around Drew Hartwell any longer. I'd already kissed him twice in moments of weakness. I needed to get away from him, and fast.

And Sonny's guinea pigs were the perfect excuse.

"Do you have any tools?" he asked. "Any way of breaking into her place?"

"No. But—"

"I do. Let me just go get them." He turned and started heading back up the steps to his house.

"Oh," I said, realizing I still had an excuse to get out of this situation. "But there's no way we can take your truck. The roads are really bad. You won't believe how many power lines and trees are down. It took me over an hour just to get out here—"

"That's okay," he tossed back over his shoulder. "We can take your scooter."

My scooter?

This was getting worse and worse. If we took my scooter, that meant he'd be sitting behind me—if he even let me drive, which, knowing him, he probably wouldn't, which was going to lead to a whole other argument—and since the seat on my scooter wasn't that big, that meant—assuming I won the argument over who was driving—the front of his body was going to be pressed up against my back, and that I was going to feel *all* of him against me, because my scooter didn't have a handle in the back for an extra passenger to hold on to, so he was going to have to hold on to me. And then . . .

No. Just no. This could not happen.

Determined not to allow this, I grasped at whatever excuse I could think of to stop it . . . and realized several were panting on the steps below and beside me.

"But . . . but what about your dogs?" I pointed at the Bobs. "You can't leave them behind!"

Drew was standing on the top step. He turned to squint down at me, shading his eyes from the sun. "Of course I can. They just came in from a half-hour run on the beach. They've had their breakfast. They're dogs. They'll be fine."

"But . . . but . . ." Think, Bree. Think! "The house—aren't you afraid of looters?"

He laughed. "You've been listening to my uncle, haven't you?"

I didn't want to mention the pistol Ed had given me, which I still had in my backpack. Instead, I said only, "He did seem concerned."

"Who's going to find their way out here?" Drew asked, gesturing toward the debris-strewn beach. "Unless they have a boat. But it'd have to be a pretty big boat to navigate its way through those waters."

I told myself to calm down. Just because we'd shared a couple of kisses and were probably going to share a scooter didn't mean it was inevitable that we'd be sharing anything else.

Except that I couldn't get the way those kisses had made my body feel—like it was alive for the first time in months—out of my mind.

This was the problem. I was starting to worry I *wanted* to share something else. And that was only going to lead to—

"But I only have one helmet, so—"

"Relax, Fresh Water." His rakish grin did the same unsettling thing to my insides that his kisses had. "There's never been anyone I've trusted more than you to drive safely. And I've done a lot riskier things in my life than ride around without a helmet on the back of a girl's scooter."

I was sure this was true.

But I was even more sure that I was the one taking the bigger risk.

CHAPTER TWENTY-TWO

Most communities enjoy prompt and efficient recovery from large storms. Various emergency-response teams are trained to take immediate action to restore necessary services.

It wasn't as bad as I thought it was going to be, having him sitting behind me on the scooter. For one thing, I was wearing my backpack—there wasn't room for it under my seat once he'd stuffed his tool bag in there.

So there was a natural barrier between me and that electrical-charge-inducing skin of his.

But for another thing, he kept his hands to himself—well, except for the fact that he had to hold on to something, and that something was me. He didn't have any other choice.

Still, after swinging one of his long, lean legs over the seat and making himself comfortable behind me, he asked, politely, "Is this okay?" before settling his big tanned hands on my hips.

And it was okay. Surprisingly so. I nodded and said,

"That's good," relief flooding through me. I'd been feeling a lot of anxiety about what was going to happen when he got on the scooter.

But suddenly it all seemed to ebb away. I even sort of liked having him back there, his long hairy legs wrapping around me, radiating so much masculine energy. With the bright sunshine beating down on us, and the wind still whipping at us, it made me feel almost happy . . . and definitely secure. Even when he kept pointing at hazards in the road that I could plainly see—such as someone's deflated swan pool floatie—and calling, "Look out!" in my ear, I could only laugh.

"Oh my God. You are literally the worst backseat driver."

"Well, you're the worst front-seat driver. You were headed straight for it!"

"I was not."

"You were, too. Has anyone ever told you that you need glasses? Because you do."

The streets were actually a lot easier to navigate going back into town than they'd been on my way out to the beach. That's because all the people I'd seen out in their yards, cleaning, had also been busy picking up the refuse that had fallen across the roads, including tree debris. There was nothing they could do about downed power lines, but we saw a few crews from the electric company working on those. It was amazing to me how many people hadn't evacuated. All those times I'd ridden my bike across town, to and from the Mermaid, ahead of the storm, the place had seemed deserted.

But it hadn't been. The residents of Little Bridge had merely been hunkering down, waiting for Marilyn to pass, so they could begin the hurricane-recovery process.

In some places, however, this was going to take more than a little bit of sweeping and cutting. When I pulled up in front of my apartment building, I was horrified to see that the frangipani wasn't the only tree that had been lost to the storm. An enormous mahogany that had graced the yard of a neighbor had fallen across the road, crushing a car parked beneath it, directly in front of the entrance to my building's courtyard.

"Oh, God," I said, dismayed by the sight.

Drew chose to be optimistic. "It's probably not that bad. I'm sure your apartment is fine."

He was wrong. Beyond the gate was an even greater disaster. The storm surge from the harbor had reached the apartment building. I could see the dark line where the water had risen, only about three inches up the pink stucco walls.

Still, the leaves and branches of the frangipani—not to mention the dirt where it had been planted—had been churned around the courtyard like bits of food in a dishwasher, except with nowhere to drain.

Now frangipani—and mud—was stuck to everything . . . except for my neighbors, Patrick and Bill, who had the door to their apartment open and were carefully removing from it everything that had been drenched in the flood.

"Bree!" Patrick cried when he saw me. "Aren't you a sight for sore eyes?"

All three of their dogs had rushed over to greet us when

we entered the courtyard, and now Drew and I were fending off happy pug tongue lashings.

"Hi," I said, gently pushing away Brenda Walsh, their eldest pug, as I hurried over to greet the couple. "I'm so sorry. Is it bad?"

"Could have been worse." Bill, holding a sodden box of what looked like record albums, returned the kiss I gave him on the cheek. "Here it was only a couple of inches. At the Cascabel, it was four feet! All that beautiful art deco lobby furniture was absolutely ruined. Not to mention, the elevators stopped working. We had to carry the babies down all those flights of stairs in the dark."

I ignored the told-you-so look that Drew flashed me.

"I'm so sorry," I said again. "That must have been terrible."

"You made the right decision not to stay there with us," Patrick said. "Honestly, we should have known better. But we were just so enchanted with the idea of not evacuating this time."

"Brandon Walsh!" Patrick shouted at the pug that was slowly and deliberately humping Drew's leg. "You stop that this instant!"

"Oh, that's all right." Drew gave his leg a soft shake, and Brandon (all three pugs were named after characters from the old television show *90210,* of which Patrick and Bill were fond) trotted jauntily away. "I have dogs myself."

"Do you?" Patrick was giving Drew an appraising look. I knew exactly what he was thinking just from his tone and the way his eyebrows were raised: that Drew and I were sleeping together. Patrick had been teasing me from the moment I'd moved into the apartment complex, practically, for not having had a Little Bridge hookup, and now he suspected he'd finally caught me with one. "I don't recall having seen you around here before—and believe me, with those shoulders, I'd remember. Are you the reason Bree chose not to spend the hurricane in luxury at the Cascabel with us?"

"No, he's not." I hurried to change the subject. "He's just here to help me break into Lydia's apartment. Sonny's guinea pigs are in there. His cousin Sean was supposed to look after them, but he evacuated, and I have no idea if they're dead or alive."

Bill looked alarmed. "R2-D2 and C-3PO? Well, what are you doing just standing there? Go save them!"

Drew seemed amused by the exchange. I sent him an aggravated look and pointed at my landlady's door. "You heard the man."

Still grinning, he said, "Yes, ma'am. Right away," and crossed the tree-branch-strewn courtyard, then bent to examine Lydia's lock.

While Drew's back was turned, Patrick elbowed me. "So?" he whispered. "What's the deal? Spill, sweetie, spill."

I rolled my eyes. *There is no deal,* I mouthed.

Liar, Patrick mouthed back. *I can feel the sparks.* He silently mimed the moment from his drag performance when one of his characters—Joan of Arc—is engulfed in imaginary flames.

Ignoring him and the uncanny way he'd sensed the truth about what was going on between Drew and me (was it that obvious?), I said aloud, "I'm so glad my roommate and I had enough sense to move our stuff off the floor so it wouldn't get ruined."

Patrick, recovering from his make-believe conflagration, threw me a sour look as Bill cried, "Oh, I know. What were we thinking, leaving all this stuff on the floor?" He nudged one of the boxes of record albums with his foot. "Normally we'd have remembered, but this time we were in such a hurry to get to the hotel, we completely forgot."

Drew, over by Lydia's front door, straightened up. "This is a dead bolt," he said, flatly.

"So?"

"So, I can't break into a place with a dead bolt. And this one is top of the line, with side panels."

I blinked at him. I knew what he meant—more than a few of my dad's clients had been burglars, and they'd given me lessons in lock picking while my unsuspecting father was otherwise occupied. So I knew a dead bolt with side panels was bad news.

But I wasn't sure how it would keep out someone with a chain saw. "What does that even mean?"

"That means we should go back to my aunt and uncle's place and use their landline to call your friend and ask her if she's got a spare key hidden around here somewhere, because otherwise we're never getting through this door. I can't even get through a window with the kind of shutters she uses. They're all bolted into the ground, and I didn't bring a drill."

"Drew, we don't have time," I said instead. "Can't you see

that water line? The tidal surge got in there. Sonny keeps his guinea pigs in a wire cage on the floor. Those animals could be dying as we speak!"

"I'm pretty sure guinea pigs can swim, Bree. And the water's gone now."

"Sure, but the poor little things are probably suffering from shock or hypothermia or both—"

"They don't have hypothermia. The water was eighty-six degrees. That's how the storm got so strong. You see, the two ingredients you need to fuel a hurricane are warm waters and wind—"

"Um, if I might interrupt." Patrick approached us, Donna Martin—his silver pug—in his arms, and mercifully cut Drew off before he could explain to me how hurricanes form, a fact I already knew, having had the Weather Channel on twenty-four-seven before the power went out. "All of the bathrooms in this unit were built with jalousie windows."

I had no idea what Patrick was talking about, but from the way his dark eyebrows lifted, Drew appeared interested. "Really?"

"Oh, yes." Seeing my puzzled expression, Patrick explained, "That window in your bathroom with the louvered panes?"

I wrinkled my nose. "Oh. Yeah. What's up with that?"

I hated that window. The individual glass slats were ancient and discolored and hardly let in enough light for me to see by when I was putting on my makeup. Worse, because the fittings were so old, the panes were loose, and so allowed steamy tropical air to flow into the bathroom instead of keeping it out.

Drew said, "It's called a jalousie." To Patrick, he said, "What about it?"

"Well, since those windows are so small and in the back of the building," Patrick said, "and therefore more protected from the winds, Lydia never bothered to have shutters made for them."

Drew looked even more interested. "So they aren't boarded up? Are they big enough for a person to crawl through?"

"Oh, certainly." Bill hurried over, Brenda and Brandon Walsh trotting at his heels. "I squeezed through ours once when Patrick lost our keys over at the tea dance by the dock—"

"You're the one who lost the keys, Bill."

"Um, no, I distinctly recall that it was you, Pat. Remember, you were the one who insisted on wearing that smoking jacket with the hole in the—"

"Sweetheart, that was you."

Drew reached out and grabbed my wrist. "Come on."

The next thing I knew, we were rounding the side of the building and picking our way past multiple recycling bins and trash cans—the lids of which had been carefully strapped down with tape by Sonny to keep them from blowing away in the storm—and locked-up bicycles, until we reached a small louvered window in the middle of the stucco wall.

"Bingo," Drew said, and bent to retrieve a screwdriver from his tool kit.

"What are you going to do?"

"This is why jalousies fell out of fashion," Drew said, using the screwdriver to bend one of the metal brackets holding the lowest louver in place. "They're fine on porches and breezeways, but for windows to home interiors, not only are they energy inefficient, but"—he popped the second bracket, and the panel of glass fell noiselessly into his hand—"they can also be a security nightmare."

I swallowed as he handed the heavy glass pane to me, then went to work on the next louver. "You mean . . . this whole time, somebody could have broken into my bathroom window just by removing the louvers?"

He threw me an amused glance. "Well, yes. It's not very common, but it happens. But I thought you didn't believe in Mean World Syndrome."

I blinked at him as he handed me another glass pane. "What?"

"Isn't that what you told me the other night? That the world is not this dangerous and unforgiving place that people like your mother are always trying to convince everyone that it is."

I frowned. "Oh, that. Right. But a little common sense—like not having windows that are super easy to break into—never hurt anybody."

He grinned as he turned back to his work. "True. Well, if you want, I could talk to your landlady when she gets back. There's a company that makes new, energy-efficient jalousies that also lock in place. That way the building wouldn't lose its historic charm, and you'd feel more secure."

"Oh," I said, as he piled another heavy slab of glass into my arms. "Yeah, thanks. That would be great."

"Don't mention it."

I wondered why he was being so nice to me. It couldn't only be that he wanted to get into my pants. There were girls all over the island throwing themselves at him who were much prettier than me, and who'd made it clear—within my hearing—that they'd be willing to fulfill his every sexual fantasy, whereas I was pretty obviously a ball of nervous uptight neuroses. Why wasn't he hanging out with one of those other girls? It was unlikely that all of them had evacuated.

And I was fairly sure the vast majority of them weren't going to make him follow them around, break into apartments, and rescue their landlady's son's guinea pigs, either. There had to be easier ways for him to get laid.

Shortly following the words "Don't mention it," he pulled out the final louver.

"There," he said, looking with satisfaction at my landlady's now gaping window. "Are you ready?"

"For what?" I lowered the heavy pile of glass to the soft dirt at my feet. Several geckos scampered away, anxious not to be squashed.

"To climb in there." He nodded at the window while interlacing his fingers, preparing to give me a boost.

I took a wary step backward. "Me? Why do *I* have to do it?"

"Because I'll never fit through there." His dark eyebrows furrowed. "I thought you were the one who was so worried about saving your friend's guinea pigs. Are you backing out on me now?"

"No." I threw a nervous glance at the darkened window. "I've just never broken into anyone's apartment before."

"Oh, but you were fine with me doing it? What, are you worried about what the gossip sites are going to say when they find out—*Judge Justine's Daughter Caught Breaking and Entering?*"

"Shhhh." I instinctively glanced around.

He laughed. "Uh, sorry. Do you think there are paparazzi hiding in the bushes?"

Embarrassed, I shook my head. "Of course not." I swallowed and laid a hand on the windowsill, pointedly ignoring his cupped fingers. "I can do it myself."

"Oh, you can?" He lifted an incredulous eyebrow. "Excuse me. I thought you might need a little boost."

"No, no." I shook my head. "I've got this."

"All righty, then." He straightened and stepped back, watching as I struggled to lift myself through the window, which turned out to be higher from the ground than I'd thought. After several unsuccessful attempts to push myself over the sill, I finally turned to look at him.

"Perhaps," I said, blushing, "I might need a little help."

"Yeah," he said, pushing himself from the side of the building where he'd been leaning, watching my struggles with some amusement. "I was wondering when you were going to ask. What's the trouble, exactly? You don't trust me not to drop you? Or you're afraid of falling even more deeply and irrevocably in love with me than you already are?"

My blush grew even deeper as I glared at him.

"Gee, I don't know. Maybe I'm just not in the habit of having to rely on tool jockeys who drink beer for breakfast and are too lazy to think up individual names for their dogs."

He hooted. "Ouch! Lazy? Is that really how you think of me?"

"It is." I wasn't going to mention how precisely he'd nailed it—that I'd already lost control of myself around him and kissed him twice. I didn't want to go for a third time, much less lose my heart to him, even though I was starting to worry it might be too late. "Look, can we talk about my trust issues later? For now I just need to get in there."

"No problem." He cupped his fingers again for me to slip my foot into. "You've got other issues, too, just to let you know, but we'll let those slide for now."

I hesitated before laying a hand on his shoulder. "What?"

"Well, I've just found that people are rarely comfortable admitting their *real* problems during self-analysis."

He straightened up so I was face-to-face with him. "Oh, really?"

"Really. So it isn't only that you don't trust me. It's something else." I found myself staring at his lips. They looked so highly kissable. "Don't worry, though. We'll get to it, eventually."

I shook my head. Because of course he was right. It was *myself* that I didn't trust . . . around him.

But I was never going to admit that.

"Could we just—" I pointed at the window behind him.

"Oh, sure," he said.

That's when he lifted me high enough for me to catch the edge of the windowsill.

"Got it?" he asked.

"Got it."

I was preparing to push myself through the small opening, not realizing that he had a similar intention—of helping me through it with a push of his own.

"Ow!"

My landing wasn't soft. The Petroviches kept a wicker laundry basket under their bathroom window. I pretty much destroyed it.

"You all right?" Drew called from beneath the window, having heard the crunch of wicker and my squeal as the wicker wands stabbed me in the right calf. "What was that?"

"Nothing." I bent to investigate the wound. No blood had been drawn, but the scrape was going to be tender for a while—my first hurricane-inflicted wound. "Just give me a warning next time, okay?"

"Sorry about that."

I climbed to my feet. "Go around front, I'll unlock the front door for you."

"Got it."

The apartment was dark and dank thanks to the rest of the windows being boarded up and there not being any power. But I didn't have to see Sonny's guinea pigs to know that they were alive. I could hear them squeaking excitedly from the other room, having overheard my not-so-graceful entrance into the apartment.

After unlocking the front door for Drew, I followed the

sounds into Sonny's bedroom, where I found the two little rodents—R2-D2, a black-and-white shorthaired, and C-3P0, a longhaired golden "Teddy"—darting around their cage, covered in shavings. The bedding had obviously become soaked thanks to the flood and was now sticking to the poor animals' fur.

"Oh, you poor things!" I looked around Sonny's room for something I could put the guinea pigs in in order to get them out of the mess. Fortunately Sonny had left the animals' traveling case on his bed, along with a bag of the pellets they were supposed to eat.

"Well, boys," I said to the guinea pigs as they continued to poke their little toes and noses through the mesh of their cage at me, grunting and squealing, almost as if they were trying to describe to me what they'd been through since Sonny had been gone. "Looks like you're going home with me."

"Huh." Drew was standing in the doorway with a beer in one hand—one that he'd evidently found in Lydia's refrigerator—looking down on the scene with an expression of mild disbelief on his face. I wasn't sure which he found most incredible, the fact that I was lifting a trembling, grunting R2-D2 into the traveling case, or that he was in the situation at all.

"What," he asked, "are you doing with that rat?"

"They're guinea pigs, not rats."

"If you say so. What are you doing to them?"

"Water leaked in here and got the bedding of their cage all wet. Now it's sticking to their fur. They're going to need a bath, I think."

"Are you even supposed to bathe guinea pigs?"

"I don't know," I said. "Are you supposed to take beers out of the refrigerators of people you don't even know?"

He glanced down at the beer in his hand. "Hey, if I don't drink it, it's just going to get hot and explode in there. I'm doing your friend a favor. You want one?"

"No," I said. "I'm taking these guinea pigs back to your aunt's house, and then I'll see if I can reach Sonny's mom and find out whether or not you're supposed to give guinea pigs a bath."

"Well." Drew eyed the animal carrier. "Lu's going to love that."

"I think she will, actually. She likes animals. She's already taken in a pair of rabbits, a parrot, and my cat. Two little guinea pigs aren't going to make a difference."

He let out a laugh. "Whatever you say."

"Well, I can't leave them here," I said defensively. "There's no power. It must be ninety degrees in here. It stinks, and it's filthy."

"I'm not disagreeing with you, ergo the beer. But . . ."

I glared at him. "Listen, if you don't like it, you can leave. I'm sure there must be more important things for you to be doing right now. Aren't you supposed to be a carpenter? Shouldn't you be out making emergency repairs on someone's house?"

"Probably," he said, a slow grin beginning to creep across his handsome face. "Too bad there's no cell service, so no one can reach me."

"Fine. Well, if you want I can drop you back at your

house first, before I go to your aunt's, so you won't have to face her if you're so afraid of what you think she's going to say if I show up there with two so-called rats."

"Oh, no." The grin broadened. "I'm sticking around so I can watch how the rest of this plays out. You're not getting rid of me that easy, Fresh Water."

And the weird thing was that even though his words should have annoyed me, I sort of liked hearing them.

That's when I should have realized the true extent of the hurricane's damage.

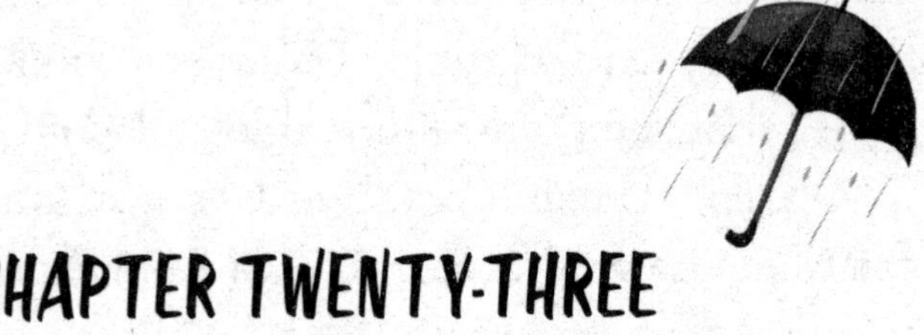

CHAPTER TWENTY-THREE

The Little Bridge Aqueduct Authority reports pressure is increasing down its main transmission line as crews continue to shut off leaks. Anyone who sees water coming out of broken lines should contact the LBAA.

"Drew!"

Aunt Lu's scream upon seeing her nephew enter her home was almost as loud as the howls of Hurricane Marilyn had been, but significantly more joyful.

As the older woman threw her arms around his neck, I could see that she had tears in her eyes.

And they were not, as Drew had tried to tease me, tears at the fact that I was bringing "rats" into her home, but of happiness because I'd returned her beloved nephew to her.

Leaving the family to their tender reunion—through which I could hear Drew saying, over and over again, "Come on, now, Lu, everything is fine"—I headed to my room in the library to check on Gary . . .

Only to find him—and all my other stuff—gone.

"Um." I didn't want to interrupt such an intimate moment with questions about the whereabouts of my cat, let alone my clothing, but my heart had begun to beat practically out of my chest, particularly about Gary. According to the people at the animal shelter, it can take a cat days to get to know the inside of a new home well enough to feel comfortable in it, weeks not to get lost in a new neighborhood (the shelter preferred that new owners not allow their cats out of the house at all). If someone had let Gary outside, I might never see him again. "Does anyone know where Gary is?"

"Oh." Aunt Lu was drying her eyes on the edge of a dish towel. "He got so lonely in there while you were gone. We could hear him crying."

This was not boding well. I had to fight to keep my tone even. "So . . . ?"

"So Nevaeh and Katie took him upstairs with them. They're playing with him in Nevaeh's room."

"Oh." Relief washed over me. "Thanks."

While this didn't exactly explain where the rest of my stuff had disappeared to, it didn't particularly surprise me. It sounded, in fact, like typical Gary behavior. After his lonely days in the animal shelter, he loved being the center of attention, and whenever he wasn't, he did whatever he had to in order to ensure that he was. This generally consisted of persistent—but cute—mewing.

I popped into the laundry room to get the guinea pigs settled. The rabbits had been moved back to their outdoor pen, so it was simple enough to put Sonny's pets into the cage the rabbits had been using, swapping out the rabbit food for guinea pig food. I made some bedding for the guinea pigs out of torn newspaper (the Hartwells had piles and piles of the *Little Bridge Gazette,* since there'd been no recycling pickup due to the evacuation order). Then I hurried upstairs to see what was up with Gary.

I hadn't been to the second floor of the Hartwell home before, but it was like the first, heavily wainscoted and wallpapered. Only here, the ceiling in the hallway at the top of the stairs had been painted by a nineteenth-century muralist: a bright blue sky with fluffy white clouds floating by. Here and there cherubic angels peeked out from behind the clouds, and bluebirds darted, ribbons streaming from their beaks. With the sun pouring in from the French doors along the second-floor terrace, it looked, quite literally, like heaven.

And in the room of the girl whose name was heaven spelled backward, I found my cat purring in a sunny spot on the canopy bed, a tiny doll tiara on his head.

"Oh, Bree," Nevaeh said, when she noticed me in the partially opened doorway. "Isn't Gary the cutest? He's been such a good boy."

Katie had her cell phone out and was taking photos of my cat from different angles. "We're totally going to make your cat a social media star," she informed me. "After the Internet comes back on."

"Like Grumpy Cat," Nevaeh said. "Only Gary's not grumpy. He's a little prince. Aren't you, baby?"

Gary, in his absolute element, let out a little meow at me, as if both questioning where I'd been and asking why I'd been so slack in making him the social media star that he so clearly was.

"That's great," I said, because it was. "If anyone deserves to be an Internet sensation, it's Gary. Nevaeh, I just thought I'd let you know that your uncle Drew got through the storm just fine. He's downstairs if you want to say hi to him."

"Oh, good." Nevaeh was completely absorbed with looking through her drawers for Gary's next costume. "I'll come down and tell him hi in a minute. I knew he was going to be fine. I don't know why everyone was so worried. He spent, like, ages storm-proofing that house."

"Um," I said. "Okay."

I was reminded of my own teenage years, when family drama had seemed much less important than the dramas going on within my circle of friends.

"You know Uncle Ed wants us to go over to the café in a little bit to start serving food to all the people who don't have power or didn't stock up, or whatever," she went on. "He's over there now, getting stuff ready."

"Okay," I said. "Well, there are some guinea pigs downstairs that I brought over from a friend's house. They need a little TLC and probably a bath. They nearly drowned in the flooding from Marilyn. So maybe you guys could help me—"

"What?" Katie nearly dropped her phone. "Guinea pigs?"

"Oh my God." Nevaeh's eyes widened. "I love guinea pigs!"

I thought the two girls were going to bowl me over in their haste to get down the stairs to see Sonny's pets. Though suddenly abandoned, Gary didn't appear particularly upset. He only bent his head toward a paw that appeared to need licking, his tiara sliding off as he began grooming.

"Yeah, I know," I said, and—removing the tiara and then cradling him in my arms the way Drew had done—I followed the girls downstairs. "You'll always be a star to me, big boy."

Gary purred happily, still enjoying his newfound fame.

Mrs. Hartwell was waiting for me in the library, looking nervous.

"Oh, Bree," she said, twisting her hands as I went to deposit Gary back on the inflatable mattress where he belonged.

Except that I'd forgotten. The air mattress was gone. So was all the bedding I'd used the night before. Of course my things were gone, including Gary's litter box. Was it in Nevaeh's room? I hadn't thought to look.

What was going on? Now that the storm was over, did Mrs. Hartwell expect me to go back to my apartment? That made perfect sense, of course, except . . . well, there was no power there, and when I'd opened the door to take a quick look inside to survey the damage, the place had reeked of damp.

I didn't mind going back, of course, but . . .

"I don't think I'll ever be able to thank you enough for bringing Drew home to me," Mrs. Hartwell was saying.

"Oh, you're welcome, Mrs. Har—Lucy." I smiled at her as Gary made a beeline for his favorite chair, the pink-silk-cushioned love seat. Mrs. Hartwell, however, didn't seem to care. "It was nothing, though, really. And Ed's the one who donated the gas. Could I just ask you quickly what happened to the stuff I had in here? It's no problem except that Gary's litter box—"

"Oh, I wanted to talk to you about that, Bree."

Wait. What? This did not sound good. Had I done something wrong? From the anxious look on her face, it appeared as if I had . . .

"Bree, this morning, while you were gone, the sheriff stopped by—"

"The sheriff?"

What on earth could the sheriff have wanted with me? I hadn't disobeyed any laws.

Well, except for breaking into my landlady's house. But that had been in order to rescue her son's guinea pigs! And I'm sure she'd have wanted me to do that.

And I hadn't done it alone. I had had a partner in crime.

"Where's your nephew?" I asked quickly.

"Drew? Oh, he's out back, looking at the pool. It really is going to need a lot of work if we're ever going to get it back to the way it was. But we're so fortunate that's really the only damage we suffered. So many have it so much worse."

"Sure. Well, listen, if it's about the guinea pigs, Drew can help explain. See, he saw Sean Petrovich driving out of town last night. And Sean said he'd take care of them. But then Sean evacuated at the last minute with his girlfriend. So what was I supposed to do? I couldn't leave them to die. They're living creatures, just like the rest of us."

Mrs. Hartwell stared at me, looking bemused. "Honey, I don't have any idea what you're talking about."

"You don't?" I was confused. "But you said the sheriff—?"

"Oh, yes. Sheriff Hartwell stopped by this morning because he says he's been receiving emergency calls all day on his satellite phone from the governor. Apparently, you're a very important young lady. Bree, why didn't you tell us that your mother is Judge Justine from the radio?"

CHAPTER TWENTY-FOUR

> Little Bridge Island remains closed to anyone who is not currently in residence or is working in an official capacity with the hurricane relief effort. There will be no exceptions by order of the Sheriff's Office.

I sat on the pink-silk-cushioned love seat, staring at the keypad to the Hartwells' landline.

I knew by heart the number I was supposed to dial. I just really, really didn't want to press it.

Instead, I took out my cell phone and looked up the number of my landlady, Lydia Petrovich. Then I pressed the buttons on the landline, dialing her instead.

She answered on the second ring.

"Hello?"

"Lydia? Hi, it's Sabrina Beckham, your tenant in—"

"Bree!" She sounded relieved to hear from me. "Oh, Bree, sweetheart, how are you? Where are you?"

"I'm in Little Bridge, Lydia, and I just wanted to tell you—"

"You're in *Little Bridge*? But how can that be? On television they're saying that—"

I smiled. "I know what they're saying on TV, Lydia. But it's not true. I mean, the apartment building did flood a little, and a few houses along the beach were destroyed, along with the bridge to the mainland. But for the most part, we didn't receive that much damage."

I heard her tell someone on her side of the phone everything I'd just said, only in Russian. When she came back on, she sounded excited. "When you say the apartment building flooded a little, how much do you mean?"

"Only a few inches. And please tell Sonny not to worry about R2-D2 and C-3PO, because I got them out. They're just fine."

Her tone sharpened. "What do you mean *you* got them out? What happened to Sean? Sean was supposed to look after them."

"Well . . ." As matter-of-factly as I could, I told Lydia what had happened with Sean.

But even though I'd been careful not to cast Sean as the bad guy, Lydia was spitting mad by the time I got through. Most of what she said, however, I didn't understand, since I don't know many Russian curse words.

"Lydia, Lydia." I tried to calm her down. "Please. The storm was really, really bad at that point. It was only natural that he was scared. Let's try not to judge. We don't know what was going through his head."

"I know exactly what was going through his head," she cried. "Helping himself and himself only, because he's a spoiled little brat, just like his mother, my sister, and he always has been. Of course I will judge him. When that bridge opens back up and I get my hands on him, he's going to wish he was never born, that—"

"Well, it's over now," I interrupted in my most soothing voice. "And it all turned out okay. Your son's guinea pigs are fine, okay? So let's concentrate on that."

"Mom," I heard Sonny saying in the background, "what's going on?"

"Nothing," she told him, in a calmer voice. "Everything's fine. Your little piggies are fine. Bree saved them."

"Bree? What about Sean?"

"Never mind about Sean. He—" There was another long pause while I overheard the mother and son discussing something animatedly in Russian. I heard the name Chett mentioned frequently.

Finally Lydia came back on the line with me. "Bree, I know it's a lot to ask, but could you do us another favor? You're the only person we've heard from who's still on the island, with cell service being out."

"Of course. Anything you need."

"Chett, one of Sonny's friends from the community college, evacuated as well, and left behind his bird. He thought he'd only be gone a day or so. But now, with the bridge out—"

"Of course," I said. "I understand."

I was lying. I didn't understand how anyone could evacuate and leave their pets behind without someone to look after them.

But, like I'd told Lydia, I wasn't there to judge.

Instead, I reached for a pen and a pad of paper that sat near the Hartwells' landline. The pad said *HOME* in fancy cursive across the top.

"Give me Chett's phone number, and I'll get in touch with him about his bird."

"Oh, you're such an angel, Bree," Lydia said, and gave me the information.

After I'd said good-bye and hung up, I looked at Gary. Displaced from his favorite seat, he regarded me resentfully from the Persian carpet.

"What have you got to be so upset about?" I asked. "You're living in the lap of luxury. I'm the one with problems."

Gary yawned, then turned his head to lazily lick a paw.

Sighing, I dialed Chett's number. He answered on the first ring. "Hello?"

"Hi, Chett? This is Bree, Sonny's frie—"

"I know who you are, ma'am." Chett spoke with a Southern accent, his voice breathless and impossibly young. "Sonny already let me know that you'd be calling."

"Oh." Sonny must have texted Chett while I'd still been on the phone with his mother. "Okay. Well, so he must have told you that—"

"Yeah, that you're in Little Bridge, and you said you'd check on my birds?"

"Um . . . birds, as in more than one?"

"Yeah, I have eight of 'em?" Chett's voice rose at the end of his sentences to make it sound like he was asking a question, even when he wasn't. "They're cockatiels. I put 'em in the attic because I was afraid it was going to flood. But now I heard on the news that it didn't, it was more of a wind event? I live on Roosevelt, so maybe you would know. Did it flood over there?"

I was still trying to absorb the bombshell he'd just dropped on me. "Did you say you have *eight* cockatiels?"

"Yeah, eight of them. I left 'em plenty of food and water, but if the power is out I imagine it's getting really hot in that attic. Cockatiels are sensitive to heat. Do you think you could go over there and check on them? I rent a room at 804 Roosevelt. There's a key under the welcome mat in front of the door. I'm in room three. You shouldn't have any problem getting in."

"Um . . . okay."

"I can't thank you enough, ma'am, this is real nice of you. Also, I know a bunch of other people from the college who can't get back to their pets, either. Would you mind if I gave you their names?"

I hesitated with my pen poised over the *HOME* notepad. "A bunch of other people who left their pets behind?"

"Well, yes, ma'am, I know it sounds bad, but we're students so it wasn't like we could afford hotel rooms or anything. We're all staying at this one girl's grandma's condo in Boca, but her grandma said we couldn't bring pets on account of she's allergic to animal dander. We thought it would be okay to leave our animals behind because we'd only be gone a little while. We didn't know the bridge was going to—"

I cut him off, as I could sense a growing hysteria in his voice. "It's okay. I'm not judging you. I know you love your pets."

"We do, ma'am." I could hear tears in his voice now. "We do love our pets. My 'tiels are my life. I thought I'd be right back, but then when I tried to drive back this morning, the sheriff—"

"It's okay," I repeated gently. "Just give me your friends' addresses and . . . uh, well, I guess what kind of pets they have, and how I can get into their homes, and if they have spare keys under the mat, like you do, or any other way I might be able to get into their place."

Chett happily obliged. By the time he was finished, I had filled a whole page of the *HOME* notepad.

I also had writer's cramp.

"So will you call us?" he asked eagerly. "Will you call us and let us know how it goes? Because I'm real worried about my birds. They're just the sweetest things."

"I'll call you, Chett," I said. "Don't worry."

All I could think about was how much gas all of this was going to take. Ed was going to kill me.

But since Ed was also an animal lover, I knew he'd be happy to donate to the cause.

Probably.

Speaking of which, I knew I had one last—and much more difficult—call to make. Which I did as soon as I'd hung up with Chett, finally dialing the number I'd been avoiding for so long.

"Mom?" I asked when she picked up.

She sounded like her usual self—her voice throaty from all the cigarettes she'd smoked before I was born, and still occasionally sneaked in times of stress. "Sabrina, finally. You don't know what I've been going through these past twenty-four hours, not knowing whether you were dead or alive."

"Mom, it hasn't even been twenty-four hours since the storm hit."

"You know what I mean. Where are you? Who are these people you're staying with? How are they treating you?"

"They were treating me just fine until you had to go and call the governor and make him send the sheriff over here and blow my cover. No one here knew I was your daughter until then."

"Why? What do you mean? Oh my God, Bree." She lowered her voice. "Have you been kidnapped? Are they listening in? Just say yes or no."

"Mom, no, don't be ridiculous. It's the opposite, in fact."

"What does that mean?"

"It means that unlike you, Mother, I wasn't asking for special treatment. But now my hostess has moved all my stuff into her best guest room. She's practically falling over herself to be nice to me. Not that she wasn't nice before, but now I've got an en suite bathroom all to myself . . . and my cat."

"Well, what's wrong with that?"

"Mom, don't you get it? I want people to like me for me, not because I'm Judge Justine's daughter."

"People *do* like you for you, Sabrina. You're a kind, smart, pretty girl. And if my being who I am happens to help . . ."

well, what's so wrong with that? Why, those people ought to show a little gratitude to you. It's because of me that the longest runway at the Little Bridge airport is going to be cleared as soon as tomorrow."

It took a second for that to register. "What?"

"That's right. The governor has promised that even if they can't get anything else done, that, at least, will be finished as a special favor to me, and your uncle Steen swears he's going to have a plane there ready to pick you up—"

"Mom." I cringed. "No. I don't want that. I mean, yes, the runway is nice, the people here need it. But do not send a plane for me."

"Sabrina, have you lost your mind? The governor says they don't expect to have that bridge fixed or power or cell service up and running there for at least another week!"

"I know, Mom, but I've got everything I need."

"Sabrina, don't be ridiculous. The governor tells me there isn't a functioning hospital down there for a hundred miles. What if something should happen to you? You could step on a nail and get lockjaw, or something. No, it's simply too dangerous. Steen and I are coming down there as soon as the runway is cleared, and that's all there is to it."

I felt as if someone had poured a cold beer down my back. "Mom, no. Do not come here."

"Well, someone has to, honey. If you don't have the common sense to get out of there, then—"

"Mom. You can clear all the runways you want—I'm sure everyone will appreciate it. But I'm not leaving."

"Sabrina. Look. I understand that you're still angry

about your father and me not telling you about your donor mother. And you have a right to be. But haven't you punished me enough? Isn't it about time that you let that go? This is a very dangerous situation, and—"

"I know it is, Mom. And I swear to you that my not wanting to leave yet has nothing to do with you not telling me about my donor mother."

"It doesn't?"

"No, of course not. I'm not even angry with you about that anymore. I'm mad that you didn't believe me about Kyle—"

"Oh, honey, I told you, I believed you. I just think you overreacted. You know, I was at a Christmas party once with the president of AMC Radio, and you wouldn't believe where he put his—"

"Mom, I'm sorry, but I don't want to talk about any of that right now. I actually do need your help. Just not the kind of help you're offering."

"Well, what kind of help do you need, then?"

"I need you to go online—since I can't, because we don't have the Internet—and post a message to every social media outlet that you can think of that anyone who's evacuated from Little Bridge Island and left a pet behind needs to contact your office. Tell them to call your office and leave their name, address, type of pet, the pet's needs, and a way we can get into their home. Make sure they don't post this information online—they have to leave it verbally with whoever picks up at your office when they call. If there really are looters, we don't want them knowing which houses are sitting empty and how to break into them. These people have to feel that their private information is safe with you. Then I'll call you back in a little while to get the data you've collected, and we can go from there."

There was silence on the other end of the phone. I waited tensely until finally my mother said, "Sabrina. What are you talking about?"

"I'm talking about all the people from this island who evacuated and left their pets behind and now can't get back to them because the bridge is out. You need to help me reach them before all their pets die."

"Sabrina." My mother's voice was tight. She sounded furious. "That is ridiculous."

"What? Why is it ridiculous?"

"Because those people should never have left their pets behind in the first place. Why should you go to all the trouble of helping them?"

"Because if I don't they'll die, Mom. And anyway, things happen. Don't they? Like people panic and evacuate and then the bridge blows out and they can't get back to their homes. And parents use a donor egg to have a baby and then never tell the kid, but eventually the kid finds out anyway. Do you think maybe we shouldn't judge people so harshly for their poor decisions?"

My mom made a croaking noise. "Sabrina—"

"Most of these people were just scared, Mom. Most of them were just doing the best they could. Many of them were only thinking of their children or their family or friends. Let's try to help them without judging them. Okay?"

"But . . . I just don't understand. It seems like so much work. Why do *you* have to be the one to do it?"

I sighed. Sometimes I felt like I was never going to understand my mother, and she was never going to understand me. But that didn't mean I didn't love her.

"Because," I said, "I'm here. And I'm not doing anything else. And I'm your daughter, and you have millions of followers on your social media. They, in turn, will spread the word to other people on social media, until it finally gets to the actual evacuees from Little Bridge who we're offering this service to. And then we'll be able to save these animals, and also prevent a possible potential health hazard. Okay? Can you just have someone do this, please? It would mean a lot to me, and I actually think it might do wonders for your reputation. It could even win you some new fans."

"Sabrina." My mom's voice sounded choked. "I—"

"Mom. Could you just do it? Will you do this *one* thing your daughter is asking you to do?"

There was silence again over the phone. And then finally my mother said, quietly, "Yes. Yes, Sabrina, of course. Tell me again what it is you want me to do."

CHAPTER TWENTY-FIVE

The Little Bridge Electric Company continues to make progress bringing power back to its customers. Some homes have experienced saltwater intrusion and won't be able to accept power until repairs are made. Progress will be slower in the hardest-hit areas where transmission poles were lost.

I explained it again.

"And remember," I added when I was done. "It's important that they don't feel judged for having left their pets behind. If they do, they won't call in. We want to save as many animals as we can, so the *why* of how it happened isn't important."

"I got it," my mother said. "No judgments."

"No judgments." I nodded, even though she couldn't see me. "Will you do it today? Like right now, when you hang up?"

"I'll call Shawna right now and have her do it." Shawna

was my mother's longtime—and long-suffering—assistant. "And, honey—"

"Yes, Mom?"

"I . . . I like you like this."

"Like what?"

"So . . . passionate."

"What?"

"It's true. You haven't seemed actually to care about anything since . . . well, in a long time." She tactfully avoided mentioning Caleb's—and Kyle's—name. "Except running away. You cared about that."

I smiled wryly. "Thanks, Mom."

"But now for the first time in quite a while you seem to care about something else . . . helping others, which, if I remember correctly, was why you went to law school in the first place—"

"Mom," I said in a warning voice. "Don't get your hopes up. I'm not going back to law school."

"I know, I know. I'm just saying, at least you're doing something that you feel passionate about, and not just wasting your time waitressing—"

Someday, I really needed to tell her about my paintings. But this was not the day.

"—even if I'm not very happy about where you're doing it. Did you know that most deaths from hurricanes occur after the storm has passed?"

"I do know that, Mom," I said. "Thanks. That's why I really appreciate whatever help you can—"

"Sabrina."

I looked up at the sound of the deep voice calling my name to see Drew Hartwell leaning against the door frame to the library. As always, he looked good. Good enough to make my heart give a flip inside my chest. He'd found a new clean linen shirt—did he keep a collection of these in every place he'd ever lived?—though he'd buttoned it as haphazardly as all the others, revealing far more tanned chest and abdominal muscles than should be legal.

In one hand he held the bowl of hurricane dip I'd made. Beneath his arm was tucked a bag of chips.

But on his handsome face was an expression of urgency.

I could not imagine what kind of chip-oriented emergency necessitated my getting off the phone, but his raised eyebrows and frown seemed to indicate that there was one.

"Uh, Mom," I said, "I have to go. This is the only phone line in the house, and I think someone else needs to use it."

"Oh, of course, honey. But I want you to know that I'm still coming tomorrow, or at least as soon as they can get that runway cleared."

"Uh-huh," I said, as Drew rolled a chip in the air, indicating that I needed to speed up the conversation. "Okay. Bye-bye now."

"Can I use this number to call you back, if I need to?"

"Better let me call you." A picture of my mom calling and Ed answering the phone entered my head. The vision was not pretty. "Bye, Mom. Love you."

"Love you, too, sweetie . . ."

"What?" I demanded of Drew as I slammed down the

phone. The fact that the mere sight of his lean body, lounging in the doorway, had caused my heart to do jumping jacks inside my chest was making me angry. I was an adult woman who should not be ruled by her hormones.

"Oh, nothing." He lowered the chip he'd been using to direct the speed of my conversation into the bowl of dip, then put it into his mouth. "I could tell you needed rescuing, is all."

I glared at him. "I did not need rescuing. I never need rescuing."

"Oh, really? 'Don't get your hopes up, I'm not going back to law school'? That was part of a normal, happy, everyday conversation—"

I held up a hand to stop him from continuing. "That was my mother. I was calling to let her know I'm all right."

"And the first thing she wanted to know is when you're going back to law school?"

"It wasn't the first thing she wanted to know. But yes, as you've probably guessed, my mother can be a little controlling. Speaking of which, do you always go around snooping on other people's phone calls?"

"When they're yours, I do." He dunked another chip into the dip, then ate it. "How else am I going to find out anything about you? For a woman, you aren't exactly communicative, you know. For instance, when were you going to tell me that you went to law school?"

I stood up. "Never, because it's none of your business."

"Ouch, Fresh Water!" He grabbed his chest as if wounded. "That hurts. After all we've been through together?"

"See, that's the thing." I crossed the room until I was standing directly in front of him. "You keep calling me Fresh Water like you think I'm so innocent." Reaching into the bag of chips he was holding beneath his arm, I purposefully let my hand brush against the tender and sensitive skin of his inner bicep while keeping my gaze locked on his. "But I'm not, you know."

"Oh, you're not?" His tone was teasing . . . but I was standing close enough that I heard his quick inhale at my touch.

"No." I plunged the chip I'd grabbed into the bowl he was holding, then raised it deliberately to my lips. "See this dip?"

His gaze was on the chip, which meant it was on my lips, since I was holding the chip in front of my lips. "Yeah."

"I made it." I slid the chip into my mouth, enjoying the explosion of flavor on my tongue, and chewed. "Pretty good for an alleged Fresh Water, huh?"

He couldn't seem to look away from my lips. "I'll admit I'm impressed."

What was I doing? First those kisses, now this. I needed to stay away from this guy.

On the other hand, by tomorrow my mother would probably be in town, and the sweet little temporary life I'd built in Little Bridge might be destroyed, much more thoroughly than by any hurricane. Maybe I needed to enjoy what was left of it while I still could.

"I know," I said. "It's a shame I have to go now." I watched as his gaze flicked from my mouth back up to my eyes in surprise.

"Go? Go where?"

"I have to go check on eight cockatiels, two dogs, seven cats, and a tortoise."

"Excuse me?"

"Do you have a hatchet I could borrow, by the way? One of the people who's asked me to look in on his pets thinks the only way I'll be able to get into his house is with a hatchet."

Drew's lips flattened into a grim line. He set the chips and dip down firmly on a nearby table. "If you think I'm going to let you go off by yourself on another pet rescue mission—"

I narrowed my eyes. "*Let* me?"

"We're supposed to be heading over to the café to help Ed. He's making a free hot meal for anyone who stops by. That's the real reason I came in here. Aunt Lucy told me to come get you. Or rather, now that she knows who your mother is, she told me to ask if you'd be *willing* to help out."

I smiled at that. "Well, as much as I'd love to, that's going to have to wait a bit. You won't believe how many residents of this island evacuated and left their pets behind. Now that they can't get back, someone has to go take care of them."

Drew was still frowning. "Unfortunately, I can believe it. I grew up on this island. But I don't see why the person who has to go take care of them has to be you."

I stared at him. "Do you know my mother? Because you sound exactly like her."

He stared back silently. Then after a beat or two, he said, finally, "Yeah. Okay. Well, let me go break the news to Lu, and then check the shed for some more of Ed's precious gas for the scooter. We're going to need it if we're going to be jetting all over the place, chopping down doors to rescue starving dogs and cats."

"Wait a minute . . ." I caught his arm, not simply brushing it this time. "*We*?"

He glanced down at my hand, then back into my eyes. I was uncomfortably reminded once again of how very blue the eyes of the Hartwell men were. "Of course *we*. I'm not gonna loan you my best hatchet and then let you run all around town with it, unsupervised."

"Uh-huh." I released his arm, a little reluctantly. His skin had felt warm and welcoming beneath my fingertips. And once again, there'd been sparks. Oh, there'd been sparks. "Seriously, I have to ask—isn't there something more important you should be doing with your time? I've seen you with a chain saw. Why aren't you out helping people clear streets or repair their homes?"

He looked wounded again. "Bree, you met my dogs. You saw the rapport I have with them. Do you think there's anything more important to me than the helpless animals of this earth, all of God's creatures, great and small?"

"Well, I don't really know you, so . . ."

"Of course you do. I would have thought by now you'd realized that you and I were a team back there with those rats."

"Guinea pigs."

"Whatever. Were we not a team?"

"We were definitely something."

"Okay. Fine, then." He grinned wickedly. "This is gonna be fun."

CHAPTER TWENTY-SIX

Hot meals will be served daily FREE OF CHARGE at the Mermaid Café from 12:30 P.M. until dusk from now until further notice. LITTLE BRIDGE STRONG!!!

He was right. It was fun.

Part of it was due to the fact that everyone we saw along the way—and there were people everywhere, even more than earlier, helping to clear the roads or their yards or simply taking a stroll since there was nothing else to do with no electricity or cell service or Internet, and it was too hot to remain indoors—greeted us.

Well, mainly they greeted Drew, since, as a lifelong islander, he was known to everyone.

But a few knew me as well, from the café.

Everyone raised a hand to wave a cheerful hello, then asked when I pulled over about the damage we'd seen, or shared their own storm story, and then agreed that, all in all, the hurricane had not been as bad as expected, and that—

except for the bridge washing out—the island had dodged a bullet.

But most of the fun was due to Drew himself.

Oh, he was still annoying. He'd insisted on taking "roadies" from his aunt's house, cans of beer in insulated sleeves he kept in his beloved tool kit, and that he claimed, since he wasn't driving, were safe and even appropriate for him to drink to "replace lost electrolytes" and ward off the post-storm heat and humidity.

But he was also funny, with his dry wit and (mostly) self-deprecating humor.

And it didn't hurt that he smelled good. Despite the heat and how closely we were forced to sit together on the scooter, he gave off the scent of clean laundry (thanks to the shirt he'd swiped from his aunt's house) and whatever kind of deodorant he wore.

And he was infinitely helpful with the animals. The key was right where Chett had said it would be, and if it hadn't been for Drew, I'd never have reached the cockatiels in time: the pull string to the attic door was in the ceiling, way out of my reach. I'd have needed a ladder to grab it.

Drew merely reached up a hand and pulled it down.

If we'd taken much longer to reach the cockatiels—or if it had gotten much hotter in that attic—the outcome could have been very different.

But as it was, all eight were still alive when we got there—though they weren't exactly chirpy. They perked up considerably once we moved them back down to Chett's apartment, which was cooler than the attic, despite not having air-conditioning. At least we could open the windows and let in a breeze.

We fed and watered the birds, as Chett had instructed, and then set off to check on the rest of the animals on our list. The dogs were the easiest to care for, as they were waiting for us, wild for attention, wanting only to be fed and let out to relieve themselves (a few had made messes indoors, but those were easily cleaned).

The cats were more difficult because several of them hid, and I insisted that it wasn't enough only to fill their bowls with water and food. We had to put eyes on each cat, so I could reassure their owners that it was okay . . . which wasn't easy to do in apartments with no electricity and where the windows had been boarded up. Some of the places were as dark as mausoleums, and the shyest cats—one of whom was also black—chose to hide in the shadiest reaches under the bed.

Fortunately I'd tossed Daniella's flashlight into my "pet rescue kit," which also included Gary's favorite cat treats. Eventually we were able to find each cat, establish that it was well enough to leave alone for one more night, and move on. Even the tortoise seemed to be in pretty good shape.

The only one who wasn't was me. Spending so much time in such close proximity to someone to whom I was so attracted wasn't doing me much good. It was especially annoying when he persisted in keeping his hands to himself, regardless of my many signals that it was okay now to touch me. Why not? I probably only had twenty-four hours left in Little Bridge as "Bree," the pink-haired Mermaid Café waitress, and not Sabrina Beckham, Judge Justine's daughter.

Why shouldn't he be the guy to help me enjoy it?

Except he wasn't exactly playing along . . . probably because I, like a dummy, had blurted out to him who I really was on practically my first occasion to do so.

And he, it turned out, was no fan of Judge Justine.

Welcome to the club.

The house with the shy black cat (Smokey) was our last stop on the list, and also happened to be located on a street near the Mermaid. As we were heading from it back to the scooter, we saw a barefoot blond woman wearing only a macramé beach cover-up over a bikini top and a tiny pair of jeans shorts coming down the branch-strewn street toward us, her cell phone in one hand and a small child of indeterminate sex—also shoeless and wearing only a diaper—clutching the other.

"Hey," the woman said to us. She was waving the cell phone high in the air, apparently searching for bars. It didn't seem to have dawned on her that there weren't any, and she appeared frantic about it. The child, however, was smiling at us cheerfully. "Do either of you know where the, um, Manatee Café is?"

I stared at her, thinking of all the sharp or electrified objects on which either she or her child might step, especially since she wasn't paying any attention to where they were going.

"Do you mean the Mermaid Café?" Drew asked.

"Oh, yeah, that's it." The woman lowered the phone, smiling with relief. When she smiled, the child smiled even more widely, and began chattering in a language known only to itself. "Someone said they're giving away free food, only I can't seem to get any service on my phone to check. It's the weirdest thing."

Drew cleared his throat. "Yes, well, the storm knocked out cell service to the island."

The woman seemed shocked to hear this. "Really? We didn't even know there was going to be a storm. I didn't have time to stock up on milk for little Josiah or anything. Do you think the café will have milk?"

I sucked in my breath to ask the woman how she could possibly not have known there was going to be a storm when news of it had been broadcast all over the radio, television, and Internet for days—even as much as a week—beforehand, but Drew cut me off, as if he'd known what I was going to say.

"The Mermaid's right around the corner." He pointed to make sure the woman understood. "And I'm sure they'll have plenty of milk for Josiah. We're headed there now. Why don't you let my friend here give you a lift on her scooter? I'll take Josiah."

Without waiting for a response, Drew leaned down and scooped up the toddler. Fortunately, the child seemed pleased, shrieking delightedly as he found himself suddenly dangling in midair.

I shot Drew a quick look to let him know I wasn't pleased about his volunteering me for taxi service—then realized, when his gaze met mine and then shifted quickly to the woman's feet, that he'd been thinking the same thing I had: that neither mother nor child should be walking around barefoot on that hot, storm debris–strewn pavement.

"Sure," I said, jolting my scooter off its kickstand. "I can give you a ride. It's only around the corner. Want to hop on?"

"Oh, no." The woman shook her long blond hair politely, but I could tell she was longing to say yes. Wherever she and her baby had come from, they'd walked a long way. "I wouldn't want to be an inconvenience."

I climbed onto the scooter and started the engine. "It's no inconvenience. I'm going there anyway."

"Well . . ." The woman reluctantly climbed onto the back of the motorbike, taking the helmet I handed to her. "I guess if it really isn't any trouble . . ."

"It's so close," I said, nodding at Drew, who was already halfway down the block with Josiah bouncing on his shoulders. "They're going to beat us there if we don't hurry."

They did, but only because I was so shocked when I turned the corner and saw the Mermaid that I slammed on my brakes. It wasn't because of what the storm had done to the restaurant: Drew's expert shuttering had guaranteed it was buttoned up tight against any wind damage from Marilyn, and Ed had sandbagged, preventing any storm surge flooding from the nearby harbor.

What surprised me was the size of the crowd I saw in the street outside the café. I should have expected it—there'd just been a significant weather catastrophe, and Ed was giving away free food, after all.

But I hadn't seen that many people in one place in Little Bridge since the Fourth of July fireworks display at the dock.

If things were this bad—if there were this many people in need of food and water on the island—where was the National Guard? Where was the Federal Emergency Management Agency? Where was the Red Cross, the Salvation Army, any of those people you always saw on television rushing in after a disaster to help those in need, and to whom, in the spirit of giving, my parents always donated money every year during the holidays? Where did all that money they sent go, if it wasn't to the people who needed it? Were we really just on our own?

"Is everything all right?" the woman sitting behind me asked, no doubt wondering why we were just sitting there.

"Not exact—" I started to say, then realized I shouldn't alarm my guest with my own dark thoughts, especially since she appeared to be one of the people in need. "Nope, everything's fine."

I pulled over to park without further comment but wondered how Ed and Lucy Hartwell and the others were doing, serving such an overwhelmingly large crowd.

The woman must have been thinking the same thing, since she said, "Wow," as she slipped off the helmet I'd loaned her and handed it back to me. "I guess word traveled around fast about this place."

"It sure did." Drew came up beside us to hand the woman her still happily chattering child.

I was relieved to see that most of the people in the crowd

were already holding paper plates and cups. It looked like Ed had cleaned out the freezers. I could smell the scent of grilling meat and vegetables floating on the sea breeze.

"You stay here," I said to the woman, since I was anxious to get to the café and see what I could do to help out. "One of us will bring you back a couple of plates, and some milk for Josiah."

"Oh, no," the woman said, looking mortified. "I don't want to be any more bother."

"It's okay," I said. "I work for the café." I stabbed a finger in Drew's direction. "And he's the owner's nephew."

The woman turned suddenly tear-filled eyes in Drew's direction, then reached out to grasp his hand.

"Oh, bless you," she cried. "Bless you for doing this. You are just the kindest, sweetest man." She kissed the hand she'd seized, then clutched it to her heart, possibly by accident, but also maybe on purpose, giving Drew a pretty thorough feel of her bikini-clad breasts.

I glared at her while, above her bowed head, Drew grinned at me, one eyebrow cocked mischievously, obviously enjoying my discomfort.

"I really am the kindest and the sweetest," he said. "Also the handsomest."

"Well, we have to go now," I said, taking Drew by the arm and physically propelling him away from the woman. "But we'll be back."

"One of us will," Drew assured her with a wink. "Probably not me."

"Oh." The woman looked crestfallen, even as several

other women rushed up to her, each bearing items of food and clothing that had already been donated that they wanted to give to her and her child.

"What was that?" I demanded, as I dragged him through the crowd toward the café. "I'm the one who actually works here and gave her the scooter ride. Why didn't she kiss *my* hand?"

"Do you want me to go back there and ask her?" Drew froze, grabbed my wrist, and began to drag me back toward the woman. "You're right, this is gender inequality."

I dug my heels in. "Stop it. This isn't funny."

"You're being jealous is sort of funny."

"I'm not jealous!"

"You're completely jealous."

"I'm embarrassed for my sex, is all. That woman was throwing herself at you. Also, how could she not have known a storm was coming? She has a child! It's her job to know."

"Hey, I thought we weren't judging people." He was moving again, just more slowly, and unfortunately, he'd let go of my wrist. "Isn't that what you told your mom? Why is it not all right to judge bad pet parents but all right to judge bad child parents?"

I scowled. "You're right. It's not. Everybody is just trying to do their best, I guess. Do you think that woman is trying to do her best?"

He nodded. "I do. She reminded me of my sister—Nevaeh's mom, Andrea—a little." Then, seeing my glance, he added quickly, "Not the kissing my hand part. But the not having her shit together part."

I didn't say anything right away, because I was too stunned to think of anything to say except one thing. Until finally, I could keep it to myself no longer: "Your parents named you Andrew and your sister Andrea?"

He narrowed his eyes at me. "Yeah, they did. But is that something you should really be commenting on, considering your parents named you after a type of cheese?"

I snorted. "My name's not Brie. It's Sabrina. My mom named me after the title character in her favorite movie, which is almost as bad as being named for a cheese, because it's a movie about a chauffeur's daughter who falls in love with the son of the wealthy family her dad works for."

"What's wrong with that?"

"Well, nothing, I guess, except that—"

"Bree!"

The cry came from Angela, who was working behind the line of fold-out tables that had been set up in front of the café. Without power, and therefore no air-conditioning, it was too hot to serve food from inside the building, so Ed had set up a line of grills and coolers just outside the door. In front of them, Angela, Mrs. Hartwell, Nevaeh, and the rest of the staff worked at folding tables beneath hastily set-up beach umbrellas to serve what looked like half the town the contents of the café's now nonfunctioning freezers.

"Hey." I hurried up to greet Angela. "How did your mom's place weather the storm?"

"Good. We lost a few roof tiles and a tree or two, but otherwise, it wasn't nearly as bad as we were expecting." Her face was shining from the heat, but I expected mine was looking worse, considering all the beds I'd had to crawl under looking for people's cats. "What's going on over there?" She nodded toward Drew, who was standing by one of the barbecues, observing his uncle's grilling technique. "I saw you two pull up together, along with Mary Jane Peters."

"You know that woman? We ran into her on the street. She didn't even know a storm was coming."

"Yeah, that makes sense. She's one of those ditzy yoga moms. Doesn't believe in vaccinations or television or public school."

"Oh, that explains it. I thought she was on drugs."

Angela shrugged. "No, just vegan. Lets the kid have dairy, though, if it's organic."

"Yeah, that makes sense, she's looking for milk."

Angela sighed. "We've got some that hasn't gone bad yet. I'll give it to her. But you still haven't told me what the deal is with you and Lover Boy over there."

I felt myself blush, but fortunately there was no way Angela or anyone else was going to be able to tell, since the sun was beginning to sink in the west and turning everything and everyone pink with its fiery rays.

"There's no deal. He's helping me feed all the pets that people have left behind and can't get back to on account of the bridge being out."

"Ooooh." Angela grinned. "I bet he is. And I bet he's only doing it out of the goodness of his heart, not because he wants to get into your bed. Everyone knows Drew Hartwell is a real Boy Scout."

"Shut up. He is."

"Wait, what do you mean?"

"I mean, I've made out with him twice, but that's as far as we've gotten. Although admittedly this pesky hurricane thing keeps getting in the way."

Angela grinned, obviously wanting to know more, but then was distracted by something happening at the table in front of her. "Marquise, no. It's one serving of chicken or steak or fish per person per plate. They can't have all three at once. If they want more, they can come back through the line for more once they've finished."

Marquise—Angela's handsome young nephew who often helped out at the café when we were shorthanded but couldn't work full-time because of his position as quarterback on the Little Bridge High School football team—looked frustrated. "But this gentleman here asked for chicken *and* fish," he hissed. "Look at him! I'm not going to deny the man!"

Angela leaned forward to deal with the dissatisfied customer, who already had a plate piled high with corn bread, Caesar salad, black beans and rice, and a baked potato.

"Sir," she said. "We're happily giving away all this free food today on account of the storm. But we have to make sure we have enough for everyone. We're serving chicken, fish, or steak. But you can only have one protein at a time."

"But—" The gentleman, who appeared from the weathered condition of his skin to have spent a great deal of time at sea, opened his mouth to protest, revealing a past lacking in proper dental care.

"If you finish your plate and are still hungry, of course

you can come back for more. But for now, it's one serving of chicken or fish or steak per person per plate."

The old sailor looked resigned. "Then chicken, I guess."

Marquise delicately placed a chicken leg, thigh, and breast on his plate. "Enjoy, sir. Don't forget, there's key lime pie for dessert."

The old sailor grinned toothlessly before moving on. "God bless ya, son!"

Nevaeh, who was standing beside Marquise, looked up at him from beneath her heavily made-up eyelashes and said, "You handled that really well."

Katie Hartwell, also standing nearby, hurried to add, "I think so, too."

Marquise looked confused but pleased. "Uh, thanks."

"Are you going to stick around?" Angela asked me. "We could really use your help, especially with cleanup. The trash cans are already overflowing, so people are just piling their plates wherever."

"Sure. I'll go inside and grab some trash bags."

"No!" Mrs. Hartwell appeared as if from nowhere. "I'll do that. Bree, why don't you take over my spot, handing out key limeade?"

I knew exactly what she was doing. She didn't want me taking on menial tasks anymore because I was Judge Justine's daughter. It didn't matter that I'd already spent months mopping floors and cleaning the bathrooms. "Mrs. Hartwell, it's all right. I'm fine with trash duty."

"No, no, dear, I want to get out there anyway. I need to talk to some of these people, see if they need—"

"And stand in the hot sun?" Drew was suddenly by her side. "Why don't you let me and Bree handle the trash, Lu, and you keep serving folks the drinks. You okay with that, Bree?"

I smiled at him. The sinking sun glinted on the fine hairs on his arms, bleached gold by all the time he spent outdoors. "I'm fine with that."

We'd fetched Mary Jane Peters and her son a couple of plates of food, along with some milk, and were moving through the crowd with our large garbage bags, collecting people's trash, when a man riding a horse—truly, a handsome, well-fed pinto—suddenly clattered into the parking lot.

"Uh-oh," Drew said, eyeing the tall man in the dark green uniform sitting astride the horse. "It's the cops."

I watched in some alarm as Sheriff Hartwell dismounted from his horse and began approaching the café. "What's he doing here? Do you think someone saw us breaking in to people's houses to feed their pets and thought we were robbing them and turned us in?"

Drew, smiling, looked down at me. "You really are a Fresh Water, aren't you?"

Flushing, I grasped my trash bag. "Well, you never know. What we're doing isn't exactly legal."

"It is if you have permission from the home owners." He saw the look on my face, then asked, "You *did* have permission from all the homeowners, didn't you?"

I nodded. "Of course." I mean, I'd had permission from Chett, who'd assured me that all of the homeowners were friends of his . . . how else could he have known what sort of pets they owned and how to break into their houses?

I watched with a drumming heart as Sheriff Hartwell strode closer and closer . . . and finally walked right past us, with a nod of greeting in Drew's direction, and right up to Ed, who was still working the grills he'd set up, a green bandanna wrapped around his forehead to keep sweat from dripping into the food.

"Hey, there, Ed," I overheard the sheriff say. "Nice little operation you got running here."

"Well," Ed said, modestly, "I gotta get rid of all this meat before it goes bad. Shoulda installed a generator here when I had the chance. Don't know what I was thinking."

"I understand." The sheriff sounded sympathetic. "Thing is, I'm gonna need you to shut all this down by sunset. I'm issuing an island-wide curfew from dusk to dawn. I've told my people to arrest anyone they find out of doors, no questions asked."

Ed whistled, low and long, and Drew, who'd clearly overheard as well, raised his eyebrows.

"You've got a lot of people here who are far from home right now, Sheriff," Drew said. "Word got around fast about what Ed was doing here, and people came here from as far away as Ramrod Key."

"I know that." The sheriff scratched his chin. "But there's still an hour till sunset. That's plenty of time for them to get back home."

Drew looked out over the crowd, who were happily eating and drinking. Someone had brought out a ukulele and was playing it. Several people had broken out bottles of beer, and even, by the smell wafting toward us, some herbal refreshment, despite the presence of the sheriff, who didn't seem inclined to investigate.

"Maybe it's for the best, Ed," Drew said to his uncle. "The rest of that meat will keep for tomorrow."

Ed looked down at his coolers. "True. And some people will need it even more then."

"Yes." The sheriff looked up. A lone helicopter—the first one I'd seen all day—was flying by, low and slow.

"Is that FEMA?" I asked, hopefully, thinking maybe, finally, someone from the national or even state government was paying attention to us.

The sheriff shook his head. "Sorry. No. That up there is Channel Seven out of Miami. Been buzzing around all afternoon, getting pictures for the evening news. I'm not particularly worried about looters myself, but the media's playing up the angle, and getting the folks who are stuck on the other side of the bridge all fired up about it. Curfew's the only way I could think of to keep everybody happy."

Ed nodded. "Makes sense. Okay, lemme cook off the last of this meat here and then you can let people know we have to shut down for the night."

Which is what they did—not that anyone was too happy about it. Katie Hartwell in particular expressed a few harsh words to her father when she found out her time as a volunteer working at the side of Marquise Fairweather was ending. I myself overheard her tell her father that he was "ruining everything" and that she was "never coming home."

Mrs. Hartwell, however, told the sheriff not to lose heart, and that it was probably better for Katie to continue staying with the Hartwells anyway during this time of crisis, since her father was going to be so busy.

I was stooping over, helping Mrs. Hartwell store the left-over corn bread on rolling racks, when Drew approached me and said, "Well?"

I squinted up at him. I had on my sunglasses, but the sun was lower than ever, and he was standing with his back to the light, so I couldn't make out his features and had no idea what he wanted. "Well, what?"

"Well, when are you taking me back to my place?"

I stared up at him, dumbfounded. "I have to help clean this all up. Can't you snag a ride with the sheriff, or some-body?"

"On the back of his horse? No, I can't snag a ride with the sheriff. What are you talking about?"

I rose, brushing the crumbs from my hands. "That's not his only mode of transportation. I've seen him driving around in a giant SUV."

"That's never going to get around that yacht sitting in the middle of my road. Listen, we have to go. Do you know how long it's been since my dogs have been out? They've probably trashed my place by now."

"Drew." I glanced around. I could sense that Angela and quite a few other people nearby were eavesdropping on our conversation. There wasn't anything else to do. "I'd love to drive you. But I have to get home, too. I haven't seen my cat all day—"

"Your *cat?*" Now that I was no longer stooping, I could see into Drew's face. He was wearing an expression of incredulity. "What are you worrying about that cat of yours for? He's living in the lap of luxury over there. He's got AC and those two girls fawning over him, feeding him tuna and doing photo shoots of him. Whereas my dogs are alone, cooped up in a house with no air or food or—"

"Fine." I glanced around but saw that everyone was busily working to put things away, and not listening to our conversation at all. Or pretending not to, at least. "Fine. I'll take you home."

"Good. Great. I mean, really, it seems like the least you could do since I let you use my hatchet, and I'm also the kindest, sweetest, handsomest—"

I couldn't help grinning at him. He really was the worst. Or the best, depending on how you looked at it.

CHAPTER TWENTY-SEVEN

A curfew has been instituted in Little Bridge from dusk to dawn for safety and security reasons. **Anyone out after the designated times is subject to arrest by order of the Sheriff's Office.**

Nothing had changed on Sandy Point Beach while we'd been gone. Since Drew was the only resident who hadn't evacuated, and the electrical crews were working to clean up streets farther inland, closer to the hospital and the majority of residences, this made sense. I still had to dodge downed power lines and piles of sand and seaweed on my scooter—not to mention the washed-up refrigerator and yacht—in order to get to his house.

But the view, when we finally made it, was worth it. The sinking sun was turning the few clouds that streaked the sky a rich, blazing fuchsia, and now that the last remnants of the storm had passed, the sea was finally starting to smooth out, so the clouds were reflected in the dark, glassy water beneath. The birds were still out in force, especially the gulls and pelicans, circling over the sand and surf, calling noisily to one another.

But other than that and the rhythmic whoosh of the waves, there wasn't a sound to be heard, with the exception, every so often, of the plop! of a silver-backed tarpon as it broke the water's surface, diving for unseen prey.

"Okay," I said, when I'd pulled to a stop in his sand-strewn driveway. "I guess I see now why you'd want to live all the way out here instead of in town."

"Not so crazy after all, am I?" He swung his long leg from the scooter's seat and took his canvas tool kit from the scooter's running board. "Come inside for a drink."

"And risk getting arrested for breaking curfew? No thanks."

"You've got plenty of time." He pointed at the brilliant red ball sinking low in the sky just west of us. "Sunset won't be for another half hour at least."

"It'll take me that long just to get back to your aunt's house."

"Nobody's going to arrest a pretty girl going home on a moped—especially when they realize who your mother is."

I smirked at him. "Thanks so much for that."

"Come on. What harm will one drink do?"

Of course I was tempted. How couldn't I be? A good-looking man whom I'd come to like and trust and, okay, maybe lust after a little was asking me to his home for a drink.

And what a home! Mother Nature seemed to be pulling out all the stops to apologize for her misdeeds the day before, making this sunset as dramatic and beautiful as any she'd ever created. The evening breeze was as fresh and cool as the afternoon had been hot and oppressive. Even as I stood there, trying to decide what to do, the wind tugged playfully at my hair and sent the sound of all four of Drew's dogs' eager barking down toward me. They seemed to be crying "Come on up! What are you waiting for? We miss you, Bree! We want to play!"

"Fine," I said, and lowered the kickstand of my scooter. "But only one drink. Then I really have to go."

"Great!" He looked as delighted as a kid who'd just found out he was having ice cream for dinner. "You think the view looks good from down here, wait until you see it from up there . . ."

He wasn't wrong. The view of that scarlet sun slowly sinking toward the sea, unbroken by any man-made structures, was breathtaking, and I was reminded once again of why I'd found it so hard to leave Little Bridge. I really hadn't meant to stay as long as I had. It wasn't only because of the people—who, quirky and odd as they often were, were also some of the kindest and most giving I'd ever encountered. It was also because of the sheer natural beauty of the place, the unspoiled ocean views and skyscapes that even now I felt myself itching to paint.

It didn't hurt that Drew had let out the dogs—who'd greeted us with near fanatical delight—and that they were now running up and down the beach after the yellow tennis balls that Drew was tossing them from the deck. This was upsetting the flocks of birds, causing them to rise indignantly from the clusters of seaweed strewn across the sand every time they came near. This actually made the vista even more special—at least to me.

"Okay," I said, laughing, as Drew expertly threw his seventh ball. "You really do have a good life here."

"You haven't even seen the best part yet." He disappeared into the house, then reappeared a moment later holding a bottle of red wine and two wineglasses. "I've been saving this for a special occasion."

I glanced at the label and could not help feeling impressed. It was a small-batch California cabernet that Caleb favored, and claimed was hard to find.

I'd never have expected to see such a thing in Little Bridge, particularly in Drew Hartwell's home.

"What?" I asked in a teasing tone as he began opening the bottle with a corkscrew he'd also brought from inside. "The famous Drew Hartwell drinks something besides beer?"

"Well," he said, after pouring a generous amount into my glass, "like I said, it's a special occasion."

"And what's that?"

"I finally got Bree Beckham over to my place to have a drink." He raised his glass to clink mine.

I pulled my glass away, refusing to toast something so ridiculous. "Oh, right. You never even knew who I was until the night of your aunt's hurricane party, even though I've been serving you breakfast every day for months."

"That," he said, taking a reflective sip of his wine, "is untrue. For part of that time I was unavailable." The ghost of Leighanne rose silently between us. "And for the rest of that time, you seemed . . . preoccupied." I took a sip of my wine, not wanting to think about my own ghosts. "But the truth is, I've had my eye on you for some time. I was never quite sure what was going on with your hair—"

I reached up instinctively to touch one of my pink curls. "What?"

"—but I like it. It brings out the brown in your eyes."

"Is this your thing?" I asked. "Is this what you do? You bring girls out here and give them expensive wine on your fabulous deck during amazing sunsets in order to seduce them? And then you insult them?"

He grinned. "God's honest truth, you're the first. Is it working?"

"I'll let you know. What was your shtick before you had the house? You'd drive your truck into town and park at some different lucky lady's house every night?"

"What?" He looked genuinely baffled.

"That's what everybody says. They say they used to see your pickup in front of a different house every morning."

Comprehension dawned, and he laughed. "Yeah, of course! Those were the homes where I was doing carpentry work. I usually had a couple of beers with the home owners after. I wasn't going to risk a DUI driving back home later. I'd usually just grab an Uber, or sometimes I kept my bike in the back of the truck and rode it home. Better to be safe than sorry."

I blinked, shocked at how something so innocent had

morphed into such a lurid rumor. Then again, Little Bridge was a very small town, and its residents loved to gossip.

"What about Leighanne?" I asked, carefully.

"What *about* Leighanne?"

"What was the deal with the saltshaker? I was standing right next to you in the café when she threw it at you."

"Oh, that." He sighed and looked toward the sea. "Yeah, that's the thing about this place. People either get it or they don't. You get it. Leighanne never did."

"What's that supposed to mean?"

"Well, people come here and they either love the island life or they hate it."

"Who could possibly hate it?" I asked in genuine astonishment.

But even as the words were coming out of my mouth, I remembered. My mother. My mother had always hated Little Bridge. She'd hated it almost as much as my father had loved it.

"Someone like Leighanne could hate it," he said. "I met Leighanne when I was working up in New York. Then after my parents died and my sister went into her third or fourth stint with rehab and it was clear I needed to come back to help out with Nevaeh—well, Leighanne volunteered to come with me. On paper, it should have worked—she said she liked dogs and was ready to leave the fast pace and cold winters of the city. But in reality—she couldn't stand the dogs or stand it here. The lack of seasons and the slow pace, the fact that there were so few different restaurants and stores—it all drove her crazy."

"Island fever," I murmured, remembering what Nevaeh had told me.

He looked surprised—but whether it was because I knew the term or that Leighanne had been suffering from it, I wasn't sure. "Possibly. All I know is, since there weren't any stores in town that sold the kinds of things she liked, she kept ordering things online—like the Himalayan salt—to make herself feel like she was back in New York, I guess. I kept asking, 'Why do we need this? Why do we need that?' I guess, since they made her feel better, I probably shouldn't have said anything."

"No," I said, remembering the angry look on Leighanne's face when she'd hurled the saltshaker at him. "Probably not."

"But I did, and I guess that was the straw that broke the camel's back, because the next thing I knew, she'd packed up everything she'd bought—and I mean *everything*, including the salt—and moved out."

I thought this over as I sipped the wine. It really was delicious.

"Maybe you just weren't ready to share your space," I suggested.

"Maybe." His blue-eyed gaze was bright on mine. "Or maybe I am . . . with the right person."

I felt more than a little conscious of how close we were standing to each other—his arm grazed mine as it rested on the deck railing—and also that his gaze hadn't left mine for a second. The gentle wind from the sea seemed to be pushing both of us toward each other . . . or maybe it was the wine . . . or his words: *Or maybe I am . . . with the right person.*

Was that person me? I liked dogs. I liked Little Bridge. I liked him.

But I wasn't ready for another relationship. Look at how my last one had turned out. I was as good at picking guys as I was at careers.

And anyway, what was I panicking for? He wasn't interested in me. Not like that.

"Bree," he said in a low voice, as his gaze lowered to my lips.

It was at that moment that all four dogs came bursting back up onto the deck, their run on the beach completed. Bob the beagle, who seemed to have taken a particular liking to me, dashed straight over and drove her front paws, claws extended, right into my thighs.

"Ow," I cried, buckling over and nearly dropping my wine.

"Bob!" Drew roared, not just at the beagle but at all the dogs, since none of them were behaving with particular decorum. "No! You know better than that. Get in the shower, all of you!"

I was shocked when all four dogs—led by the black Lab, who despite Drew's insistence that he was the alpha, seemed to be the actual leader of the pack—swarmed beneath an outdoor showerhead. Drew strode toward it, then switched it on. As warm water streamed down on the wriggling bodies, sand poured off them and down a drain on the deck that had clearly been installed for this purpose.

I laughed, amazed. It appeared that Drew had thought through every detail of his dream home on the beach, including his dog-washing duties.

“Sorry about that,” he said, returning to me and the glass of wine he’d abandoned when he seemed to feel that his dogs were clean enough. He’d switched off the water, and the dogs had trotted off to different sections of the deck to shake themselves dry. “Where were we?”

“Uh,” I said. “I don’t remember,” even though I did. *You’d been about to kiss me.*

And I’d been about to let you.

But before Drew could reply, Socks came slinking shyly over to us, one of the yellow tennis balls in his mouth. His black-and-white body was low to the ground in case his action garnered the wrath of his new owner—that was, after all, the kind of reaction he was used to—but his long, fringed white tail wagged slowly as he looked up at us, his dark eyes filled simultaneously with both hope and anxiety that one of us would take the ball from his mouth and throw it.

“Oh my God,” I said, looking down at the sadly abused dog. “I think I’m going to cry.”

“Yeah. He’s a good boy.” Drew reached down and took the ball from Socks’s mouth, casually—but affectionately—giving the dog a stroke on the head as he did so. “Get the ball, Bob.”

He tossed the ball to the far end of the deck, and Socks took off after it, his sleek body uncoiling like a spring, all muscle and joy.

“You can’t call them all Bob,” I insisted as I watched the dog expertly catch the ball in midair—probably one of the first times in his life he'd ever engaged in a game of one-on-one catch. "They really do each have their own unique personalities. Just because your parents named you and your sister basically the same thing doesn't mean you have to do that to your dogs."

"Are you sure it was law school you dropped out of and not psychiatry school?"

"Very funny."

Socks brought the ball back and dropped it at Drew's feet, dancing there excitedly, hoping he'd throw it again—which of course he did. Socks took off, as joyously as before, while the other dogs yawned and gazed at the newcomer disdainfully. They'd had their game of catch and were ready for supper.

"Are you sure you're not just too lazy to think up individual names for them?"

"Too lazy?" He raised an eyebrow. "That's pretty harsh for someone who claims we aren't supposed to judge people who left their pets behind during a hurricane."

"Point taken. But it would be pretty easy to personalize their names. This one"—I'd put my wine on the deck railing and was petting Socks, since he'd brought me the ball—"could be Bobby Socks."

Drew groaned.

"And the beagle could be Bobby Sue, since she's a girl."

Drew threw me a disbelieving look. "I'm not renaming my dogs."

"It's not really renaming them. It's just individualizing

their names. The little terrier could be Bobby Lee. And the big one could be—"

Drew turned, grabbed me by both shoulders, and pulled me against him, dropping his lips to mine. For a second, I was so startled, I wasn't sure what was happening. Then I realized he was kissing me.

CHAPTER TWENTY-EIGHT

The Florida Fish & Wildlife Conservation Commission reports that a preliminary estimate of vessels that are derelict, lost, or abandoned off Little Bridge Island stands at 506. If a boat is missing, the owner should file a report with the Sheriff's Office so the vessel can be added to a database to make return easier if it is found.

And what a kiss. This was no platonic kiss between friends. It wasn't even like the kiss I'd given him earlier in the day when I'd been so glad to see that he was alive.

This was the hunger-filled kiss of a lover who'd been waiting—and thinking about—doing this for a long time. This was the kiss of someone who was trying to be gentle but had held back long enough and couldn't restrain himself any longer. This wasn't like any of the kisses I'd received from dates in the past. Those had been the kisses of boys.

This was the kiss of a man.

His hands went from my shoulders to my waist, pulling

me so close, I could feel every inch of his body through the thin fabric of his shirt . . . and his shorts. And what I felt there didn't belong to a boy, either. It was thick and hard and insistent—just like his hands, slipping under my top. My nipples went instantly stiff beneath his work-roughened fingers.

"Drew," I moaned, when he lifted his lips from mine for a moment. "Do you have any—"

He was breathing as hard as I was, his voice an unsteady rasp. "You bet I do."

"Thank God."

Then his hands went from my breasts to my waist as he hoisted me physically into the air, the dogs dancing around us, barking excitedly.

"Drew!" I threw my arms around his neck and my head back, laughing. I couldn't remember the last time I'd felt this happy. "What are you doing?"

"Taking you to my bed, of course." As the dogs barked more feverishly, he shouted, "Down, Bobs! Down!"

This only made me laugh harder. I knew I shouldn't. What if he was extremely serious about his lovemaking and got upset that I found anything about his technique—even his rambunctious dogs—amusing?

But it was impossible not to laugh when I was filled with so much joy, especially as he attempted to carry me romantically through his living area and down a hallway toward his bedroom—but nearly tripped several times over tools he'd left lying on the floor. Since the sun had sunk so low, and there was no electricity, the interior of his home was shrouded in semidarkness.

"Damn it," he cursed each time his foot came in contact with a screwdriver or an awl.

"Drew." I buried my head in his neck, trying to stifle a giggle. "I can walk. Put me down."

"No." His hold on me tightened. "I can do this!"

Finally we made it to the master bedroom, which was as sparsely furnished as the living room, save for a massive, gray-sheeted king-sized bed. This was where he deposited me.

"There," he said when I was safely on the mattress. "Now wait here."

What he wanted me to wait for, apparently, was for him to corral the dogs out of the bedroom. He closed every door leading back into the room, so they couldn't follow him—though they tried to, desperately.

Fortunately there was still a cool breeze coming into the room from the ocean via a large overhead skylight that he'd left open just above the bed. Through it, I could see the last orange rays of the setting sun arcing across the lavender sky . . . and the far-off white light of the evening's first star. I gazed at that white light, welcoming it like a beacon of hope . . . my hope for a chance to start again.

"Now," Drew said as he turned from the door. "We finally have some privacy."

My heart gave a lurch as he came toward me out of the darkness . . . but it wasn't an unpleasant lurch. It was filled with anticipatory excitement about what was about to happen.

"Yeah," I said. "Your roommates are cute, but a little demanding."

"I know, right?" Drew sat down on the bed beside me, his large hand going to rest on top of my thigh as his lips sought mine. "I'm glad we got rid of them."

It was hard to think of anything but him while he was kissing me. He seemed to fill all my senses, the woodsy scent of his overlong dark hair, the smoothness of his skin beneath my fingertips, the heavy masculine weight of him as he pressed me back against the pillows. As his heart thrummed hard against mine, all I could think was that I wanted to feel more of him against me. The fabric of his clothes was getting in the way, so I pulled at it, and as if by magic, his shirt disappeared, and the shorts soon followed. He seemed to find my clothes equally burdensome, and in what seemed like seconds, my T-shirt and shorts were gone as well, flung to the far side of the room.

Then his skin was hot against mine, *all* of his skin, his sex hard and demanding in my hand. He moaned at the contact. His calloused workman's fingers undid the clasp to my bra with admirable dexterity, freeing my breasts from their silken cage to the onslaught of his lips and tongue. Now I was the one moaning, especially when he dipped one of those strong, powerful hands between my legs and began to stroke the already soaked area at the crotch of my panties.

I knew what he was trying to do, but it wasn't helping the situation—unless he wanted things to end before they got started. I grabbed his hand, moved it up to my breasts—noting his expression of surprise—then wiggled out of my underwear.

"Where's the, uh, thing you said you have?" I asked.

"Oh." Desire had dulled his senses. It took a second for what I'd said to register. Then, when it did, he had to dig around beneath the bed in a box before he found the condom. "Right here."

I heard rather than saw him put it on. The sun had set. Except for the stars twinkling through the skylight overhead, the room was in near total darkness.

But it didn't matter. Even if I couldn't see him, I could feel, hear, smell, and taste him. And he was mine. The second he turned back toward me, I lay my hands upon his chest, pressing him back upon the bed, skimming my nipples along his furred chest as I straddled him, tasting salt when I dropped my lips to his throat.

Then, before he could say a word, I lowered myself onto him, trying to take it as slowly as possible so I could savor every delicious inch of him.

But he had other ideas, gasping and reaching out to grab my hips, rising impatiently to thrust all of him inside me at once . . . again . . . and then again.

This was not what I'd planned, since there was a lot of him and not so much of me.

But fortunately after the initial shock it felt incredible, like being rocked by a cool ocean wave on a hot day, then rocked again . . . and again. I didn't want it to stop. I rode the wave to what felt like the edge of the earth . . .

. . . until suddenly I was dropped off, into the most glorious sunset anyone had ever seen, all shimmering reds and golds and pinks, the colors washing all around and over and beneath and even through me, until I felt as if they were flying from my fingertips and toes like electric sparks . . .

I collapsed, sweaty and panting, on top of Drew's bare chest, happy about the physical pleasure I'd received, but also relieved that I could still enjoy sex with a man . . . or anyone, for that matter. It had been a while.

It took a minute or two before I became aware that he was sweaty and panting, too.

"Jesus Christ," he said, blowing away a few pink strands of my hair that had fallen across his face.

"Does that mean it was good for you, too?" I asked.

"I'm never calling you Fresh Water again," he said. "You're like an Olympic athlete of sex."

I sat up and smiled down at him, even though in the dim lighting, I was pretty sure he couldn't see me.

"Aw, thanks, Drew. That's the nicest thing you've ever said to me." I patted him on the cheek. "You're not so bad yourself."

He was still panting. "I need a drink of water," he rasped. "I think I'm suffering from dehydration."

"I'll get you one."

I swung away from him and picked my way across his clothes-strewn bedroom floor to the master bathroom, where I found a water glass and, more important, a candle and some matches he'd left there from the storm the night before. After filling the water glass from the faucet in the sink, I used the lit candle to guide my way back to the bed, where I found Drew sitting up, looking a little dazed.

"Thanks," he said, as I handed him the water glass. He drank from it thirstily.

"Should we let the dogs back in?" I could hear one or more of them whining softly outside the door.

"No," he said. "They're going to have to learn that when we have our adult time, dogs have to wait outside."

I found this remark interesting. "Oh, really? Are we going to be having adult time together again in the future?"

He set aside the water glass and pulled me to him. "I don't know about you, but I hope so. You see how I slyly caused you to miss curfew using the irresistible power of my sexuality?"

I pulled away from him, realizing he was right. "Damn it." I hit him with the closest pillow. "Now I'm going to have to spend the night here! What about Gary?"

"I already told you, Nevaeh will look after him."

"What about your aunt? She's going to wonder where I am."

His smile was cocky. "Trust me, Bree. No one's going to wonder where you are. They all know exactly where you are."

I could feel myself blushing in the candlelight. "I don't need this entire island knowing my business."

"Better get used to it," he said, with an evil laugh. "It's called living in a small town."

I tried to hit him with the pillow again, but this time he ducked. "We didn't even get any dinner," I said. "We're going to starve to death out here."

"Would I let that happen to you?" He got up, found his shorts, and put them on, sans underwear. "I grabbed a couple of Ed's steaks before we left. I'll throw them on the grill right now, and we can finish up that bottle of wine I opened."

I stared at him. "You what?"

"I grabbed a couple of steaks from one of Ed's coolers today before we left. It will only take a few minutes for me to grill them. How do you like yours, medium, medium rare?"

I hardly knew how to respond. "You knew I'd be missing curfew and staying for dinner?"

"I didn't know." He opened the bedroom door, causing an eruption of dogs. "I hoped."

CHAPTER TWENTY-NINE

Time: 10:10 P.M.
Temperature: 75°F
Wind Speed: 6 MPH
Wind Gust: 0 MPH
Precipitation: 0.0 in.

Of all the places I ever thought I'd be the night after one of the most powerful hurricanes ever to hit the Florida Keys, sitting beneath the stars on Drew Hartwell's deck, eating freshly grilled steak, was not one of them.

But there I was, a dog on either side of me, and Drew Hartwell seated right across from me, dining by the light of what Drew had informed me—since I'd never seen it before, and so hadn't recognized it—was the Milky Way.

"The Milky Way is our own galaxy, made up of billions of stars," he said, as he poured more wine into my glass. "Normally you can't see it around here because of light pollution. Man-made light at night prevents most of the population of the U.S. and Europe from seeing it."

"Wow," I said.

I didn't mind that he was mansplaining the Milky Way to me, since I didn't know anything about it. Also, I was a little bit drunk from the wine—we were on our second bottle—and it turned out he cooked a really good steak . . . just the right amount of salt and pepper, and no other seasonings—and a decent baked potato. He'd kept a little cooler himself, and there was cold butter for the potatoes as well.

Of course, there was also the fact that I was falling in love with him. Or that I'd maybe already fallen in love with him. Who knew when? It had probably happened the moment he'd stepped up and saved Socks from Rick Chance.

Or maybe it had happened before that . . . that day Leighanne had thrown that saltshaker at him, and he'd responded by doing exactly nothing. Who knew?

Daniella was going to be so disappointed in me when she found out. You weren't supposed to fall in love with the guys you slept with, especially the first guy you slept with after a bad breakup, and especially guys who lived on Little Bridge Island. They were just supposed to be guys you messed around with for fun. You never fell in love with them, and you certainly never entertained ideas about changing all of your life plans (such as mine were) for them.

I'd broken all the rules, and now I was sitting here, like an idiot, by the light of the Milky Way, eating the guy's steaks with his happy, well-fed dogs pressed all around me, listening to him talk.

God. I had it bad.

"One summer," Drew was going on, "my dad took me

out in our boat at night to fish for hogfish—this was back in the days when it was still legal to catch hogfish; they're considered overfished in this area now so Fish and Wildlife have them on the protected list—and we dropped anchor out at that mangrove by the old train trestle. And we were just sitting there, you know, in the dark, when all of a sudden, I saw this blue glow coming from beneath the boat. I swear I thought it was a spaceship coming up from beneath the deep. But do you know what it really was?"

I grinned at him soppily. "I have no idea."

"Bioluminescence. Living lights. They're single-celled organisms called dinoflagellates that live in warm marine water. You can only see them at night in certain areas, and only when you disturb the water's surface. Sometimes they're floating there so thick, you can write your name in them on the top of the water with the tip of your finger. So that's what my dad and I did. I mean, it doesn't last long, but it's pretty cool. I'll take you out in my boat and show you sometime."

"Wow," I said, hugging my knees with pleasure. He was going to show me sometime. I was going to stick around in Little Bridge long enough for him to show me that. "I'd love that. That's a great story."

"So when are you going to tell me your story?" His eyes were very bright in the candlelight.

I was too drunk on love and wine to be startled, but I was a little confused. "What story?"

"About what really brought you to Little Bridge."

"I already did. I told you, I needed a break."

"Yeah, you did say that. You said you were taking a break to work through some things. What kind of things? I know you dropped out of law school. Why?"

Suddenly my happy little cloud of endorphin-induced joy burst. It was bound to happen, of course.

I just hadn't thought it would be this soon.

"There were a lot of reasons," I said, slowly. "My dad passed away from cancer this past Christmas . . . I told you that. After that, I just sort of realized my heart wasn't in it. School, I mean. I was still going to class, but not as often as I should have, and my grades started to slip—"

"That's natural." Drew's blue eyes had narrowed with concern for me. "You'd just been through the death of someone close to you."

"Yeah. And I probably should have asked for the semester off. But I didn't think of it. No one in my family has ever asked for time off for anything except our annual family vacation here—to Little Bridge—so it just never occurred to me . . . until things got to be too much."

Tears filled my eyes. I knew what was coming next, and I absolutely did not want to go there.

But I also knew I had to. He'd been honest with me, so I knew I owed him the same.

"What about that guy you were talking to on the phone the other day—Caleb, I think you called him?" he asked. "The one who wanted to fly in a private jet to come get you? Is he one of the things that got to be too much?"

I exhaled shakily.

"Yeah," I said, staring down at my empty plate. It was

easier to look at my plate than at Drew's face, even though I knew I had nothing to feel ashamed of. None of it had been my fault. I don't know why it was still so hard for me to talk about it. "Well, Cal and his best friend, Kyle. See, what happened was . . . we were all in law school together. The two of them graduated last spring, but since I wasn't going to class so much anymore after my dad died, we were still hanging out together all the time, especially me and Cal. I had my own place, but it was in the law school dorm—you remember what I told you, about my mom and her Mean World Syndrome. She was totally paranoid about me having my own place. And it turned out she was right . . . except that the person I ended up needing to be afraid of wasn't some rando from the street, it was Cal's best friend, Kyle."

Drew's spine straightened so abruptly that I heard a cracking sound. I gave him a wan smile. "It's okay. Nothing happened. I mean, something happened, but nothing prosecutable. Because I wasn't actually physically harmed, only psychologically. I just had trouble sleeping for a while. I had to get up a million times a night to make sure my bedroom door was locked. But really, the worst part of it was, that afterward, no one believed me. Or at least, no one believed me about how upsetting it was, because it was Kyle who did it, and Kyle was always doing stupid things when he was drunk. And what he did this time was, the night of the Super Bowl, he got so wasted that he ended up spending the night on Cal's couch. I was sleeping over, too, but in Cal's room. Cal went out the next morning to get bagels and juice and stuff for breakfast while I was still asleep. He'd only been gone for about five minutes and I'd fallen back asleep, before Kyle came stumbling into our room, still drunk, I think, and completely naked, and jumped onto me—"

Drew leaned forward and enunciated each word with staccato precision. "Just tell me where this guy lives, and I will go up there and kill him."

Now I was laughing. It was nice to laugh about something that had, for so many months, been such a source of anxiety and fear. "It's crazy, right? Like we lived in a frat house, or something. I was like, 'Get off of me, you perv,' and all of that, only he wouldn't. I could barely move, because he's about six foot three and weighs a ton, and I was all tangled up beneath the sheets. I couldn't so much as raise a fist to punch him. Even when I told him if he didn't get off, I'd scream, and the neighbors would call the police, he just laughed, because of course Cal's apartment is completely soundproofed. Also, like I said, he was still drunk from the night before, trying to kiss me and get under the covers with me. So finally I did the only thing I could think of, which was say that if he got off me, I'd go out with him. Don't ask me why, but that's what finally sank into his alcohol-soaked brain, and why he finally got up and left—because I promised I'd sleep with him if he took me on a proper date, and that a quickie while my boyfriend, his best friend, was gone wasn't the best way for us to start the new, beautiful relationship he apparently thought we were going to have."

Drew was shaking his head. "So tell me that when your boyfriend got home, he tore the guy a new one."

"No. I told Cal about it as soon as he got back—by then Kyle had left for his own room and was taking, as he put it, a cold shower, and I was shoving everything I owned into one of Cal's suitcases, because all I could think of doing was getting the hell out of there—and Cal just laughed it off. He said I was overreacting."

Drew blinked. "Overreacting?"

"Yeah. He said I knew perfectly well that Kyle had a substance-abuse problem, and we all needed to cut him some slack, because he was doing the best he could. He said it was really petty of me to be so judgmental of someone who was struggling so hard to get his life together."

Drew frowned. "Tell me that you judged that guy with extreme prejudice."

I looked down at my empty plate. "Honestly? I didn't know what to do. Not at first. I mean, I'd just lost my dad. And . . . and this other thing had happened, as well. I didn't want to lose my boyfriend, too."

"What other thing?"

"After my dad passed away, a friend of mine got me one of those DNA ancestry testing kits for Christmas. She thought it would cheer me up. We could both do one, she said, and compare our results. So we did. Right before the Kyle thing, I got my results, which was another reason I was doing so badly in school. They revealed that I'm fifty-two percent British, Irish, and Scottish . . . which was expected, since my father's ancestors are from there. But the rest of my results were almost all Scandinavian."

Drew shrugged. "I don't get it. You have something against our Nordic friends?"

"No. But my mom's ancestors are strictly Sephardic Jews, with roots in North Africa and Spain. She's always bragging about it."

He looked puzzled. "What are you saying? Your mom's a liar?"

"Not about that. About me. I'm not her biological daughter."

He blinked at me. "Whoa."

"Yeah. As soon as I asked my mom about it, she confessed that she had fertility issues, so she and my dad had used an egg donor to conceive me. They never told me because . . . well, apparently there just never seemed to be a good time, and I can be overly sensitive."

Drew gave a wry smile and lifted his glass. "To family," he said. "Can't live with them, can't live without them."

I clinked my glass to his. "To family."

We both sipped.

"No wonder you ran away," he said. "Not only had you lost a father, but you must have also felt as if you'd lost a mother, and then, after what happened with this Kyle person—"

"I felt as if I'd lost my boyfriend, too," I said. "Especially when he blamed me for being so judgmental of Kyle. My mother said the same thing, too, at first."

Drew whistled. "Well, good riddance to all of them." He

reached out to pour more wine into my glass. "You did the right thing, especially coming here. This is the best place in the world to heal from old wounds and start life over. But the school thing—is that forever? You definitely don't strike me as a quitter. You had a rough semester, but you're one of the smartest people I've ever met, so you could easily make up the work if you wanted to go back."

My eyes filled with tears once more. He'd tossed me so many compliments at once—and not the kind Caleb always had, about my beauty, but about my character and intelligence—that I hardly knew how to handle it. I lifted my wineglass and brought it swiftly to my lips, hoping the bowl of the enormous glass would hide my suddenly shining eyes.

"I don't know. I guess I grew up thinking I should be a lawyer because my mom and dad were, and helping people is something I'm definitely interested in. But in my heart—"

He nodded. "I get it. In your heart, you're an artist. No one who's seen those paintings of yours could ever think otherwise." He raised his glass toward mine. "Cheers to having the sense to follow your true path."

I laughed—a half sob, half laugh, because I was still fighting back tears—and leaned forward to clink my glass to his. "Thanks. But that's the problem. I don't know what my true path is. So far it seems to have led me toward waitressing and a hurricane."

He looked slightly hurt. "And me."

"And you," I said, this time laughing without a hint of tears.

"On the other hand," Drew said, gazing up at the stars, "now you have two moms. Not many people can say that."

"That's true," I said. "And I'm pretty sure my egg donor mom is the one from whom I inherited my artistic talent. I was able to see her application. It was an open donation, meaning that she checked off that she had no problem with me contacting her once I came of age."

"That's great," Drew said, looking interested. "Did you look her up?"

I shook my head. "No. Not yet. My mom really pressured me to. I think she thought maybe it would make things better between us. But I just haven't felt ready. Maybe when things get more . . . settled."

"Hmmm." He grinned and reached for me, pulling me against him. "If there's anything I can do to help you settle things, let me know."

"Aw." This so warmed my heart, I leaned up to kiss him.

I'd only meant it to be a playful kiss across his cheek. But he turned his head so that the kiss landed on his mouth.

And just like every other time, the second his lips met mine, fireworks seemed to go off inside my shorts. It was all I could do not to launch myself at him, I so badly wanted to be in his arms . . . and his bed.

I needn't have worried, however, since he was apparently feeling the same way about me. A second later, he scooped me up from the deck chair and carried me back into his room—no trouble tripping over tools this time, since we'd lit plenty of candles to light the way.

Unfortunately, in our ardor, we forgot to put away the leftovers, so the Bobs climbed up onto the table and feasted on what was left of our steaks.

But that was all right, we decided when we discovered our empty plates, much later. They deserved a treat, too. The way we were feeling, the whole world did.

CHAPTER THIRTY

> Residents are encouraged to dispose of the following hurricane debris at the designated landfill: yard waste, appliances, furniture, and any hazardous materials, including paint, fuel, and batteries. (No sludge will be accepted.)

When I woke the next morning, it was to the gentle, rhythmic sound of ocean waves lapping at the shore. Ocean waves, an unfamiliar grinding noise, and . . . voices?

At first, I thought the voices belonged to the gulls, chattering away out on the beach as they'd been doing the whole time I'd been at Drew's house.

But the more conscious I grew, the more I realized these voices were forming words. And that one of them sounded a lot like Drew's.

I sat up, looking around Drew's bedroom. Sun was pouring in through the skylight. I had no idea what time it was because his only clock was digital, and without power the screen was blank, as was the screen to my cell phone.

Drew's side of the bed was empty, his clothes gone. The only sign that he'd been there were the flung-back sheets and the sliding glass door, which was open. Since no dogs were piled on the bed beside me, I could only assume he'd taken them down onto the beach with him. That's where the voices appeared to be coming from.

Wrapping myself in the sheet, I padded onto the deck to see if I could tell what was going on. Though it had to be quite early—the sun wasn't that high in the sky—it was already blazing hot. Shading my eyes with my hand, I peered down at the water . . .

. . . and nearly died of shock.

The romantic private beach that Drew and I had been sharing was now crawling with SUVs, bulldozers, and white trucks from the Little Bridge Electric Company.

How I'd managed to sleep through that, I couldn't imagine. Apparently, I'd been worn out by so much good sex.

I saw a number of people in orange jumpsuits scraping at the piles of seaweed with rakes. Drew appeared to be talking to their leader, who was too far away for me to recognize. I hurried back inside and jumped into the shower.

When I descended onto the beach, a mug of coffee in my hand—Drew had thoughtfully left a potful on the grill, along with half a breakfast burrito, which I'd ravenously consumed—I soon saw whom he was talking to. It was Ryan Martinez, the deputy sheriff. The men in orange jumpsuits who were cleaning up the piles of seaweed were prisoners he was supervising. Prisoners from the Little Bridge jail!

I nearly choked on my coffee when I realized it.

"Good morning there, Bree," Ryan said amiably. He'd seen me approaching first, since Drew's back was toward me. Drew spun around, then grinned happily to see me, even though I was choking.

"Hey, Bree," he said.

I'd recovered myself enough to notice that Ryan's lips were twitching with amusement at the sight of my wet hair and coffee mug. I had no doubt that word of the fact that I'd clearly spent the night with Drew Hartwell would soon be spread all over the island, despite the fact that there was no cell service. On Little Bridge Island there was something faster than texting or social media. Ryan would undoubtedly go home later and tell his girlfriend what he'd seen, then she'd tell everyone she knew, they'd tell everyone they knew, and so on.

This was called the Coconut Express, and I was about to become its leading headline.

I didn't care, and apparently neither did Drew, since he wrapped an arm around my waist and pulled me to his side, giving me a hearty kiss on the top of my head.

"Sleep well?" he asked.

I grinned up at him. I couldn't help it. I was happier than I could ever remember being.

"Great," I said. I indicated the coffee mug. "I could get used to breakfast on the barbie."

"Best there is," Drew said, with an equally wide grin.

Ryan cleared his throat, looking politely away from the two love-struck idiots beside him. This drew his attention to one prisoner who was also staring at us, so he shouted,

"Hobart! What do you think this is, spring break? Get back to work!"

When he turned back toward me, he must have noticed that I was staring curiously at the orange-suited workmen, since he explained, "Governor instructed us last night to let the inmates accused of nonviolent, low-level crimes do hurricane recovery work. The sheriff has a big group of them over at the airport right now, clearing runways."

Fortunately I hadn't taken another sip of coffee, or I'd have choked again. "Really? Is this, uh, a normal procedure?"

Of course I knew the answer already. It wasn't. The governor was only doing it because of my mother.

"Well, it's not typical," Ryan said. "But it's happened before. The prisoners like it. They can get about three days off their sentence for every thirty days they work . . . but we're not talking about a ton of time since there's not that much work for them to do, and their sentences run less than a year to begin with."

Hmmm, that made sense. But it seemed to work out well for everyone involved . . . except maybe for Rick Chance, who was operating a rake near us, and was staring in the direction of Socks. All of Drew's dogs were leaping happily in and out between the waves, chasing tennis balls that Drew was casually throwing to them.

But Socks was the most excited about it.

"Is that my dog?" Rick asked in tones of disbelief, apparently astonished at the transformation of this sleek, confident creature before him, and the dirty, pathetic one that had lain for so many months beneath his bar stool.

The sheriff's deputy was quick to retort, before Drew could say a word, "In your statement you said you didn't have a dog, Rick."

Rick turned swiftly back to his raking. "I don't. I don't."

"Then try to keep your story straight." To me, Ryan said, "Drew told me you're running some kind of pet rescue for all the people who are stuck on the other side of the bridge?"

Startled, I said, "Oh! Yes. I am." I couldn't believe that Drew had been talking about me. "I mean, if it's all right with you—"

"'Course it's all right," the sheriff's deputy said. "I think it's great. According to the engineers, it might be eight, ten days before we can get that bridge repaired. We're gonna need all the help we can get—"

"Eight or ten days!" I was shocked. Most of the homes I'd already visited had left only enough food for two or three days. "We're going to run out of pet food. Do you think Frank over at the Emporium is going to reopen soon?"

Drew was frowning. "Frank and his family evacuated, as well."

I was horrified. "Where am I going to get food for all the dogs and cats people left behind?" I glanced at the sheriff's deputy. "Do you think Frank would mind if I broke into his store and took what I needed, then left an IOU?"

Ryan was already shaking his head *no* in disbelief when Drew laid an arm around my shoulders. "We'd better leave the nice officer to his work, don't you think, Bree?" he said, gently steering me in the direction of his house. "Be seeing you, Ryan. Thanks for the help."

"Don't mention it." The sheriff's deputy looked out at his rough-and-tumble crew, one of whom was taking an impromptu break to lean on his rake and flirt with one of the female electric workers. "Hobart!" The sheriff bellowed. "Back to work!"

Drew whistled to his dogs, who tore themselves away from the birds and sand and came loping after us. "Looks like we've got a big day ahead of us," he said, his lips in my hair.

"We?" I loved the heavy weight of his arm around my shoulders. Even more, I loved the intimate way he dipped his head down to whisper in my ear.

"Of course we. You don't think I'm going to let you run around town, getting all the glory for rescuing every pet in Little Bridge and keep it all to yourself, do you?"

This time, I didn't mind when he said the word *let*. I loved his possessiveness.

I wrapped my arm around his waist and hugged him. "I wouldn't have it any other way."

CHAPTER THIRTY-ONE

ARE YOU AN EVACUEE OF HURRICANE MARILYN? IS YOUR HOME IN LITTLE BRIDGE ISLAND? DID YOU LEAVE A PET BEHIND?

We know that you didn't expect to be gone for this long, or that the storm was going to be this bad!

Call the offices of JUDGE JUSTINE and leave a message giving your name, address, type of pet(s), their needs, and a way we can get into your home to care for your beloved Fifi or Fido!

We will feed, water, and care for your animals WITHOUT JUDGMENT!

BECAUSE JUDGE JUSTINE CARES!

Twenty-seven. That's how many people had contacted my mother's office since she'd posted the information about the Little Bridge Hurricane Marilyn Emergency Pet Rescue Mission. Twenty-seven!

I couldn't believe there were that many people stranded outside the island who'd left their pets behind . . . but there were apparently more coming.

"Shawna's faxing them over later," Mrs. Hartwell said. She was making copies of the pages she already had. "I hope you don't mind about the copies, but I think it's a good idea if we draw up a schedule. That way, we'll not only know where you are at any given moment, and be able to find you, but we'll also make sure all the animals are fed and walked every day around the same time."

Although everything she was saying made sense, the only thing I could focus on was: "Fax?"

"Yes, from your mother's office. We decided it would be easier if they just faxed over the names and addresses instead of reading them off. That way, we wouldn't have to sit there, writing everything down by hand."

That wasn't exactly what I meant. "You have a fax machine?"

"Well, yes, of course, for the business. It makes ordering stock so much easier." She stuck a sheaf of papers in my hands. On the top was a fax cover page addressed to Sabrina Beckham, care of the Hartwells. It was listed as being from Shawna Mitchell, personal assistant to Judge Justine Beckham. Peeking beneath it, I saw several pages of neatly typed names, addresses, and notes about pets, their needs, and how to break into their owners' homes.

"What's this, Aunt Lu?" Drew asked. Along one side of

the library, Mrs. Hartwell had hung a large bulletin board. On it, she'd stuck a map of Little Bridge Island. The map was dotted with brightly colored pushpins, each connected with color-coordinated yarn. "Your murder board?"

"Certainly not." Mrs. Hartwell looked down at the list in her hands. "Each pushpin represents a different pet in need. The yellow pins are dogs, red are cats, green are fish or reptiles, and blue are birds. One person has a potbellied pig, so I used white for that. Anyway, I thought this would be a nice, easy way for you to keep track of all the homes you needed to get to, as well as which neighborhood they're in. As you can see, most of them are over on the Gulf side. But you have a fair number over here, on the Atlantic Ocean side, too."

Drew stood there, grinning at me, apparently thrilled by his aunt's take-charge attitude.

"Oh, and Ed said to tell you to use this." Mrs. Hartwell handed me a small black object.

"A walkie-talkie?"

"That's right." She beamed. "It's Drew's from when he was a boy, but it still works. It has a range of over a mile. As new calls come in, we can reach you and let you know."

Drew's grin was huge. "Wow. Just, wow, Aunt Lucy. Isn't that great? You've thought of everything."

I had slightly different feelings—of mortification. "I'm so sorry about all this—especially that I, um, wasn't here to take all these messages for you."

It seemed to me to be the elephant in the room . . . the fact that I'd been gone all night, then rolled in that morning with her nephew, both of us sporting damp hair and huge, silly grins.

But Mrs. Hartwell seemed nothing but delighted.

"It's my pleasure! We can't let the animals go hungry, can we?" Mrs. Hartwell beamed at us. "Now why don't you grab something to eat from the kitchen if you're hungry—there's leftover lobster enchiladas that I just heated up—and then you better get on your way. You have a lot of people's pets to take care of!"

We did as she suggested—the enchiladas were as delicious as I'd known they'd be—after I stopped upstairs to change into fresh clothes and give Gary his medication.

Gary pretended not to know me at first—I'd never been away from him overnight before—but soon came around when I rolled him over and gave him belly rubs (and some breakfast).

I didn't want to think too far into the future . . . it was nice to be enjoying the here and now for a change. But what was going to happen if, down the road, things got serious with Drew?

Not that they were going to. This was just a casual fling, probably.

But what if it turned into something deeper? How would Gary get along with the Bobs? He got along well with Patrick and Bill's pugs, so it wasn't beyond reason he'd be okay with Drew's dogs.

But would Drew's dogs be okay with *him*? They'd have to be, or there'd be no Drew. That was all.

Why was I thinking about these things after having spent

only one night with the guy? Why did I overthink everything? No wonder my parents had never told me the truth about my conception. What was wrong with me? Why couldn't I ever just enjoy anything for what it was?

"Oh, hey." Nevaeh paused in the doorway to my room, which I'd left open. "There you are. Where were you last night?"

Ugh, awkward. Of course my new boyfriend's niece would ask that.

"I was, uh, around."

"Well, you totally missed it." Fortunately, it turned out Nevaeh was too wrapped up in her own little world to care much about mine. She came into the room and flopped onto the bed. "Marquise and his brother Prince came by to help with the coolers from the restaurant, and these people down the street set up a fire pit in their front yard and they invited us to come toast marshmallows, so we went and Marquise told me I have pretty eyes. It was so romantic."

I smiled at her, remembering what it was like to be a teenager with a crush. "That's sweet. Do you like him?"

She looked surprised by the question. "Sure. Everyone does. He's super popular." Then she frowned. "Katie likes him, too. Katie *really* likes him."

"Well, be yourself. No boy could help but like you if you act like yourself around him."

She rolled over with a sigh, then reached out to scratch Gary under the chin. "Everyone is always saying that, but I don't understand what that means, act like yourself. I'm fifteen. I don't even know who I am!"

I couldn't help letting out a laugh. "I know who you are. You're Nevaeh Montero, soon-to-be high school sophomore, who, from what I hear, gets almost straight As, cares a lot about her family, and works her butt off at her aunt and uncle's restaurant."

She sighed. "Yeah, you see? If there were any justice in the world, all the boys would love me. I get great grades and have an actual job. What man wouldn't prefer a smart woman with her own cash?"

If only it worked that way, I thought. Instead, I said, "From your lips to God's ears. Can you do me a favor and look after Gary again for me today? I have to go take care of other people's pets with your uncle Drew."

"Sure." Nevaeh stuck her finger in Gary's direction, and he rubbed his head against it. "You've been hanging out with my uncle Drew a lot lately. Do you like him or something?"

I couldn't suppress a grin. "I do. Would it be weird for you if he and I . . . hung out?"

She smiled. "No. I think it would be good. It's about time he finally had a normal girlfriend."

I wasn't certain I liked being called "normal," nor was I sure it was a ringing endorsement. But considering the source, it was probably the best I was going to get.

"Thanks, Nevaeh," I said, and bounced from the bed just as Drew popped his head into the room.

"What are you two yakking about in here?"

"You," Nevaeh said, without a second's hesitation.

"Why would I think it would be anything else?" Drew

tossed something onto the floor. Two somethings, actually. "Here, Bree, try these on."

I stared. "Hiking boots?"

"Yeah, they're my sister's. You look like you two probably wear the same size shoe. Considering what we're going to be doing today, I think you need some sturdier footwear."

I recoiled. "Oh, no. I'll be just fine in my sneakers."

"Do you remember that laundry basket that attacked you at your landlady's? If you'd had on those boots that thing never would have stood a chance. Try them on."

Realizing he had a point, I reluctantly laced on his sister's Timberlands. And was disappointed when they fit just fine.

"Oh, my mom's shoes look good on you," Nevaeh commented. "You look kinda like a pink-haired Lara Croft."

I chose to take this as a compliment. "Okay," I said. "Well, we'd better go. We have a lot of pets to look after."

"I'd offer to come with," Nevaeh said, "but Uncle Ed says he needs me at the café again today. He's serving food all day until curfew." Her tone suggested she was making a great sacrifice, but I wasn't fooled.

"And I suppose Marquise will be there, too," I teased.

She turned away with a shrug. "I don't know. Maybe."

But I saw that she'd flat-ironed her hair to an extra sheen, belying her indifference.

Grabbing Drew's tool kit and all the extra pet food we could scrounge from the Hartwells, as well as their generous neighbors, we got back on my scooter and jetted to the first few houses on Mrs. Hartwell's list.

There didn't appear to be any sort of common denominator among the people who'd left their pets behind. It wasn't merely students like Sonny and Chett. It also turned out to be wealthy but slightly senile widows who lived in mansions like Mrs. Hartwell's and who'd left their beloved cats in the care of ne'er-do-well sons who'd abandoned them. Or large and loving families who had been unable to find room in their car for their enormous fish tank (both cat and fish turned out to be fine, if ravenous).

Then there were the homes in which we found no sign of pets at all. No food bowls, no litter boxes, no leashes, squeaky toys, or pet hair. These turned out to belong to people who'd lied to get on the list in order to have their homes checked for damage. Because there was no other way to communicate with anyone on the island—unless you knew someone with a landline or a satellite phone—a few people had said they had a pet in order to get us to go and check to see if their house was still standing, having seen all the dramatic reports on the news about the severe damage sustained by the island.

These people, we decided, would receive no answers to their questions as punishment for wasting our time.

For other homes, however, the news was not so good, nor the reasons behind the owner's decision to leave their pets behind so easy to understand.

"Hey, I know this house," Drew said, as we pulled up beside a small "Conch" home close to the marina. Called "Conch" homes because they'd been built in the late nineteenth century by Bahamian immigrants, the houses were known for their timber framing, large windows, and high ceilings, all constructed to allow cooling in the days before air-conditioning.

"Oh, really?" I glanced down at the list that had been faxed to us. "You know Duane Conner?"

"Yeah, I know Duane." Drew was already off the back of my scooter and heading toward the house. "He's got two pit bull mixes. I see him all the time with them down at the dog beach."

I pulled off my helmet. It was a hot day, and I'd been sweating beneath it. "There's a dog beach? I thought you lived on the dog beach."

"No, there's another beach, over on the Gulf side, where everyone's allowed to let their dogs off leash. Duane takes his dogs there all the time. They're good dogs, just a little rough unless Duane is around to handle them. Are you sure that information is right?" He stood in the middle of the storm-ravaged yard, staring at the house. "Duane would never evacuate without Turbo and Orion."

I checked the list. "It says here that Duane was out of town when the storm hit, and he left his dogs in the care of his brother, Max, and that Max called and said he freaked out and took off without them."

Drew shook his head angrily the second he heard the name Max. "Damn it. Yeah, that would explain it. Max has always been less than reliable. Okay, come on. How are we supposed to get inside?"

"We aren't," I said, a feeling of dread growing in my stomach. "It says Max may have left the dogs tied to the back porch."

Drew swore.

But that's where we found them—after climbing over a back fence. Two very sad-looking pit bull mixes. It was clear by the water line along the house that the floodwaters had reached the porch, and that the dogs had been forced during the storm to swim for a while.

The waters had then receded, and the dogs were fine now.

But they'd had no food for some time, since whatever Max had left out for them had floated away in the flood.

The dogs were overcome at the sight of us, barking and crying with joy.

"Next time I see him, I'm going to kill Max," Drew said, as he saw the bedraggled mutts, their backsides wiggling with pathetic excitement.

I pressed my lips together to keep myself from saying anything I'd regret.

"At least he was honest," I said, instead, tipping over the bag of dry cat food we'd brought with us into the dogs' bowls. It was the only food we had left and was courtesy of Mrs. Hartwell. She saved it for the feral cats from the church down the street, both of whom were fine and accounted for.

The dogs didn't care what kind of food it was. They devoured it eagerly, then looked up, anxious for more.

"At least he told Duane the truth about abandoning the dogs, and Duane called us."

"I don't care if Max told him the truth," Drew said, untying the dogs' leashes from the back porch railing. "I'm still killing him. And we're taking them. They're my dogs now."

"No, they're not." Drew said this at practically every home we visited. "You can take them for a walk, or even take them back to your aunt's, if you want, until their owner gets back into town. But you can't keep every pet we find."

"I'm keeping them until Duane gets back. I'm not surrendering them to anyone but Duane. And if I see that idiot Max, I'm killing him!"

"At least Max told his brother the truth, so he could call us," I repeated.

I didn't want to think about how many animal owners hadn't seen or heard about my mom's online post, and so hadn't contacted us yet.

It was as I was telling myself firmly not to think about this that I heard a rumble. It seemed to be coming from the sky. I looked up just in time to see it . . . a large, dark gray jet plane. It was flying awfully low. It was the first man-made object I'd seen overhead since the hurricane, and it was flying awfully low.

"Military cargo jet," Drew said, answering my unuttered question. "They must have gotten the runway cleared."

"FEMA?" I asked hopefully. If it was FEMA, there was a chance it might be carrying pet food.

"Doubt it. They usually send military personnel first. But it's good news, anyway."

It wasn't to me. It meant that my mother might make good on her threat about arriving.

"How many is this, anyway?" Drew asked, tapping the list I'd pulled from my backpack.

"Oh." I checked. "Twenty. We have seven more to go. Then we should probably head back to your aunt's and see if there've been any more faxes. I'm sure there have."

He looked dismayed. "*More*? There can't possibly be more."

I smiled at him. "Why? Are you ready to go back to restoring historic windows?"

He scowled at me, picking up the leashes of the now considerably happier dogs. "Not on your life. I love our new business . . . even if we're not getting paid. I'd just like it better if it involved less starving animals, and more time with you, preferably in my bed."

I smiled. "I think that could be arranged—after we've finished checking the rest of these houses."

The rest of the pets on our list were fine, only in need of a little TLC—like one tuxedo cat who wanted only to sit on our laps and be petted (it turned out a neighbor had been looking in on her, but had been unable to communicate with the owner to tell her so). In the next house, a poodle was similarly being cared for by neighbors, and wanted only to play fetch with us, because she was so bored. Each had been left with enough food to get them by for at least another day . . . but beyond that, we were in trouble.

"I really think," I was saying to Drew as we climbed the steps to the last house on our list, his friend's pitties in tow—he'd insisted on taking them with us—"that we should break into Frank's and take what we need. I know he wouldn't mind. He's a pet lover himself. I've heard he has a boxer."

I'd had to raise my voice, because as I was speaking, another plane flew overhead. There'd been a steady stream of cargo jets, floatplanes, and helicopters flying by, so many that it was nearly impossible to hear oneself think. It felt like Casablanca, as portrayed in the classic old movie of the same title, only with all the flights arriving, not departing, and all the palm trees missing their fronds.

The home we were visiting was a stately older Victorian house much like Drew's aunt and uncle's. Painted a lovely shade of blue with cream trim, it didn't appear to have suffered much hurricane damage at all. Its storm shutters were already thrown back, which was odd for a home whose owners had apparently evacuated, and there was a newish set of white wicker chairs sitting on the porch.

"We're not breaking into Frank's," Drew said, as the dogs scrambled eagerly up the porch steps ahead of him. "CVS will probably reopen soon. Even though the last thing I want to do is give my hard-earned money to a corporate conglomerate, we can buy food—"

It was as he was saying this that a figure I hadn't noticed before rose from one of the porch chairs and stepped in front of me.

"Hello, Sabrina," Caleb said.

CHAPTER THIRTY-TWO

Due to flooding and damage caused by Hurricane Marilyn, the Florida Department of Health (DOH) is advising residents to take precautions against unclean water. Your tap water may contain disease-causing organisms and may not be safe to drink. BE SAFE NOT SORRY!

I was so startled, I nearly fell back off the porch.

"Wh-what are you doing here?"

My mind was whirling. This didn't make any sense. What was Caleb doing in Little Bridge? How had he known I'd be at this house? And why was he wearing white jeans and a pink Lacoste shirt in a hurricane-recovery zone?

"You know why I'm here, Sabrina," Caleb said. His handsome, expressive face was filled with angst. "How else was I supposed to see you? You won't take my calls. You won't answer my texts. You—"

"There's no cell service."

"I meant before."

Before he could take another step toward me, Drew came striding up, seized Caleb by the collar of his shirt, and pushed him back against the home's decoratively painted front door.

"Hello, there," Drew said, with deceptive cheerfulness, as both the pitties immediately thrust their noses into Caleb's crotch and began to paw at him, barking excitedly. "Have you met my new dogs?"

Caleb was wincing and trying to break free, but there was nowhere he could go with Drew pressing him so firmly against the door, and the pitties' hot breath on his middle section. "I-I don't know you. You got the wrong guy, man."

"I don't think I do," Drew said, his face just inches from Cal's. "Your name is Caleb, isn't it?"

Caleb, still trying to squirm away since Drew was in his face and the dogs were in his private parts, threw a glance of appeal at me. "Sabrina, who is this guy?"

"This is my new friend Drew." My heart was still hammering from the surprise encounter, but it was slowing down a little, and I felt able to make introductions, the tall, dark, handsome man to the tall, blond, handsome man. "Drew, this is Caleb. Caleb, Drew."

"Hey, man," Drew said, relaxing his hold on Cal's collar slightly, though the dogs continued to bark and paw at him. "Maybe you can explain something to me. See, we're supposed to be feeding a cat at this house. Or maybe it's a dog. What is it, Bree, a cat or a dog?"

I checked the list. "It's a cat."

"Yeah," Drew said, relaxing his hold completely on Caleb,

since the dogs were managing to keep him cornered. "But then we get here, and we find you instead. Where's the cat, Cal?"

Caleb looked terrified. "There's no cat, okay? I saw the judge's post last night online and seized an opportunity. This is my second cousin's house. He said I could borrow it anytime I wanted—"

I shook my head, amazed. "How did you even get here?"

"Flew into Miami this morning, then took a floatplane. They're letting anyone land as long as they bring food or medical supplies. We brought a bunch of antibiotics. I know a doctor. Look, Bree, can you get this guy to call off his dogs? I really need to—"

"*We?*" Something cold had clutched at my heart. "Who is *we?*"

Caleb sighed. "Fine, okay. Kyle is here, too."

The cold thing turned to icy panic. "What? I thought he was in rehab!"

"He was. He got out."

"*Got out?* Or signed himself out?"

"He signed himself out. Look, I really don't like dogs, could you just—"

"Hold these." Drew handed me the dogs' leashes, then confronted Caleb. "Where is that douchebag?"

"Look, it's not what you think. Kyle's changed. He admits what he did to you, and that he made a mistake. That's the whole reason he's here. He wants to make amends."

"He can make them to me," Drew said, shoving his chin in Caleb's face.

"Jesus, Sabrina, who *is* this guy?" Caleb demanded. "Call him off, will you?"

I'd successfully dragged the dogs away—though it hadn't been easy, since they were so strong—and was busy tying their leashes to the porch railing. "No. He's my friend. And he's a lot better friend to me than you ever were. He knows all about what happened, and he doesn't think I overreacted."

Cal, seeming to feel that he was out of at least 50 percent of the danger he'd been in now that the dogs were tied up, sagged against the door, though he still managed to look sheepish. "Look, it wasn't that I thought you overreacted. I just thought you could be a little more compassionate. You know Kyle's always had a substance abuse problem—"

"So that means he should be allowed to go around assaulting women in their sleep?" Drew demanded.

"N-no. Not at all." Cal's eyes were as wide as nickels. "You're right. That shouldn't be an excuse. It's just that occasionally he acts a little—"

I couldn't stand to hear any more. "Where is he?"

Drew looked at me like I was crazy. "You're not actually going to talk to him, are you?"

"Yes," I said. "I am." To Caleb, I asked again, "Where is he?"

Caleb looked nervous. "He's inside. In the kitchen. But, Bree, I think I should come with—"

"Stay here and keep an eye on him," I said to Drew. "I'll be right back."

Drew shook his head. "Oh, no. I'm not letting you go in there alone."

I shouldered my backpack. "I'll be fine. Trust me. I need to do this."

Drew's look of alarm didn't decrease much, but something in my face must have told him how serious I was, since he stopped arguing. "Okay. But at least take the dogs."

"No." I shook my head and patted the backpack. "This will be enough. Whatever you hear, do not come inside."

Caleb glanced worriedly from me to Drew. "What's that supposed to mean?"

Drew shrugged. "It means she's got some things to settle."

I smiled at him, surprised that he remembered. "Right."

"So whatever she says, goes. Bree"—Drew dug into one of his many pockets, then threw a small black object he'd found inside it toward me—"here."

I caught it. It was the walkie-talkie his aunt had given us.

"Oh," I said. "Great, thanks." I had no intention of using it, but I put it into my backpack anyway. "If I'm not out in five minutes, you can send in the dogs."

Drew nodded. He seemed more comforted by this than by the presence of the walkie-talkie. "Okay."

"Wait." Caleb did not seem comforted at all. "What? What does that mean, send in the dogs? I don't understand. What's going on? What's any of that supposed to mean?"

"Don't worry about it," Drew said. "Just stay out here with me if you don't want to get hurt."

"Hurt?" I heard Caleb bleat as I moved behind him to open the front door. "She's going to hurt someone?"

"Maybe." Drew sounded bored. "What are you going to do about it, call the cops? Don't you think *that* might be overreacting a little? If you want to run down the middle of the street yelling for the police, please, be my guest. I won't stop you. The dogs might, but I won't."

I closed the door behind me. The air inside the house was cool, and I realized the place had a working generator, but a much quieter one than the Hartwells'. The home was decorated in the same soft beach tones as the front of the house, cream and bluish gray. The décor was modern, but in the chicest of tastes, the pine walls stripped of paint and glossed to a high sheen, the way I'd always imagined the inside of an old-fashioned coffin might look. All of the electronics were high end, but discreetly hidden within alcoves and wall panels so as not to clash with the nineteenth-century architecture.

Late-afternoon sunlight was streaming into the kitchen at the back of the house from a set of glass French doors that had been thrown open to reveal a long dipping pool that hadn't seemed to have sustained any damage from the storm—or, if it had, someone had been paid to clean it up. Along the back of the pool was a high, black-tiled wall, from which poured a waterfall that was already back in working order, consuming precious electric energy from the generator.

Kyle's back was to me. He was mixing a pitcher of margaritas.

"So rehab worked out well for you, I see," I said sarcastically from the doorway.

He spun around, surprised, then gave me a big smile. He, too, was dressed in the height of Hamptons elegance, tight white jeans and a beige cashmere sweater thrown casually over his shoulders, only his shirt was yellow. He was maybe even a little blonder than Cal, and definitely tanner. Rehab had suited him.

"Sabrina!" he cried. "I like what you've done to your hair."

"Do you? I'm glad." I reached into my backpack and pulled out the gun Ed had loaned me. As Kyle watched, wide-eyed, I drew back the safety and pointed it at him.

"Get on the floor," I said.

He burst out laughing. "You can't be serious."

I aimed the gun at a bottle of Cuervo sitting on the counter behind him and pulled the trigger. The bottle exploded into a thousand pieces of glass, none of which likely hit him, considering the trajectory of the bullet, which went sailing through the bottle, then past the French doors and into the black-tiled wall behind the waterfall.

Kyle yelled anyway and threw his arms over his head protectively.

"Get on the floor," I said again, when he was done yelling. I could hardly hear my own voice, thanks to the deafening sound of the shot.

"Oh my God," Kyle cried. "You're crazy, you stupid bitch! You could have killed me!"

"No," I said calmly, "but I will, if you aren't more polite to me. Now get on the ground, or next time I'll aim for you and not the tequila."

Reluctantly, his hands in the air, he sank to his knees. This was clearly difficult for him, because his jeans were so form-fitting.

"I'm sorry." He seemed to be taking me more seriously now. "I didn't mean to call you a bitch."

"I should hope not, especially since I understand you came here to make amends."

"Yes!" He looked like he'd only just remembered. "Step nine! I'm here to make amends to those I have harmed through my drinking."

"Yeah," I said. "Except that's sort of hard to believe considering the fact that you're drinking right now."

"Well." He glanced at the shards of glass covering the black tile floor behind him. "I know. This looks bad. But no one is perfect."

"That's true," I said. "And who am I to judge? Except that in your particular case, I'm going to. I don't accept your apology, Kyle."

"Sabrina. Honestly. This is all a huge misunderstanding. Please let me explain. You see, that morning at Caleb's, I wasn't myself. I was drunk, or got some bad weed, or was sleepwalking, or something."

"Really? And my telling you to get off me didn't wake you up?"

"Well, you didn't tell me to get off. You told me that you wanted me to take you to dinner—"

"How interesting," I said, "that you were so drunk, and yet you remember that."

He looked confused. "So you never wanted me to take you to dinner? Because I actually sort of thought that you and I always had a thing—"

"No, Kyle, we did not, and we do not. I only said that to

get you away from me. Women will say a lot of things they don't mean, it turns out, to get a huge slime bag like you off them. But here's something I do mean: if I ever, ever hear about you touching any girl—or any person, of any sex—against their will, I will find you, wherever you are, and I will kill you. And I won't get caught, because I happen to know how to dispose of bodies in places where no one will find them. And even if they did, I'm pretty sure there isn't a jury in this country that would convict me, because you're such a jerk, everyone would be glad that you're dead anyway. Do you understand me, Kyle?"

He was nodding his head vigorously. "Yes. Yes, I do. But can I still just say that I'm really, really sorry? That morning, that wasn't me . . . it was the drugs talking. And the booze. I really, really think you're blowing this whole thing out of proportion. Nothing actually happened—"

"*Nothing?*" I nearly shot him then and there. "*Nothing?* I think you mean to you. Nothing happened to *you*. I haven't been able to sleep because of what happened that morning. I dropped out of law school because of it." I stepped closer and closer to him, each time bringing the mouth of the pistol nearer his head. "I moved to an entirely different state because of it. I've fought with my mother for months because of it. You may not have hurt me physically, Kyle, but you and Cal and everybody else who kept saying *nothing* happened completely twisted me up inside, making me think I was the one who was wrong to be so upset over what you kept calling *nothing*. But you know what? I wasn't wrong. Because it wasn't *nothing*. And you know what the worst part of it all was? To get away from that *nothing,* I had to agree to go out with you, just so you would get your stupid, stinking, disgusting body off of me, when the truth is, you're the last person in the world I would ever go anywhere with. And all this time, in your stupid pea brain, you actually thought I *liked* you? Are you insane?"

The mouth of the gun was directly parallel to his temple. Kyle knelt, frozen, too frightened to move a muscle.

"No," he said. "I'm pretty sure I know now that you don't like me, and that you and I are never going out. I'm sorry, Sabrina. I really am sorry."

Because he finally sounded sincere, I turned the safety on the gun back on, then dropped it back into my bag.

"Good," I said. "Never come near me again. Understood?"

He swallowed. It appeared that I had really gotten through to him. "Y-yes."

"Great. Good-bye forever."

I turned and left the house. Outside, Drew was leaning against one of the porch rails examining his cuticles while Caleb was sitting back in the porch chair, uneasily eyeing the pitties, who were panting heavily while sitting and staring at him.

Drew looked up as I came out. "Everything go okay?" he asked brightly.

I smiled at him. "I think we came to a pretty good understanding. Thanks for asking."

Caleb nearly exploded from his seat—but kept a safe distance away from us, due to the pit bulls.

"What was that sound?" His eyes were nearly bulging from his head, and his face was shining with nervous sweat. "Was that a gunshot? Did you shoot him?"

"Don't be ridiculous." I scooped some of my hair from the back of my neck. It was terribly hot outside. "He's fine. But I did explain to him that I don't accept his apology, and that I don't want to be friends with him anymore, or you, either, Caleb. I don't like either of you, and I especially don't like this sneaking around, lying thing the two of you did to get in touch with me. It was really dishonest, and it wasted our time"—I pointed at Drew and then at myself—"while we're trying to get some really important rescue work done. So please don't ever contact me again." I looked at Drew. "Are you ready to go?"

He lifted his lanky frame from the porch railing with a shrug. "Yeah, I guess."

"Fine," I said, and began untying the dogs. "Good-bye, Cal."

"Wait." Cal looked confused. "That's it? You're just . . . going?"

"Yes, we're just going." I had to hand the leashes over to Drew, because the dogs were too strong for me. Apparently, they were familiar with the word *go,* and upon hearing it, were ready to take off. They'd practically yanked my arm out of its socket rocketing down the porch steps. "I've moved on, Cal. I suggest you do the *same*."

"But—"

I'd turned my back on him and started down the path through the home's front yard toward the sidewalk. Along the way, Drew reached out and took my hand. I didn't look back, even though Caleb kept calling, "Sabrina! Sabrina, I need to— Sabrina!"

"Keep walking," Drew said, under his breath.

"I know," I whispered back. "You don't need to tell me."

"There's something wrong with that guy."

"Duh."

"Why did you ever go out with him?"

"Um, I could ask you the same thing about Ms. Pink Salt."

"At least she didn't wear Lacoste."

"Shut up. That's still a thing in some places."

"Where?"

"I don't know."

"Sabrina!"

We made it to the corner where we'd parked the scooter without either Caleb or Kyle chasing after us. I was riding the scooter—slowly—while Drew walked the dogs so as not to traumatize them by making them run alongside the motorbike.

"So what happened in there?" Drew asked. "Did you shoot that guy, I hope?"

"No. I shot a bottle of tequila."

He winced. "No! Good stuff?"

"Cuervo."

He shook his head. "They're probably going to tell the cops. Your ex seems like the type."

"I don't think so. And even if they do, don't you think the sheriff has a little more to do right now than worry about a pink-haired waitress who shot a bottle of tequila in some snowbird's house?"

He considered this. "You're right. In about six months, he might get around to looking into it. But even then, what's he going to do? Charge you for illegal discharge of a weapon? Hell, half the town shoots off their guns into the sky every New Year's Eve."

I thought about the bullet I'd lodged in the back of the waterfall, then decided that Caleb could pay for its removal, if his second cousin ever noticed it was there.

"Thanks for being there for me," I said, reaching out to squeeze his hand. "I know that was . . . weird."

He looked surprised. "What are you talking about? I was ready to beat that guy's head in. I don't know why you didn't let me. Now would have been the perfect time to do it, too. No cops, no accountability."

"But it's my problem," I said. "It felt good to settle it myself."

It did, too. Even if the way I'd done it might have been questionable, I felt a strange sense of peace, and no anxiety whatsoever.

It was an unfamiliar sensation. But good. Really good.

"Yeah," Drew said. "You do seem sort of . . . calm."

"That's thanks to you," I said. "Now let's get back to your aunt's place and see if there's anyone new on the list. Then we need to go back to Chett's and his friends' to check on their animals. They all need to be fed and walked again."

"God, you know all the right things to say to get a guy in the mood for romance."

I laughed. I was still laughing, in the best mood I could remember being in in a long time—and that was saying something, considering how happy I'd been last night—when I walked up the front steps of his aunt's house.

Right up until the moment the Hartwells' front door was flung open, and my mother walked out of it, threw her arms wide, and cried, "Sabrina!"

CHAPTER THIRTY-THREE

Bottled water and MREs are being provided by FEMA in the Publix parking lot on a rotating schedule. Both are available from 7 A.M.—9 A.M., 11 A.M.—1 P.M., and 5 P.M. to 7 P.M. This schedule is subject to change.

"Oh my God." I froze in my tracks.

My mother was wearing a flight suit. Literally, a gray flight suit like the kind astronauts wear. Only hers was silk and probably Armani.

"Sabrina, sweetheart!"

My mother flung her arms around me.

She was soft and smelled as she always did, of Chanel No. 5. Being hugged by my mother triggered something deep inside me, a memory I hadn't thought of in a long, long time. It took me a few seconds to realize what that memory was, and then, like a lightning bolt, it hit me: home.

But it was also so strange to see my mother on Little Bridge Island. She looked so out of place, with her pale blond blowout and her manicure and her carefully made-up face. Not to mention the flight suit.

I wasn't sure, after the incident not ten minutes earlier with Caleb and Kyle, how many more out-of-town visitors I could take.

"Sweetheart, I was so worried about you. Are you all right?" She pulled back to look at me, allowing me to steal a glance at Drew. He was trying not to laugh over by the gumbo-limbo. I could have killed him. "Oh, sweetheart. Your hair. It's so . . . *bright*."

"I'm fine, Mom," I said from between gritted teeth. "What are you doing here? And what are you wearing?"

"Oh, sweetie," she said, taking my hand. Her skin felt cool because she'd been inside with the air-conditioning for so long. "You'll never believe it. Your uncle Steen got us a cargo plane. Because you know they weren't going to let us land the jet here, because this place has been declared a national disaster zone by the governor. So we had to bring recovery supplies. But don't you worry, we brought plenty of things for your new little friends, plenty of good, healthy things, like bottled water and fresh vegetables and diapers and some of those things, what are they called—"

"MREs."

She'd pulled me inside now, into the living room, where her lawyer, Steen, dressed in a business suit, was sitting on the couch with a satellite phone in his hand.

"Meals Ready to Eat," he elaborated, with a brief smile at me. "Hello, Sabrina."

"Um, hi." I really could not deal with seeing so many

people from my New York world in my Little Bridge world in one day. Not on this day, of all days, when I was so happy because of Drew. It wasn't fair.

Even worse, there was another person, a stranger they appeared to have dragged with them, sitting on the other end of the couch. She was a small woman in her early fifties with a severe blond pixie cut who was at least wearing more sensible clothes—khaki shorts with a collared shirt and no-nonsense boots like mine—than either my mother or Steen.

She was sipping a cup of coffee that Mrs. Hartwell, standing nervously in the corner, had apparently poured for her, while staring owlishly at the rest of us through somewhat thick glasses, probably wondering how on earth she'd gotten herself into this mess. Since she was holding a blissfully purring Gary on her lap, I assumed that she was at least somewhat happy, because no one could hold a purring Gary on their lap and not feel happy.

Still, I pitied her, whoever she was, for having been sucked into this mess.

And not just her—poor Mrs. Hartwell, as well. This was the last thing that poor lady needed, to have to entertain Judge Justine while also recovering from a hurricane. The least I could do was try to hurry along her visit.

"Mom," I said. "Thanks so much. I'm sure everyone appreciates it. But where exactly—"

"Oh, I gave it all to that sheriff down at the airport when we landed," my mother said breezily, not allowing me to finish my question. "He said they're going to start handing it out this afternoon in the parking lot of some grocery store."

"That's right." Mrs. Hartwell pointed uneasily to Ed's radio, which was sitting on the coffee table. "They said this morning on Head and the Toad Licker that they'd be starting food giveaways in the parking lot of the Publix at three this afternoon for anyone in need."

"And not only food for humans." My mom looked inordinately proud of herself. "Pet food, too, Sabrina, thanks to this lady, here." She pointed at the shy woman on the couch holding Gary on her lap. "Do you know who this woman is?"

Obviously, I had no idea. "Um, no, Mom."

"This," my mother said, proudly, "is your biological mother, Sabrina. Dr. Iris Svenson!"

CHAPTER THIRTY-FOUR

Free Pet Emergency Care Available in Little Bridge

The Veterinary Emergency Response Team opens today for all pet emergencies at the Animal Clinic. We have a fully operational hospital, including an operating room.

All emergency care is available at no charge. This team will remain in place until our local veterinarians are back up and running.

Care is available for ANIMALS ONLY.

My knees seemed suddenly to have gone out from under me. It was a good thing we were in the living room, where there were a lot of chairs. I sat down heavily in one of them near the end of the couch, my mind whirling.

My mother. The woman holding Gary on her lap was my mother.

"Wait." Mrs. Hartwell looked confused. "You have two mothers, Bree?"

"No." Dr. Svenson adjusted her thick glasses, but never stopped stroking Gary, who was flexing and unflexing his front claws in delight, careful not to sink them into her bare knees. He never bothered to take such care when he was sitting with me. "She does not have two mothers, only one. It's more correct to say that I am Sabrina's donor mother. I donated the egg from which Sabrina was conceived. Mrs. Beckham actually gave birth to and raised her, so she is Sabrina's real mother."

Mrs. Hartwell still looked confused. "Oh."

Drew, who was resting a comforting hand on my shoulder, gave it a reassuring squeeze. "I'll explain it to her sometime," he whispered in my ear.

I wasn't really listening. I had more important things to worry about.

"Mom." I could not believe she'd done this. Not that I wasn't happy to meet my donor mother. I just hadn't planned on meeting her *now,* in this way, with my hair in a sweaty pony while wearing a pair of borrowed Timberland boots after I'd just pulled a gun on my ex-boyfriend's best friend. "Was this really necessary?"

"Well, of course it was, Sabrina!" My mom was clearly upset that her little surprise hadn't gone over well. "Besides being your mother, Dr. Svenson is a very distinguished veterinarian and animal nutritionist! She works for the Veterinary Scientific Advisory Group! I still don't understand exactly what that is, but I'm sure it's very, very important."

Dr. Svenson gave me a timid smile that looked a little familiar somehow—until I realized, with a shock, that it was my own. "The VSAG is a group that works to develop cooperative relationships between the veterinary community and various other groups to enhance their services."

Of course. Of *course* my donor mother was a veterinarian. What else would she be?

I smiled back at her—or tried to, anyway.

"I'm very glad to meet you," I said, extending my right hand, though I'm pretty sure my fingers were shaking. "I'm so sorry about my mom. She's a lot."

"Oh, I know." Dr. Svenson slipped her hand into mine and gave it a gentle squeeze, while Gary, disturbed that no one was petting him, let out a grumble. "I met her before, you know. And your dad. I quite liked them. That's why I chose them. I thought they'd be good for . . . well, you. I didn't know you then, of course, but . . . well, it seems to have worked out. You look . . . happy."

My eyes filled with tears. It wasn't only because of what she'd said. It was her touch, as well. Even though it was simply her fingers closing around mine, it felt exactly like the hug I'd received earlier on the porch from my mom: like coming home.

But how was that possible? I didn't even know this person.

And yet it felt as if I'd known her my entire life. Maybe because I had: I was half her, after all.

"I *am* happy," I said, squeezing her hand, not caring if she noticed my tears or shaking fingers. "Thank you. Thank you for what you did for me. I'm really, really happy."

She smiled—a much less timid smile this time, more like

mine when I was genuinely pleased about something—and said, "That makes me glad. And no need to thank me. I was financially compensated by your parents for my time, and I used that compensation to help defer the costs of my education. There was an element of selfishness to the act, too, I suppose. I knew I was never going to have children of my own, because I'm not a maternal sort of person. But it's a basic human instinct to want to see your DNA passed on. So helping a couple seeking a child of their own seemed the most logical way to go about it."

Well, okay. Maybe we didn't have *that* much in common.

At least until Gary, thoroughly disgusted that no one was petting him, reached up and swiped at both our hands with a velvet paw, and let out a dissatisfied meow. Dr. Svenson looked down at him and laughed.

"And I like your cat very much," she said, stroking an ecstatic-looking Gary behind his ear.

"Thanks," I said, laughing as well. "I rescued him from the local animal shelter. Can you believe he'd been there for years and no one wanted him?"

"Their loss is your gain. I notice he has no teeth. Stomatitis?"

"Yes!" I couldn't believe she recognized the illness. But then again, she was a vet. "The surgery cost me twelve hundred dollars, but he's been so much happier ever since."

"Yes, it's amazing how well feline stomatitis patients do after tooth extraction."

"And you'll never guess what Dr. Svenson's done, Sabrina," my mom cried, clapping her hands to get our attention. She clearly felt she was losing her audience, and for my mom, that was never a good thing. "Because she's an animal nutritionist and part of this big veterinary organization, or whatever it is, she has the numbers to the heads of all the pet food companies. So she got all of them to donate food to the Hurricane Marilyn recovery fund! We brought giant bags of dog food, cat food, rabbit food, cat litter—you name it!"

"That is so great," I said, smiling at my two moms. "We're so grateful. You can't even believe how much we need that donation. We were basically down to one bag of cat food, and we were giving it to dogs."

It was the *we* that finally got my mom to notice Drew, standing behind my chair. Maybe she'd have eventually noticed him without it, but it was the *we* that got her, and possibly the fact that he was standing so close, with one hand still hovering protectively on my shoulder.

"Oh," she said, giving him an appraising look. I watched her take in his long, darkly tanned limbs—bare, of course, because he was wearing his usual low-slung cargo shorts—and flat, lightly-haired stomach, since his linen shirt was, as usual, barely buttoned due to the heat. "And you are?"

"Mom, this is my, er, friend Drew Hartwell." I had recovered myself sufficiently to rise from the puffy chair and make introductions. "Drew, this is my mother, Judge Justine Beckham."

"How do you do?" Drew leaned forward to shake the hand of my tiny, flight-suited mother.

"How do you do?" Mom's blue-eyed gaze took in every

part of Drew that she'd missed while examining him from farther away. "Are you a special friend of my daughter's?"

"Mom." How could my mother still have the ability to mortify me after all these years?

But Drew took her, as he seemed to do everything else in life, in stride.

"Why, yes, I am." Grinning in that infuriating, adorably wry way he had, he laid an arm around my shoulders, then steered me around so that I was facing both of my mothers. "I'm very happy to meet both of you ladies, because you seem very special to Bree, and recently, Bree's become very special to me."

I raised my eyes to the ceiling. Oh my God. Please make it stop.

Dr. Svenson nodded calmly at Drew while still petting Gary. "So nice to meet you."

My mother, however, could barely contain herself. "Well, that's just lovely, Drew. You know, Sabrina hasn't had a special friend in a while, and honestly, we've been a bit worried about her, haven't we, Steen? Steen!"

Steen looked up from his satellite phone, on which he'd been texting. "What?"

"This is Steen Frederickson, *my* special friend," Mom said, reaching a hand toward Steen, who obediently crossed the room to take it, though he didn't really look up from the screen of his phone. "You don't mind, do you, Sabrina? I've been so lonely without Daddy, and Steen's always been so good to us."

I smiled. I was surprised it had taken my mom this long to find a "special friend." She'd never been the kind of person who liked being alone with her own thoughts. I was just glad the person she'd chosen was someone as steady and sensible as Steen.

"No," I said, reaching out to take her hand. "I'm glad for you both."

"Well!" Mrs. Hartwell, who'd been standing in the corner watching my little family drama unfold before her like it was a reality show, clapped her hands in delight. "Isn't this wonderful? I'd say it calls for a celebration!"

Drew squeezed my shoulders. "It sure does! How about some tequila?"

Grimacing, I elbowed him in the ribs.

"Don't be ridiculous, Drew," his aunt said. "I meant lunch. My husband and niece are down at our restaurant serving free food to this entire island, practically, and other restaurants have joined us in donating their food, as well, to serve before it spoils. Would any of you like to meet me down there, to share a meal? They've cleared our street, so I'd be happy to take you in our minivan."

I glanced at my mother to see her reaction, since she had never set foot in a minivan in her life.

"Why, I think that would be lovely," she said. "We'd be happy to, wouldn't we, Steen?"

"I'm starving," Steen said, finally putting away his phone. "I'd love it."

"I'd be happy to come." Dr. Svenson gently pushed Gary

from her lap—though he protested quite vocally—and rose to her feet. "So long as they have vegetarian options."

"They will," I assured her.

"Well." Mrs. Hartwell beamed. "Let's go, then! Let me just go find my purse."

She hustled back toward the kitchen, while Drew tugged on my hand and pulled me out into the hallway.

"What?" I asked as he pressed me up against the wall, out of sight of the others.

"Nothing." He swept a few loose strands of hair from my face, then leaned down to kiss me. As usual, it felt as if fireworks were going off inside my body. "Just, I get it, now."

"Get what?" I wrapped my arms around his neck and stood on tiptoe to kiss him some more.

"Why you are the way you are—completely insane."

"Thanks for the compliment. What explanation do we have for why you're the way you are?"

"You mean so kind, sweet, and handsome?"

"I mean such a raving lunatic."

"Oh, I was dropped on my head frequently as a child."

"Yeah," I said, thoroughly enjoying the feel of his long, hard body as it pressed me against the wall. "I can tell."

"After lunch, and when we get all the rest of those damned animals fed, can I take you back to my place and ravage you again?"

"I was counting on it."

"What about your mothers?"

"Don't invite them."

“Okay, good.” He kissed me again, then nibbled on my lower lip. “I was hoping you’d say that.”

There was a cough from the hallway, and we turned our heads to see my two mothers, Steen, and Drew’s aunt staring at us.

“Um,” Mrs. Hartwell said. “We’re ready to go if you two are.”

Drew and I burst out laughing.

EPILOGUE

Four Months Later

Time: 8:22 P.M.
Temperature: 72°F
Wind Speed: 5 MPH
Wind Gust: 0 MPH
Precipitation: 0.0 in.

The Mermaid was lit up for the holidays.

Christmas lights of every color imaginable had been strung not only around the windows and doors, but all across the ceiling, in and around the mermaid Barbies, and especially around the counter and serving pass-through, too.

The place was packed, even though it was only a Thursday night . . . but it was the Thursday night before Christmas, and Little Bridge was stuffed near to bursting with visitors from the mainland, anxious to escape the winter cold up north. The Little Bridge tourist council had worked overtime to advertise the fact that the island had fully recovered from Hurricane Marilyn and was ready to take the vacation dollars of anyone willing to spend their winter break in the Florida Keys.

And it had worked. There was not a single vacancy to be found in any hotel on the island. Even the RV park was packed.

And I was loving every minute of it.

"How's it going?" Drew asked as I flitted past his counter stool for a third time in as many minutes.

"Um, kind of weird. I just sold another one."

He lifted his beer. "Why is that weird? I'm not the type to say I told you so—"

"Except you so are."

"—but I told you so. You should have priced them higher."

I collapsed onto the stool next to his—the only reason it was empty was because he was guarding it. Otherwise, it would have been filled in a second, the place was so packed with happy revelers.

And the only reason I could sit without Ed yelling at me was because I wasn't working at the Mermaid.

Oh, I hadn't given up my breakfast shift. Angela and I still toiled away every Tuesday through Saturday from six in the morning until two in the afternoon—although school had started, so Nevaeh had joined her fellow tenth-graders in class. I only saw her when I went to the Hartwells', or when she filled an occasional shift.

I was at the Mermaid tonight not to work, but because

it was a special occasion—the café's very first art opening. And the art was mine.

And it was selling.

Probably a little too quickly. Drew was right, I'd priced my paintings too low. Since they were small and therefore, as he'd suggested, highly portable in a carry-on bag, and also depicted exactly what tourists—and let's face it, all the rest of us—loved so much about Little Bridge, the beautiful wide blue sea and colorfully clouded skies, they were selling fast.

This was an ego boost, certainly.

But it was also confirmation of something my donor mom had told me—we emailed occasionally. Not too much, since she really wasn't, as she'd said, the maternal type. She was simply a nice friend to have, who knew a lot about the kinds of things I was interested in, like one half of my genetic history, animals, and art:

"Find what it is you love to do," she'd advised, "and then do that thing as much as you can. . . . That really is the meaning of life. I love to paint, too, but I wouldn't like to make a living at it. I think that might spoil my love for it. But if that interests you, you should go for it."

Now someone told me.

Not that I didn't still appreciate my birth mother. I spoke to her on the phone practically every day. She'd planned on being here, in fact, for my first "gallery" opening, but a nor'easter in the New York area had prevented her plane from taking off.

I was secretly a little glad. I had enough to worry about without entertaining Judge Justine for the holiday weekend.

"Seven." I held up my fingers to show Drew how many paintings I'd sold. "I've sold seven already, and it's not even eight o'clock."

"See?" He grinned with happiness for me. "Aren't you glad you held some back? I bet if you took the rest to a real gallery, you'd make even more—"

I waved a hand to silence him. "Shush. I'm not trying to make a career out of this yet. I just want to have fun with it for now."

"When do we ever not have fun?"

It was true. Since the morning after the storm, I'd been having nothing but fun with Drew Hartwell—with the slight exception of that incident with Kyle and Caleb.

But there'd been no fallout from that. I'd never heard from either of them again and didn't expect to. I was living a new life now, and wished them nothing but luck with theirs . . .

Unless, of course, I heard they were making life miserable for someone else. Then I might have to take action.

"But do you think people are buying them because they're good?" I asked him. "Or because I'm the girl that saved so many people's pets after the hurricane, and they want to show their gratitude?"

Drew rolled his eyes. "Bree, look around. Half the people in here aren't even from Little Bridge, and don't know who you are. They're buying them because they're good."

"I don't know." I chewed my lower lip. "I mean, it's fine

either way. But it would be really great if people were buying them because they actually thought—"

"Byotch!" Daniella appeared as if from nowhere and wrapped her arms around my neck. She was wearing a pair of light-up reindeer antlers, a sequined baseball jacket, and fishnet stockings under a green minidress. "You're so fricking awesome! The paintings look so great! I miss your stupid face so much!"

"Thanks," I said, trying to unwrap myself from her stranglehold. "I miss your stupid face so much, too. But you seem to know where to find me."

"Yeah. It's okay." She smiled blearily at Drew. She may have consumed a few too many of the café's special holiday drink, a Mermaid Moscow Mule. "I like your stupid face, too." Daniella directed this to Drew. "So you can have her. And the Gare."

"I promise to take good care of them both," Drew faithfully swore, raising his beer in a solemn oath.

"You better." Daniella saw something behind me and pointed. "But her! I love *her* stupid face!"

"I should hope so." Angela came up, a Bloody Mermaid in her hand. "Bree, have you seen how well those paintings of yours are selling? You're going to get famous soon and leave us to go back to New York to become the next celebrity artist, aren't you?"

I looked at Drew and grinned. "Um, I don't think so. But I appreciate the thought. How's my apartment?"

Angela smiled. "It's my apartment now, thank you very much. And it certainly beats living with my mother.

Although I will say there's never a dull moment with this one. How's it going, Daniella?"

"Frickin' awesome." Daniella looked down at the glass of water Ed had just silently handed to her over the counter. "What's this?" She sipped the water. "Ooh! Refreshing."

"You little sneak."

I looked up to see Patrick and Bill standing in front of me, wearing clashing Christmas sweaters.

"How could you not tell us," Patrick demanded, "that you're a classically trained artiste?"

"Um," I said. "I wouldn't say classically trained—"

"Nevertheless," Patrick said, "we've purchased one of your paintings—*Sunset Over Sandy Point,* I believe it's called."

I stole a quick glance at Drew and saw that he was smiling. "Good choice," I said. "That's one of my favorites."

"Yes, I thought it was the best. We're going to hang it over the television. That way, whenever we're tired of watching the news or whatever dreadful thing it is that's on, we only have to look up, and we'll be instantly soothed."

"I think that's a great idea," I said.

"And every time we look at it," Bill said, "we'll think of you. How is our favorite feline friend doing over in his new digs?"

"Very well, actually."

I couldn't help but smile. Gary had pretty much taken over Drew's house. His many years of living at the animal shelter must have given him plenty of experience in keeping other animals in line, including dogs, because from the outset, he'd shown no fear of the Bobs. Instead, he'd quickly asserted himself as the new alpha, with a paw to the muzzle of any dog he felt had disrespected him. He alone slept with the humans in our bed, though he did allow the dogs to pile onto the couch beside us.

He had no interest in the beach, however. The deck was his domain, where I was growing a small bed of grass for him—a suggestion from the animal shelter, where I now volunteered several times a week—since he'd so enjoyed chewing and rolling on the grass beneath the dear, departed frangipani.

"You'll have to bring Brandon Walsh and the girls over for a visit sometime," I said. "I'm sure Gary would enjoy seeing them."

Patrick gasped. "We'd love that!"

And then they were swallowed up in the throng of new well-wishers who came hurrying up to congratulate me on the show, which by the end of the evening had sold out. As Drew and I walked along the festively lit harbor toward his pickup to go home, he reached out to take my hand.

"Happy?"

"Of course!"

"But?"

"There's no but."

"Then why are you so quiet? You're not still worrying that all those people only liked your paintings because you saved their pets, are you?"

"No." I looked out at the marina, where a lot of the boat owners had decorated their boats with Christmas lights, turning their masts into brightly lit angels or Christmas trees. “I just . . . I was just wishing my dad was still alive, so he could have seen this. And met you.”

Drew stopped in his tracks and turned to face me, his expression soft. “I was thinking the same thing about my parents, and you.”

We looked up at each other in the twinkling lights as nearby, the water gently lapped against the harbor wall.

“Don’t judge me,” I said, looking up into his handsome face, “but sometimes I feel like my dad knows. Does that sound weird?”

Drew reached out and gathered me into his arms. “No,” he said. “That doesn’t sound weird at all.”

ACKNOWLEDGMENTS

I'm so grateful to so many people who helped in the creation of this book. I'm sure I'll leave someone out (if so, I'm so sorry!) but here are a few who went above and beyond:

My friends Beth Ader, Jennifer Brown, Gwen Esbenson, Michele Jaffe, and Rachel Vail. I owe you all big time.

All the amazing people at my longtime publisher, HarperCollins, but especially my editor Carrie Feron; publicity director Pamela Jaffee; and welcome new team member, Asanté Simons.

My longtime agent and friend, Laura Langlie.

My media support team, without whom I would be lost: Thank you, Janey Lee, Heidi Shon, and Nancy Bender.

Key West resident Brittany Davis, who courageously rescued dozens of pets in the aftermath of Hurricane Irma.

And of course my husband Benjamin Egnatz, with whom I'd evacuate (or stay home) anytime!

About the author

Read on

Insights,
Interviews
& More . . .

About the author

Meet Meg Cabot

Lisa DeTullio Russell

MEG CABOT was born in Bloomington, Indiana. In addition to her adult contemporary fiction, she is the author of the bestselling young adult fiction series *The Princess Diaries*. Over 25 million copies of her novels for children and adults have sold worldwide. Meg lives in Key West, Florida, with her husband.

Hurricane Survival Snacks

Preparing for a hurricane? First, obey all instructions from local law enforcement, including those to evacuate!

But even if you're just sheltering in place for a quiet night at home, don't forget the snacks! The only good part of a hurricane is the sense of community it brings about. The best snacks I've ever had were those that came from other people's refrigerators (that we needed to eat fast, before they spoiled), hunkering down with friends and neighbors. These include my neighbors' homemade smoked brisket, defrosted grilled lobster tails, and just about every kind of cheese, chips, and dips imaginable.

The rest came from my house, simple recipes made with love for people we cared about while going through a crisis, including some of the food Drew and Bree enjoyed during Hurricane Marilyn in *No Judgments*. ▸

Hurricane Dip

I first enjoyed this dip at a good friend's Kentucky Derby party, so it's officially known in my circle as "Kentucky Dip," but we now make it whenever there's a storm (if we made it more often, our cardiologists would be upset).

8 ounces mayonnaise
 (preferably Hellmann's)
8 ounces cream cheese
8 ounces sour cream
Hickory-smoked barbecue sauce
 (preferably Kraft) to taste

1. Cream the mayonnaise, cream cheese, and sour cream until smooth (electric hand mixer preferable for easiest results).
2. Add the barbecue sauce.
3. Stir until orange/light beige (sorry to not be more precise, it's a home recipe).
4. Chill, preferably overnight. Serve with chips or crudités or use as a sandwich spread!

Lemon Pudding Cake

This lemon pudding cake is an old family recipe of my husband's and is perfect for hurricanes because it stays moist while not needing to be refrigerated. It's a simple recipe and can be made for all occasions, not just weather disasters.

1 package yellow cake mix
(can be gluten free)
1 package instant lemon pudding
2 cups powdered sugar
4 eggs
¾ cup water
¾ cup vegetable oil
⅓ cup lemon juice (⅓ cup concentrated orange juice may be substituted)
3 tbsp butter (optional)

1. Preheat oven to 350°F.
2. Beat cake and pudding mix together with eggs until smooth.
3. Blend in water and oil and mix thoroughly.
4. Pour into a greased Bundt or 9 x 13-inch cake pan.
5. Bake 45 to 50 minutes or until toothpick comes out clean.
6. Remove to cool on rack. ►

Lemon Pudding Cake ***(continued)***

7. While cake is cooling, mix ⅓ cup fresh lemon juice (⅓ cup concentrated orange juice may be substituted) and 2 cups powdered sugar to create glaze (3 tbsp butter may be added if icing is preferred over glaze).
8. Poke small to medium-sized holes in warm cake with fork or toothpick for glaze. Skip this step if icing is preferred.
9. Drizzle glaze/icing over cake.
10. Let set 2 hours or overnight.

Enjoy!

And remember . . . hope for the best, prepare for the worst!

Stay tuned for a new Little Bridge Island story coming in 2020!

The Sheriff and the Librarian

Meg Cabot

Molly Montgomery couldn't be more thrilled about starting her new life as head of Children's Services at Little Bridge Island's brand-new public library. Happy to have left her problematic ex behind on the mainland, her new life feels like heaven . . . at least until she finds a newborn baby in the library's public restroom. Then suddenly she begins to wonder if life in Little Bridge isn't exactly paradise.

But when Sheriff John Hartwell answers Molly's 911 call, things begin to look up. He couldn't be kinder (or better looking) and handles the baby—and the hunt for its missing mother—with far more sensitivity and understanding than Molly would have expected from someone who never reads fiction.

Maybe there's more to this tall, taciturn sheriff than meets the eye.

Recently divorced John Hartwell has been having trouble adjusting to single life as well as single parenthood. ▸

The Sheriff and the Librarian ***(continued)***

It doesn't help that his teenaged daughter, Katie, hates Little Bridge Island and wants to move to the mainland to live with her mom.

But something in the sympathetic, smiling eyes of Molly Montgomery gives John hope that things on Little Bridge might be looking up after all—for both himself and, maybe, Katie.

But can two such different people ever find happiness together?